Devilishly Sexy

Devilishly Sexy

KATHY LOVE

BRAVA

KENSINGTON PUBLISHING CORP.

www.kensingtonbooks.com

BRAVA BOOKS are published by

Kensington Publishing Corp.
119 West 40th Street
New York, NY 10018

All Kensington titles, imprints, and distributed lines are
available at special quantity discounts for bulk purchases
for sales promotions, premiums, fund-raising, educational,
or institutional use. Special book excerpts or customized
printings can also be created to fit specific needs. For
details, write or phone the office of the Kensington
special sales manager: Kensington Publishing Corp.,
119 West 40th Street, New York, NY 10018, attn:
Special Sales Department; phone: 1-800-221-2647.

BRAVA and the B logo are Reg. U.S. Pat. & TM Off.

ISBN-13: 978-0-7582-8365-8
ISBN-10: 0-7582-8365-2

First Printing: June 2012

10 9 8 7 6 5 4 3 2 1

Printed in the United States of America

Chapter One

He couldn't suppress the low growl of satisfaction as he thrust, plunging deep in one smooth stroke, fully, to the hilt.

"God, that feels so good," he groaned, his eyes rolling in their sockets with pure exaltation.

His rough words were answered with a low, desperate moan that filled him with more delight.

It had been far too long. No man should go so long without this. This moment of pure ecstasy. And he wasn't too humble to know he was damned good at it. *Damned good*.

He pulled out, positioned himself again, his fingers tightening around the thick girth in his hand, heavy and hot. A fine shaft, if there ever was one. He couldn't help taking a moment to admire it in his hand. Beautiful. An old, dear friend.

Then he sank it in again with unerring accuracy. Deep to the hilt once more. And that was all it took.

He remained totally still, allowing himself to feel that moment of total surrender. The shudder, a tiny, almost imperceptible quiver, then complete release.

He stared at the limp body pinned to the wall by his

sheer, unrestrained strength. Eyes closed, head flung back, lips parted in a silent cry.

Now that was true beauty.

Finally he pulled out, and before the object of his determined onslaught could start to sag into a boneless, spent heap, he grasped his powerful shank for the very last stroke. The most satisfying of them all.

With a powerful sweep of his arms, he struck and a gush of warm stickiness covered his hands, his forearms. Even his chest and face. He didn't care.

He watched with a strange combination of pleasure and utter dispassion as his target's head disconnected from his body, flying through the air. It rolled across the cracked and oil-stained concrete and came to a wobbling stop under a parked car.

The headless body crumpled slowly down the concrete wall with a faint thud.

Michael pulled in a deep, satisfied breath. God, it was good to be back.

"Holy shit," came a voice from behind him.

Michael spun, his sword raised, blood gleaming along the edge of the long, sharpened iron of the blade. But as soon as Michael saw who had joined him, he grinned and lowered his weapon.

"Gabriel," he greeted his longtime friend. Seeing his old comrade still filled him with a sense of amazement. To finally be free.

He jerked his head toward his prey, smiling with pride. "Not too shabby for being out of the game for so long, huh?"

Gabriel gaped at the decapitated body with a look of horror that Michael would have expected from a normal human. Not from one of his brethren.

"You killed him," Gabriel finally said as if he couldn't believe it.

Michael made a face, confused. "Yeah. That's what we do. Kill demons."

Gabriel looked away from the body of the dead demon, and for a moment, Michael thought he saw something akin to pity in his eyes. Then the tall blond shook his head and said in the way one sibling might speak to another about a parent, "Eugene isn't going to be happy about this."

His sense of satisfaction vanished, leaving Michael somewhere between deflated and annoyed.

Eugene. His *boss*, quote, unquote.

Gabriel gave Michael another dismayed look, then reached for the small handheld electronic gizmo that sat in a holster on his hip. He tapped the rectangle a few times, then held it to his ear, waiting.

Michael watched, half-wondering if Gabriel was tattling to Eugene right this minute, and half-trying to recall what that small device was called. It was a phone, but it had a certain name. What the hell was it? A . . . cell? Yeah, cell, that was it. A cell phone.

"Hey, Simon," Gabriel said after a moment, answering Michael's first question. Simon, another of his brethren. Not Eugene. That was a good thing.

"Yeah, we've got a big problem out here in the parking garage. Level three, section . . ." Gabriel glanced around him until he located the large letter painted on the wall in yellow paint. "E."

Gabriel nodded. "Yeah. Yeah, it's Michael again."

Again. Michael frowned. Here he was glad to be back with his brethren, but clearly they just saw him as a nuisance.

"Send out the cleaning crew." His old friend's voice did not sound even remotely pleased.

Michael's frown deepened. He waited as Gabriel

made a few more curt responses, then hung up the phone.

Gabriel stared at Michael for a moment, before he sighed and said, "Michael, you know this isn't how we handle the diabolically challenged now."

Michael gaped at his friend. "What the hell kind of jive talk is that? That"—he pointed with his sword toward the headless heap—"is a demon."

Gabriel barely glanced in that direction, then said in a low voice, almost as if he was embarrassed, "Don't say that. We don't call them that anymore."

"Don't say *demon*? I sure as hell am not saying 'diabolically challenged.' That's retarded."

"No," Gabriel said. "Don't say 'jive talking.' No one says that anymore. And you really shouldn't say 'retarded' either. It's not PC."

PC? What the hell did that mean?

Michael lowered his sword. Defeat and frustration pressed down on his chest, making it hard for him to breathe. How the hell was he supposed to fit back into this world?

Gabriel regarded him, the embarrassment in his eyes turning to something that looked far too much like pity.

Michael gritted his teeth, irritated at how lost he felt in that moment.

"Listen," Gabriel said, his tone no longer dismayed at all. Michael suddenly longed for dismay rather than the pity he now heard. "I'm going to have to report this incident to Eugene."

Eugene. Of course.

"No need," Michael said, his own tone hard and cool. "I will go tell him what happened right now." He started in the direction of the stairwell at the bottom of the garage ramp.

"Michael."

Michael stopped to look back at his oldest friend. Or rather the man who had once been his oldest friend. It was amazing that even though they had damned near an eternity to live, Michael's lost thirty-three years, a span of time that should have been nothing more than a mere blink of the eye, could be an eternity in its own right.

Gabriel pursed his lips. "You can't go talk to Eugene."

Really? Was this more damned rhetoric? Gabriel had to report him? He couldn't go talk to Eugene like a man responsible for his own actions? This was bullshit.

"I think I'm capable enough to talk to the man myself without you running interference." Michael strode more determinedly toward the stairs.

"It's not that," Gabriel called after him. "You are covered in blood and carrying a massive sword. That might attract a little attention in the hallways of an office building."

Michael came to a halt, looking down at himself, realizing Gabriel was right. Maybe he wasn't capable. Not in this new world.

"I've got some gym clothes in my car," Gabriel said, his voice back to sympathetic, and Michael wanted to growl with complete frustration. Instead he straightened his spine and turned back to his once good friend.

"Great, where are they?"

Michael looked at himself in the men's room mirror. Maybe he should reconsider the offer of borrowing Gabriel's clothes. Gabriel was a large man, but not as tall and brawny as Michael. That was more than obvious from the way Gabriel's T-shirt threatened to expose Michael's stomach every time he moved his arms. Not to mention the way Gabriel's sweatpants clung to his legs more like leggings than the baggy sweats they were intended to be. Add to that Michael's work boots and he looked like a complete—well, complete turkey.

He already wasn't being taken seriously, and this wasn't going to help. He'd be seen as the poor chump who'd been out of the game for far too long. Maybe he was.

No, he belonged with The Brethren. They were his family, and being a demon slayer was who he was. No amount of lost time could change that.

He tugged at the shirt, trying to stretch it. Okay, so this look wouldn't help his credibility, but he wasn't a man who shirked his responsibilities, and he was responsible for the slaying of a demon. He was certain Gabriel had already reported to Eugene what had happened. So he'd go into that office, dressed like a total idiot and present his case like a man. Like a slayer.

Sighing and pulling at the skintight shirt again, he headed for the exit of the men's room. He pushed open the door with a confident shove. Hell, if he was going to walk down the hall in this ridiculous getup, he might as well own it. Of course, it was a little easier to be self-assured here, in an empty, back hallway unused by the majority of the people in the building.

He strode in the direction of the elevators that would take him down to the lower level of the building, where Eugene waited. The hallway was quiet except for the low hum of the air-conditioning. So when the elevator at the end of the hallway dinged, the sound was almost startlingly loud.

He came to a stop in front of it, waiting. Finally, the

metal doors parted to reveal a lone woman. Or at least he thought she was alone—until she spoke, her tone angered.

"Will you just be quiet?"

Michael leaned forward, wondering if someone stood to the side, just out of sight. Nope, no one.

"Do you ever stop?" the woman demanded, still oblivious to Michael watching her. Then she waited as if she was listening to "the other person's" response.

"Oh, for God's sake, just give it a rest!"

Okay, it was pretty clear that the woman believed she was talking to someone.

Then Michael recalled the earpiece he'd seen Gabriel and several other members of the DIA wearing. A blue something. Blue teeth? Tooth? That couldn't be it. That didn't even make any sense.

Anyway, that had to be what was going on. She *was* talking to someone, and she was clearly so wrapped up in her conversation that she didn't even notice him, until the door started to close, and he stuck a hand in to stop it.

"Oh," she said, her eyes widening in surprise. The prettiest eyes Michael could recall ever seeing. A beautiful color somewhere between green and blue and fringed with long, black lashes.

"I'm sorry," she murmured, her cheeks coloring a warm pink. She seemed to gather herself, her shoulders straightening, revealing that she was a rather tall woman, maybe five foot eight or nine—at least in heels. She was dressed immaculately in a white silk blouse and fitted black skirt. Expensive and well tailored. Of course that wasn't unusual in this building, given that it was the home of *HOT!* magazine, the United States' number-one selling fashion magazine. People tended to dress well and expensively.

Well, except for him. He glanced down at his own outfit.

Although her clothes were spotless and unwrinkled, her long dark hair looked far less tidy, as if she'd been repeatedly running her hands through it. As though hearing his thoughts, she ran a hand through the tumbled locks, which didn't do much to straighten them. But it did manage to make her look more tousled and lovely.

Michael's body reacted instantly. He fought the urge to look down at himself. He just hoped the tight sweatpants weren't revealing his reaction.

If they did, she didn't seem to notice. She was too busy gathering herself, her posture straightening further. Then she stepped out of the elevator, twisting slightly to edge past him.

When they were practically touching, she seemed to notice how he was dressed. A frown creased her brow as her pretty eyes scanned his outfit. Her original embarrassment was replaced now by a moment of unconcealed confusion. In that moment one of the heels of her open-toed pumps snagged on the carpet and she lurched forward, directly toward him.

He started to reach for her, but before he could touch her, she managed, by sheer will, to balance herself and actually step away from him. As if his touch was the last thing she'd want.

He glanced down at himself. Yeah, he'd be a little wary too.

"I'm—" She couldn't seem to stop her beautiful eyes from roaming over him again, her face even more nonplussed, if that was possible. In fact, her expression might have been comical, if Michael didn't feel so damned ridiculous.

"I'm sorry," she said again after a moment, but he

wasn't sure what exactly she was apologizing for, her clumsiness or her reaction to him. Either way, she didn't owe him an apology. Neither was her fault.

But again, before he could react, she glanced around herself as if she had no idea where she was or why she'd been on her way down to this floor. Then she nodded, seeming to remember what she'd been about to do. "I—I have to, umm, go this way."

She gestured vaguely in the direction from which Michael had just come.

Before Michael could even say anything, the woman hurried away as if someone was chasing her.

Maybe she was afraid someone as crazy looking as he was could have the potential to follow her. He suspected he looked like a crazy person who might have wandered in off the streets. Or off the set of some horrible roller-skating movie. Crop top and skintight pants. Yeah, that screamed skates and disco. Both of which, Michael had been informed, were now considered retro.

He glanced in her direction again as she fled down the hall. And although he wasn't sure over the hum of the air-conditioning, he thought he heard her mutter, "Just leave me the hell alone."

And he realized when she'd been brushing back her hair, he hadn't noticed one of those earpiece things. But that didn't mean she'd actually been talking to herself. And he was pretty sure she had been talking to someone with that last comment. Him.

Liza McLane clenched her teeth, fighting back the scream that threatened to erupt from her throat and potentially never stop. She couldn't take it anymore. No more!

She couldn't even ride an elevator like a normal human being. And then there was her meeting with that man outside the elevator.

She felt her cheeks burn at the thought of her behavior. And of her body's crazy reaction to him. He had been seriously hunky—even in his weird, *far too small* ensemble. And what had been up with the feathered hair à la John Travolta . . . or actually more like Shaun Cassidy.

Maybe *HOT!* was doing a seventies photo shoot. She hadn't heard about it, but he definitely looked like he could be a model.

Mmm, you should have let me see him.

Liza clenched her teeth tighter and picked up her pace.

Clearly, the man must be a 9 on the hotness Richter scale, because even God himself knows, I have never felt you react this way. Dare I say it, but I believe Miss Dormant Below the Waist seems to be having a little activity down there.

Shut up, she thought in a sharp hiss.

You should have touched him, so I could take a little gander myself. You know I'm always interested in a nice, sexy male. And even Heaven knows I haven't gotten any action being around you. This guy must have been a real specimen.

Before she could catch herself, she growled out, "Just leave me alone." Then she fought back a groan, praying that the badly dressed dreamboat had already gotten onto the elevator and hadn't heard her talking to herself yet again.

Oh, if only she were just talking to herself.

She didn't risk looking back, just in case. He probably thought she was utterly mad as it was.

Instead she kept focused on her mission.

Please tell me he was the tall, dark, and handsome type. I do so love those. A longing sigh echoed through Liza's head. *But let's face it, at this point, I'd settle for anything. How do you live without a good fu—*

"Shut up," she practically hollered as she stepped out of the *HOT!* building. Thankfully, the small alleyway that led from the building out to the main sidewalk was empty. If only the hallway had been too.

Another long-suffering sigh filled her head.

You do realize that if you got laid on a regular basis, neither of us would be so cranky. There was a pause. *Just sayin'.*

Liza told herself not to react, to stay focused on the task at hand. Getting to Duane Reade's. Pronto.

But not for the first time, she did wonder how her life had gotten so messed up. It was bad enough that she had to be possessed by a damned demon. But somehow she'd managed to get taken over by a demon who was gay, bitchy, boy crazy, and sounded remarkably like Uncle Arthur from *Bewitched*.

Was it really a mystery why she didn't get laid?

Chapter Two

Michael shifted, willing himself not to tug at his shirt, even as he felt the hem creeping up his abdomen. It didn't help that the silence in the room was getting absolutely unbearable, but he was determined to remain collected and as dignified as possible. Even essentially wearing a crop top.

Crop top or no, he didn't have anything to feel regretful over. After all, he'd only been doing his job. The job he'd been created to do, and he wasn't going to show a hint of uncertainty or remorse.

Beside him, Gabriel didn't feel the same need to remain stoic. He maintained a respectful posture, hands behind his back, shoulders straight, but Michael noticed he kept shifting his weight from one foot to the other. Subtle, but there. His brethren was nervous—and Michael didn't think it was for himself. Gabriel expected Michael to get in trouble. Big trouble.

Damn, he wanted to pull down this ridiculous shirt.

But he remained still, his gaze meeting his "boss's" eerie, pale blue stare directly.

Those eerie eyes were the only extraordinary thing about Eugene, the head of the DIA, the Demon Intelligence Agency. Otherwise, the man who now controlled all demon recognizance looked like any average guy. Average height, average build, nondescript hair, nothing out of the ordinary whatsoever. Except those eyes.

Michael didn't know what had happened over the past thirty-three years, but it sure seemed to him like something really odd had to have gone down for this guy to become the head of such a crucial and elite world security agency.

Another creep of cloth as the tight T-shirt crawled farther up Michael's midriff.

Okay, enough of this horrible silence. Just as Michael opened his mouth to speak, Eugene finally stopped his unnerving staring, and simply stated, in a voice that was neither deep nor high, nor loud nor soft-spoken, "I realize you are only recently reunited with your team, and many of the policies have changed, but I do not believe I have to explain to you what a breach of procedure your current action was. I would have thought you'd have known that after I spoke to you about the incident last week."

The incident. Michael yet again saw that killing as simply doing his job. But he'd already said that last week. Apparently the DIA didn't see ridding the world of demons as a part of their job these days. Apparently the DIA just observed them. That would certainly keep humanity safe.

Irritation filled him, but he squelched it, straightening to his full six foot five. Then he said calmly, "While I do realize things have changed in my absence, I cannot believe that they have changed so much that casting a demon back to Hell is a breach of policy. After all, isn't that exactly what the DIA was developed to do?"

Eugene was silent for a moment, then shifted in his seat. He reached for a small black remote on his desk, and the wall behind him flickered to life like a huge television screen.

For a brief moment, the new—well, new to him—technology startled Michael. But that surprise was quickly lost once he recalled what that screen meant.

Shit, here we go again. Michael should have just kept his mouth shut.

"I know we've been through the DIA's objectives, but clearly you still are not understanding," Eugene said in his calm, nondescript voice.

Great. Mind-numbing statistics. Again.

Eugene pressed a small button on the remote, and a list of the DIA's goals appeared, bullet-marked and prioritized.

In that voice that shouldn't have been objectionable in any way, yet managed to infuriate Michael, Eugene began reading off the list.

"To protect humanity from the evil powers of the demonic realm."

"I believe that is exactly what I was doing," Michael pointed out, even though he knew it wasn't proper protocol to interrupt a superior. But frankly, it was hard to see this guy as his superior. Hell, they all called him by his first name. Probably based on another crazy theory that equality would make the team more efficient, or some shit.

But then when Michael last served the DIA, The Brethren hadn't had superiors anyway. They'd been considered the most elite of the DIA, and they made their own rules. The Brethren of Slayers had been an entity unto themselves, trusted to do the right thing. The correct and moral thing.

Now Michael didn't feel like he was even trusted to

dress himself. Gabriel's T-shirt crept farther up his stomach. Okay, in this brave, crappy new world maybe he couldn't be.

Shit.

"You are still considered our most elite task force," Eugene stated, his eerie eyes clearly struggling not to look down at Michael's exposed midriff. "But things have changed greatly since 1979."

Eugene rattled through the rest of the goals, all of which took more power away from The Brethren. Or at least that was how Michael saw it. How could things go so wrong in a mere thirty-three years?

Eugene turned his eerie gaze toward him again. "I know you don't understand our methods right now. But you will."

Michael frowned slightly, getting the feeling, not for the first time, that Eugene was somehow reading his mind.

Eugene, however, gave no indication that he was hearing his thoughts, but rather turned all his attention back to the screen. He clicked the remote again, and Michael suppressed another groan. Not the damned pie charts again.

Eugene glanced from the large screen toward Michael, eyebrow raised.

See? Had Eugene heard that? Or had Michael only thought he'd contained his groan of frustration? He honestly wasn't sure—of either.

"I know you don't want to see the pie charts again, but they are the best way to show the progress we've made in demon recognizance," Eugene stated, his even, standard tone only taking on a slight edge of sharpness.

Michael didn't react. He simply stared at the graph he'd seen many, many times.

The chart in front of him showed the percentage of demons that had been cast back to Hell. The percentage of possessed, which were now referred to as "diabolically challenged" who had been "rehabilitated." Even the percentage of full-fledged demons who'd been "rehabilitated" too.

Only one tiny sliver of the pie, small and bright red, showed how many of the demons had been slain. Killed. Cast from Heaven, Hell, and Earth forever.

And as far as Michael was concerned, that whole damned chart should be a giant circle of bright red. Michael did not believe the possessed could be rehabilitated. Evil was all-encompassing and seeped into the very being of the humans the demons possessed. And as far as rehabilitating demons, that was asinine. And casting them back to Hell—well, that was a temporary fix, wasn't it? Demons were like cockroaches. You might be able to drive them out, but they would always be back.

But the DIA had access to the best damned exterminators in the business. Two of them standing right there.

Michael glanced at Gabriel. Gabriel remained expressionless. His eyes on the chart, his once strong conviction as to what he was on this earth to do totally gone.

Brainwashed. Totally brainwashed.

Eugene sighed, his frustration clear now. Well, at least someone aside from Michael was feeling something. Eugene pressed his remote, and the screen faded back to the white of the surrounding wall.

"You know, I had hoped to reintroduce you to your team right away. But I'm starting to think that isn't going to be a realistic possibility. At least not right now."

Michael frowned, his full attention now on his

"boss." Was he being taken out of the game? Completely?

Eugene fell silent again in his annoying, utterly calm way. Michael couldn't stop himself from glancing back toward Gabriel. His fellow brethren shifted slightly again, and even though Michael almost didn't recognize the man next to him now, he could tell Gabriel was anxious for him. Maybe some loyalty, some bond still existed between them.

A small comfort now that he suspected he was going to be let go. Perhaps the first of The Brethren of Slayers to be "fired," for lack of a better word.

But what Eugene said was almost worse.

"I think the best place for you right now is the mailroom."

Michael stared at his "boss."

The mailroom. Shit.

Michael could feel Gabriel's glances as they left the DIA's offices, hidden below the lowest level of the *HOT!* building and protected from the demon world by a thick layer of copper in the walls, floors, and ceiling. Hidden deep below what the rest of the world thought was the basement of the building, otherwise known as the mailroom. The lowest level of the *HOT!* magazine building. And as far as Michael was concerned, also the lowest level of the DIA agency.

The mailroom was the cover for many of the DIA operatives. The place where DIA agents spied and gathered information about demons. And then, as far as Michael could tell, made charts and graphs about their findings and did absolutely nothing else, while the demons continued to take over the fashion industry . . . and eventually the world.

Michael did not want to be a part of this ineffectual, worthless team. He wanted to fight the damned demons. Take them out. Put a stop to what was the biggest, organized demon takeover he'd ever seen in his centuries of demon slaying.

As they entered the elevator and Gabriel pressed the button that would take them up to the mailroom, he finally seemed to find his voice.

"You got off lucky, you know."

Michael shot his team member a sidelong glance of his own. "Oh yeah, how's that?"

Gabriel waited until the elevator door was closed before turning to him.

"Because Eugene could have retired you."

"Retired? Hasn't that been done already?" He looked pointedly toward Gabriel. "To all of us."

Gabriel's jaw set, a muscle in his cheek bunching as if holding back an irritated growl. Michael knew the feeling.

After a second, Gabriel stepped forward and pressed another button. The elevator made a dinging noise, then shimmied to a halt.

Michael turned fully to look at him, itching for a confrontation. He hadn't gotten to say nearly half of what he'd wanted to say to Eugene. But he sure as hell could and would say it to Gabriel. This was a man he'd fought beside hundreds of times. But now all Michael saw was a man who'd lost every bit of his fight. Michael would be damned if he'd end up the same way.

Nor was he going to wait for Gabriel to speak.

"We were once the front line of defense," Michael said, his voice hard, angry, disgusted. "Hell, we were once the only line. We were expected to go in and clean house. Now, we're just expected to stand around and watch, while all these DIA computer spazzes and jive turkeys gather information that is totally unnecessary."

Rather than looking ready to fight back, Gabriel had an almost pained look on his face, and Michael didn't think he was pained because he was finally realizing the truth. What the hell would get through to this guy? Was he really that damned brainwashed?

"Un-fucking-believable," Michael muttered.

Gabriel sighed. "Well, at least that slang isn't totally outdated."

Michael gaped at him, suddenly understanding that Gabriel was more concerned with his dated slang than the fact that The Brethren were all but useless members of the DIA.

"This is truly insane," Michael stated, flexing his fingers, but keeping his hands down at his sides, even though he wanted to lash out. To beat some damned sense into this man.

Gabriel glanced down at his hands, clearly well aware of Michael's agitation, but then to his surprise, stepped forward and laid a hand on his shoulder. Michael's muscles tensed, but otherwise he remained still.

"I know it's hard to understand the changes, brother," Gabriel said, his deep voice low and mellow. A voice that had calmed him in the past. Such a long time ago, it seemed. "But a lot has changed in the years you were gone. And I agree with Eugene— maybe if you see what the mailroom is doing, you will understand that we have to approach demon slaying differently these days. Some of those we thought eternally damned can be saved. I've seen it myself."

Michael stared at him, not believing what he was hearing. Not understanding how so much could have changed in a mere thirty-three years. How his one-time best friend could have changed so much.

Michael was tired of being corrected for his slang and his behavior. It definitely hadn't been his choice to be frozen in time for thirty-three years. That had been the sneaky little trick of the demon he'd been hunting. The bastard had cursed him, freezing him like Han Solo in *The Empire Strikes Back*. And ever since 1979, he'd been in a warehouse in the DIA evidence lab.

He guessed he was lucky to be here, because he didn't think anyone had expected the curse to wear off. But still, he really thought the situation he'd been in warranted a little bit of a learning curve now.

They stared at each other for a moment. Michael irritated and Gabriel almost pleading. More exasperation welled up in Michael, and he jerked out of Gabriel's hold and slammed the button that would set the elevator in motion again. At least he could lash out at that without more consequence.

Or at least he hoped he could. Maybe friggin' elevators had as many rights as demons did these days.

When they reached the basement level, Michael didn't even wait for the doors to fully open before squeezing his broad shoulders through the parting space and making a beeline through the large work-room that bustled with DIA agents posing as mail-room staff.

A slight rush of satisfaction cooled Michael's annoyance just a little as the workers/agents darted out of the way when he stormed through, parting like frightened fish at the approach of a shark.

Except they probably didn't hurry out of his way because they were intimidated by a member of The

Brethren, but simply because he was a large, pissed-off man. That realization stole a little of his pleasure.

"Michael," he heard Gabriel call from behind him, but Michael didn't slow his pace. That made him feel a little better again.

Damn, it was the small rebellions now.

He kept going, even as Gabriel's voice grew more emphatic.

Michael didn't want to hear any more. He wasn't taking a tour of the mailroom. He wasn't going to become one of the ineffectual automatons the other Brethren had become. He just needed out of this place. Out of these clothes. Away from this new world he did not understand.

Chapter Three

M ichael shoved the key into the lock of his tiny studio apartment. As he stepped into the ratty little space, melancholy mingled with the frustration still smoldering in his chest. He stopped and leaned back against the closed door, struggling to take a calming breath. To let go of these unwanted feelings.

This was his life now. A tiny, dingy apartment in a questionable part of New York City. Alone. Completely confused by this life he suddenly found himself dropped into. So very different from the life that had been taken from him.

He'd been at the top of his slaying game. The leader of The Brethren. He'd had a home in an upscale part of Manhattan. He'd dated and partied when he wasn't working. He'd had a happy, and fulfilling life. He'd known his place in the world. Things had been copasetic.

And with one misstep, one moment of letting down his guard, believing for just a moment he was powerful enough to combat anything, he'd lost it all. He'd lost thirty-three years. But despite that one misstep, the only thing he felt he understood and still had any confidence in was his job as a slayer.

And now even that was gone.

He wandered into the room, setting down the long leather bag that contained his sword. He wanted to simply toss the weapon down. Apparently it was useless to him. But years, decades, centuries of respect for the blessed weapon wouldn't allow him to treat it so cavalierly. Even though it would appear his sword was as obsolete as the one who wielded it.

He headed over to his wardrobe, struggling out of Gabriel's shirt as he went. He flung it on the worn plaid chair in the corner. The furniture had come with the apartment, the tattered, shabby pieces so old, they'd probably had their heyday in the seventies. Just like him.

Michael peeled off the equally snug sweatpants, then headed to the bathroom, a tiny space with a sink, a toilet, and a rust-stained shower stall. The minuscule room didn't even have a proper door, just an accordion-style, vinyl, sliding one, which he never bothered to close anyway, because the space would be totally claustrophobic if he did.

He turned on the shower, the hot water knob squeaking in protest, the pipes joining in with several loud bangs.

He waited for a moment for the water to warm, then shed the last remnants of his clothes and stepped into the spray.

He sighed, not even caring that the water was lukewarm at best. He stood there, limbs slack, eyes closed, but his mind didn't relax like the rest of his body.

The mailroom. He'd been back with DIA long enough to know that working in the mailroom meant he was little more than a spy, an information gatherer. Watching what the demons were doing, but not taking any active part in stopping their invasion. But then again, wasn't that all of the DIA now.

He reached for the shampoo. The bottle was labeled Herbal Essence—a brand he remembered from the seventies. But this shampoo was "revitalizing," in a purple bottle. Revitalizing. Whatever the hell that meant.

Back in the seventies this shampoo had been green and one kind for all hair types—and it smelled like its name. Herbal. This smelled like fruit—and was purple now too. What was herbal about that?

Damn, even shampoo had been so much simpler in 1979.

He finished washing his hair and body, then stepped out of the shower, the plumbing complaining just as much about being turned off.

He dried off with one of the cheap towels he'd picked up for his apartment, and the rough cloth actually felt good against his skin. Somehow reaching through the numbness that had surrounded him since leaving Eugene's office.

The mailroom. If he wanted to continue with the DIA, that was where he had to go.

He quickly threw on some clothes, needing some fresh air.

Once out on the street, he looked both ways. The streets were bustling, cars honking, traffic stop-and-go, people rushing wherever they were going. All of that was the same as his last memories of this place. But the passersby looked different somehow. The cars not any makes he knew. People talked on cell phones, or typed away on them as they walked.

But it wasn't called typing. It was called . . . texting.

It was strange how the city could be both very familiar and very foreign at the same time. He glanced both ways again, then decided it didn't really matter which way he went. He didn't have any destination in mind anyway.

He roamed the streets for a long time, seeing some things he vaguely recognized, plenty he didn't. And all the while, his mind swirled with thoughts of the world he'd left behind. And how the hell he was supposed to find a place in this one.

He wandered, for how long he wasn't sure, until he spotted a little bar on the corner. Stubby's.

Stubby's. He knew this place. The bar still existed, and it looked exactly the same as he remembered. The worn brick building, the tacky neon sign, even the chipped green paint on the door—everything was the same. A wave of relief washed over him. Finally something that hadn't changed in the time he was—indisposed.

He jogged across the street, only getting honked at once for his jaywalking, and he didn't even understand the insult that followed. What was a "mofo" anyway?

He didn't contemplate that very long. His only intent was getting back to a place he knew and understood.

He pushed open the door of the bar, the weight and resistance as well known to him as if he'd just pushed it open the day before. He stepped inside the narrow, alley-like bar and was assailed by the smell of stale smoke and beer. All that was familiar too.

He was thrilled to see that even his favorite seat at the end of the bar was empty. He strode directly toward it, settling onto the stool with a relieved sigh. The stools looked exactly the same.

God, this felt so good. So wonderfully familiar.

"What can I get you?"

Michael stopped looking around the bar, turning to grin at the bartender. His smile slipped slightly when he saw the young man waiting to take his order. His hair was cut in a shaggy, androgynous style, but that was where any semblance of seventies style ended. This kid was covered in metal studs. Two in his eyebrow. One through the septum of his nose. Another in the indentation below his bottom lip. His earlobes were stretched into wide holes held open by rims of more metal. Then there were the endless colorful tattoos covering both of his bare arms like sleeves.

This certainly wasn't the bartender Michael remembered, a cool cat named Winston with a great Afro and the craziest taste in silky, floral shirts. But Michael supposed he couldn't expect every detail to be the same. Plus, Winston had always said he was going to buy his own bar eventually. Maybe that's what he did.

Michael came out of his reminiscing to see that the new, young bartender was eyeing him as skeptically as he'd just examined the young man.

"Want a drink?"

"Um, yeah, I'll take a Pabst Blue Ribbon."

The kid frowned. "Sorry, we don't carry that."

"Since when?" PBR was always a favorite at all bars.

"I have no idea. We haven't had it since I've been here."

Michael wasn't sure how long that was, but he was willing to bet it wasn't that long, by the looks of him. Even filled with distracting metal, the kid didn't appear much over twenty.

"I'll take a Harvey Wallbanger then."

The kid made another confused face, but nodded and headed back down the bar.

Michael watched him for a moment longer, then turned his attention back to the bar. Okay, so they didn't have Pabst, but they still had the same jukebox, and the same beer and liquor signs on the walls. He sighed, again feeling at home, normal, for the first time since returning to this world.

Man, how many hours had he spent chilling in this place? All The Brethren had come here back then. They'd played pool in the back room. They'd sat at the bar and mellowed out. They'd all loved this place.

Damn, he hoped none of them would show up tonight. Then he looked around again. But there was one person he'd love to see here again.

Allie.

Allie Lewis. She'd waitressed here and knew all the guys well, but only Michael had been lucky enough to date the spunky young barmaid. She'd been a lot of fun, both in bed and out, and Michael had truly had fond feelings for her. He hadn't been willing to settle down with her. Marriage was much different for members of The Brethren than for average humans. Marriage for his kind was permanent, forever. When the proposal was made and accepted, the couple was bonded for eternity. A slayer simply knew when he'd met his soul mate.

While he'd cared for Allie, he'd known she wasn't his soul mate, but that didn't stop him from wanting to see her now. Hell, he'd love the comfort and familiarity of her smile and laughter and warm body tonight. That would truly be a godsend at this moment.

As if his longing conjured her, he heard an unforgotten sound. Allie's airy laughter.

Michael scanned the bar, trying to see Allie's honey-blond locks, her wide smile and blue eyes. The establishment wasn't crowded, so it didn't take him long to spot the woman, whose laugh he recognized instantly.

He didn't recognize the woman, however. That familiar laughter came from the rouged lips of a woman who had to be in her late fifties, if she was a day. She appeared to have long blond hair, but it wasn't like golden honey, but rather a washed-out color as if she was desperately trying to hold on to her blondness, but the gray was winning. This woman had tired, lined skin, and he suspected she tanned too much in that endless search for a youthful glow. Unfortunately now it had had the reverse effect.

She leaned over the bar to give the young bartender a peck on the cheek. The bartender winced as if he'd rather avoid the gesture of affection altogether, and Michael wondered if this woman was a regular who always demanded things like kisses on her crepey cheeks.

They spoke a moment longer, and then the bartender gestured in Michael's direction with his head. He lifted what must be Michael's drink in the air. Michael looked away, not wanting to be caught staring.

"Here you go," the tattooed bartender said, setting the orange drink in front of him.

"Thanks," he said, reaching into his pocket to hand the guy a five.

"That's nine-fifty."

Michael frowned. Damn, now that was inflation. A Harvey Wallbanger would have cost him $2.50 thirty-three years ago. Was everything destined to be drastically different?

He reached into his pocket for another five.

The bartender nodded his thanks. Michael watched him head back down the bar to talk to another patron who looked pretty much the same as he did. Tattooed, pierced, angst-ridden.

Michael took an experimental sip of his drink, pleased that at least the kid made a decent Harvey Wallbanger. Not nine dollars and fifty cents worth of decent, but it was better than he'd expected. As he took another, longer swallow, he noticed the woman at the end of the bar was now staring at him.

He finished his sip, then lowered his glass, not looking away. Under her fake tan, the woman seemed to blanch, her skin taking on an even stranger color in the dim light.

Only then, as she stared at him wide-eyed, did Michael realize he was staring into Allie Lewis's sky-blue eyes. He watched as she pushed away from the place where she leaned on the bar, and headed in his direction, their eyes never breaking contact.

Finally when she was right in front of him, her mesmerized expression, the very same expression he was sure he wore, shifted. Her blue eyes roamed his face, taking in the sight of him as if he was some long-lost love. Which, in a way, he supposed he was.

"Michael?" she finally said tentatively as if she had to be losing her mind. Her face was so different, but he'd have recognized her voice anywhere.

He managed to shake his head, even though he was still just as stunned that he was looking at her. Allie.

"Sorry, no."

A frown creased her brow, making her look older. Sadly older.

"I'm sorry. You look like a man I knew," she paused, thinking. "God, it has to be thirty years ago now."

Thirty-three, actually.

She laughed then, her pretty laugh still the same as that of the twenty-something woman he'd once known. Her blue eyes twinkled then too, also just the same as all those years ago.

"But of course, you couldn't be him."

"No," Michael said, knowing there was no way to tell her the truth.

She stared at him for a moment longer, then shook her head, still looking as if she'd seen a ghost. "Sorry to interrupt your drink."

She started to turn, and before he thought better of it, he reached out and touched her arm to stop her.

"Did you think I was Michael Archer?"

She spun back to him, her eyes wide again, shining like perfectly cut blue topazes. For a moment, she appeared almost young again. But the instant was fleeting, and she again looked more like a woman he didn't know.

"Yes."

He smiled. "I'm his . . . son." Was that really the most believable lie he could come up with? Yes.

Allie smiled, the gesture filled with something very much like relief. Michael supposed his explanation was a relief. Far better than seeing things.

"I should have guessed that," she said with another smile. "You look just like him."

"I've heard that before."

She smiled, and then to his surprise, took the stool beside him.

"I was a good friend of your father's," she told him and her smile turned wistful. He understood that expression completely. He wanted to go back to those days too.

But even as his own melancholy filled him, he managed to ask casually, "What's your name?"

"Allie Gomez . . . well, your father would have known me as Allie Lewis."

Gomez. She'd married. Of course she would have in over thirty years. Her life had gone on, just like everyone else's. Everyone but him.

As a slayer he didn't age like normal humans, so it wasn't unusual that the humans he knew aged, changed, but this was different. In his past, he ended relationships, he changed names, locations, jobs. And The Brethren were exceedingly careful not to encounter any of their past. They did the moving on.

This time everyone else had moved on, and Michael didn't like it. He didn't like seeing Allie as she was now. Totally different from his memory, with only fleeting glimpses of the woman he'd once known.

"What happened to your father?" she asked. "I mean, his friend Gabriel told me that he was transferred to a new assignment. Gosh, I haven't seen Gabriel in years and years either."

Of course he could count on Gabriel to try to smooth things over as well as he could. And it was an easy enough lie to tell her. She'd thought all of The Brethren were Secret Service, which in essence they were. They used that cover to make it easy to move on without being in touch again. Reassigned with no forwarding address. But it was still hard that he hadn't gotten to tell her that lie himself.

"Yes, he was reassigned."

Allie nodded, not asking any more. She'd learned early on in their friendship that he wouldn't give her any answers. So why would his son. Maybe his son didn't even know either.

She laughed then. "Would you believe that your father and I dated?"

Michael didn't hesitate. "Sure."

She smiled at him, the gesture almost grateful. "Well, I did look a lot different in those days. But life hasn't always been easy, and I guess its taken its toll."

"You look fine."

She smiled at him again, then waved to the bartender. She must be a regular still—or maybe she even worked here—because the tatted bartender came over immediately with a glass of white wine.

"Is she giving you a hard time?" the bartender asked sternly as he set the glass in front of her.

Michael opened his mouth to assure him she wasn't, but Allie spoke first.

"Devon, I can still spank you for being fresh."

The bartender, Devon, smiled, his big grin ruining his whole angst-filled look. His smile suddenly seemed very familiar too.

"This is my son," Allie said, and it suddenly made sense that Michael knew that smile.

"This is the son of an old friend of mine," Allie explained to Devon. She turned to Michael. "I'm sorry, I didn't get your name."

"Mi—Mark," Michael said, catching himself. "Mark."

Devon nodded. "Nice to meet you." Then he left them to wait on a new customer.

"My life hasn't always gone the way I wanted," Allie said, after taking a sip of her wine. "I lost my husband, Devon's dad, to a stupid car accident. I worked two jobs to keep Devon fed and clothed and safe. But all of that was worth it."

"I'm sorry," Michael said, wishing she'd had a different life.

But she surprised him with another of her familiar,

huge smiles. A smile that really did make her look lovely.

"I'm not. Life is about change, and survival, and making the best of whatever the fates offer you. I'm sure your father knew that."

Michael stared at this old friend, who might look different, but was still the same amazing, positive, beautiful woman he remembered.

"Yes, he does know that."

Chapter Four

"Holy shit," said Simon, the most outspoken of The Brethren, as soon as Michael stepped into the mailroom the next morning. "You look almost normal. I mean, you know, normal for this decade."

Gabriel and Jacob turned to look at what had garnered such a reaction.

Gabriel raised a suspicious eyebrow, but Jacob smiled and nodded with approval.

"Looking good."

Michael smiled back, running a hand over his newly cut hair, a style the hairdresser had assured him was popular now. Then he adjusted his plain oxford button-down shirt, and ran his hands down his black trousers as if to smooth the already wrinkle-free material. No more silky, floral disco shirts. No more bell-bottoms—which wasn't a real loss actually.

"Looking good? Isn't that a seventies phrase?" Michael teased, ignoring Gabriel's skeptical expression.

"Hey," Jacob said, "I didn't say 'Dy-no-mite.' "

Michael laughed.

"Seriously," Jacob added, "you look good. I think the twenty-first century is going to agree with you."

Michael nodded, still not looking at Gabriel. "I think you are right."

"Great," Simon muttered from behind his mug of coffee. "Michael is back, and he'll get all the chick action again."

"Damned right," Michael said, feeling like the dynamic with his fellow slayers was finally normal again. He could do this.

Then he glanced at Gabriel, who was the only one still not smiling.

"So what brought about this sudden change?" Gabriel said, jogging up behind Michael as he headed toward the mailroom's employee break room.

Michael glanced at him, entering the room. "I just realized that I have to try to fit in here."

"Really?"

"Yes, really. I know things have changed and I have to try to change along with them."

Gabriel raised that damn eyebrow again. "This is a sudden change of heart."

Michael nodded. "I know, but now I understand I can't not be a slayer. To stay in the game, I have to learn how to be a slayer now. I have to reinvent myself, just like I have other times before."

Gabriel studied him for a moment, then finally nodded. "Okay. I'm glad you are starting to understand things have changed in the last three decades, and you have a lot to learn."

Michael nodded too, wishing he felt all the conviction he managed to put into his tone. A part of him still found this new way of battling demons ludicrous. A big part, but he knew he had to give this way a try or he wouldn't be a slayer at all.

Make the best of what the fates give you.

He would do that. Even if it killed him.

"This is Elton Silver," Eugene said to Michael. "He will be showing you around the mailroom. He will show you around down here, and he will also take you to the fifteenth floor and show you around up there as well."

Michael stared at the man in front of him. Or rather down at the man. Elton Silver was a petite, almost frail-looking old man with skin like overly tanned leather and gray hair.

This would be his superior. Damn, Silver was even worse than Eugene. This man should be retired, hell, in an old folks' home, not a lead player in a war with evil.

"Elton, this is Michael. He's a part of Gabriel's team."

The stooped man stopped sorting mail only long enough to glance at Michael. With hazy eyes that reminded Michael of some ancient voodoo priest, the old man gave him an unimpressed once-over, then returned to his mailroom duties.

"Elton is the best at seeing what needs to be done up on the fifteenth floor," Eugene said.

Michael frowned for a minute. He understood what Eugene was saying. This man was a seer. He could tell who the demons were. But was he really the best, the one they sent into the middle of the devil's lair? This old man?

"He has access to the whole fifteenth floor," Eugene explained. "So you can get a full understanding of what the mailroom is dealing with."

It was on the tip of Michael's tongue to ask why The Brethren didn't just go up there with this brilliant old seer and take out every demon he sensed. But that would defeat his determination to at least learn this new way of demon hunting. He was trying to go into it as open-minded as possible.

He looked back at the slight, hunched man who would teach him how this new DIA worked.

But damn, this was going to be hard.

"That is all that we ask," Eugene said quietly from beside him.

"What?" Michael frowned at him.

"Oh, you must have missed the first part of what I said," Eugene said in his placid way. "I said all we ask is that you learn as much as you can."

Michael regarded Eugene for a moment, again feeling like the old man hadn't said that, but rather just answered his thoughts. Read his mind.

"Well, come on," Elton said, sounding just as doubtful about dealing with Michael as the slayer was to be dealing with him.

Michael glanced at Eugene, who nodded like an encouraging father.

He could do this. Keep an open mind. An open mind.

Okay, his mind was quickly closing.

Michael followed behind the doddering Elton as the man . . . delivered the mail. The very thing he'd been doing for the past two hours. He pushed his cart, leaving stacks of letters or packages—or sometimes even both, which was particularly exciting—at the desks and offices of *HOT!* employees.

Behave, Michael. Sarcasm wasn't going to help him keep an open mind. But damn. So far, he wasn't feeling any more confident that the DIA's new way of dealing with demons was working. So far, he didn't see anything happening. Period. Well, except for fairly efficient mail delivery.

Of course, Elton hadn't actually explained anything to him. In fact, aside from muttering to himself in some senile, old-man way that Michael couldn't really hear or follow, Elton hadn't said much. Period.

Michael looked around the offices and cubicles of the ultra-modern fifteenth floor. Really, with the red lights and sleek glass and chrome office furniture, broken up by velvet oversized chairs, he sort of felt like he was back in the seventies.

But again he was reminded he couldn't behave the way he would have in the seventies. With a sigh and another determined reminder to try to learn this new way of doing things, he asked, "So are all these employees—you know?"

For the first time, Elton's movements were sudden, not slow and tottering. He jerked the cart to a stop and his head snapped in Michael's direction.

"Are you trying to be overheard?" he demanded harshly through his clenched teeth.

Okay, not the right start, obviously.

"No. But I figured I should start asking you something, since you aren't offering me any info on your own."

Elton raised an eyebrow, his dark eyes still rheumy, but somehow also sharp, intent.

"I've heard of you," he said softly, his voice filled

with disdain. "Your friends talked about you like you were a legend."

Michael didn't know how to react to Elton's comment. He was surprised to hear that his team talked about him that way. Especially given how little they had backed him since his return. Michael also didn't get the feeling that Elton was impressed, or saw him as a potential legend. In fact, Elton's narrowed eyes raking over him looked far from impressed.

"I'm not sure what you find so objectionable about me," Michael said. "I'm just trying to understand what you do, and how this all works now."

Elton stared at him a moment longer, then began pushing the cart again, apparently not about to offer him any more thoughts or information.

Michael stood there a moment, debating just heading back to the mailroom. Clearly Elton didn't intend to show or tell him a thing. But just as he would have turned and stalked back to *HOT!*'s main lobby, Elton surprised him again by calling out.

"Come on. You want to know everything, right?"

Michael frowned, but nodded. He didn't understand what had just happened, but he jogged the few steps to catch up with the old man.

Elton wheeled the cart past a few more cubicles, placing mail in the bins on the desks, and Michael wondered if Elton really had any intention of sharing what the DIA was doing. Maybe he just didn't want Michael heading back to report that he wasn't sharing his knowledge.

Michael looked at the old man, again pushing the cart, or maybe using it more like a walker. Again, Michael wondered what this elderly man could really share with him.

But he followed, as he had for hours. Only after a

few more moments did he realize Elton was leading him away from the cubicles and offices. He stopped in an alcove that was far enough away so Elton could talk.

"I don't agree with all that the DIA is doing," Elton said, his deep, gravelly voice so low that Michael had to lean forward to hear him.

"You don't?" Michael was surprised.

"No," Elton stated. "I want to see all the demons killed. Destroyed."

Again, he managed to surprise Michael.

"I don't like that we have to wait around for the computer geeks and scientists and other brainiacs to figure how to save all of them."

"Save them all?"

"The ones who have lost their souls already."

Michael shook his head, not following. What was the old man talking about? Michael knew that the demons who'd taken over *HOT!* were here to gather souls and ultimately take over the human world. How could the DIA get back lost souls? Once a person made a deal with the devil, they either followed the letter of the contract and saved their souls. Or they broke the contract, and their souls were all his. There was no way to get those lost souls back. But maybe that had changed now.

"So we are just here to monitor. For the time being," Elton said. "But I have a hard time stomaching all these damned demons."

Suddenly Michael felt a kinship to the older man that he hadn't before. Elton was struggling with how things were done too. It was good to know someone else felt the same way he did.

Somehow that made dealing with the situation a little easier. To not feel that everyone thought he was completely mad.

"Sorry to be such an old grouch," Elton added, as he started pushing the cart again. "But I feel like we have the most elite team available, and every day we are losing more . . ."

He glanced around to make sure they weren't being overheard. "More people."

Michael nodded. He understood that. That was how he felt and he'd only been back for a few weeks. Elton had been doing this for years. Michael really did feel a camaraderie with the old man.

"Elton, Elton, wait."

Michael turned to see who was calling, and instantly recognized the speaker as the woman from the elevator.

"I'm sorry," she said, a little breathless, as if she'd run to catch him. Michael's pulse sped up at the sound. Strange something like that could make him react.

Although there was no denying she was beautiful.

She waved an envelope at Elton. "I need to get this in the mail today."

Elton turned too, and a smile split the man's face, revealing slightly crooked front teeth.

"Liza," he greeted the woman, "I swear you are always dashing after me with something you forgot."

The woman, Liza, smiled too, the gesture seeming somewhat . . . sad, although Michael couldn't be sure.

"I know." She sighed. "I guess I just have too much going on in my head."

Elton nodded sympathetically, then took the envelope from her. "No fear. It will be on its way today."

"Thank you, Elton. You're the best."

Liza immediately started back to wherever she'd come from, but then finally noticed Michael. She paused, frowning slightly.

"Hi," she said, almost tentatively, her green-blue eyes filled with something akin to confusion.

He nodded, suspecting that she recognized him, but couldn't place where she'd seen him.

She opened her mouth as if to say something else, but then nodded too, and hurried away. Michael watched her go, wishing she'd said something more.

"Poor Liza," Elton said and when Michael tore his gaze away from the woman's lovely retreating backside, he saw the other man was watching her too, but not with the same thoughts exactly.

Elton shook his head and began pushing the cart again.

Michael strode the few steps to walk beside him.

"So she's one of the people we are trying to help?"

Elton nodded. "Poor woman."

Michael wanted to ask more, but a tall, elegantly dressed woman brushed past them; a shorter, heavier woman, not nearly so well turned out or polished, scurried after her.

"Pardon us," the more frazzled woman said, with a pained little smile. The tall woman didn't even register that she'd all but shoved Elton out of the way.

Elton muttered something under his breath once they'd disappeared down the hallway.

"Was that—?" He didn't finish the sentence, knowing Elton would understand.

The old man nodded, "Evil. Yes, that was Finola White."

Finola White. Michael had only been back to the DIA a brief time, but he knew exactly who she was.

The devil's consort, his right hand, the head demon in charge of *HOT!* magazine and this takeover.

And despite himself, Michael's fingers flexed. If he'd had his sword, she would have been an easy kill. Over before she even knew it was coming.

But Elton had said they believed they could now save lost souls. For a moment, his mind went to Liza. She was one of those humans.

"Come on," Elton said. "I'll show you to the queen's hive."

Michael followed.

Chapter Five

So that man from the other day was a mailroom employee. Liza dropped down into her office chair, staring blankly at her cluttered desk.

He looked different today somehow. Better.

Can this be? A loud yawn echoed through her head. *Thinking about a man again. Two times in as many days. Interesting.*

Liza gritted her teeth, forcing her thoughts to remain focused on work. She looked at the mock-up of the new summer fashion review. Did it look too jumbled?

Another yawn reverberated in her head and while she winced at the sound, she didn't mind it. Yawns were good. That meant he was going to just go back to sleep.

She scanned the second page of the spread.

He had looked different. That was for certain. What had it been?

Thinking about him again? Finally something interesting. Well, maybe I should stay awake a bit longer.

"Shut up," she muttered, refocusing on her work.

Testy, testy.

She gritted her teeth. After six years, it was a wonder she had any teeth left in her head.

Six years. Damn, she was tired.

Tell me about it. I definitely could be possessing a far more interesting person.

"I wish you would."

A laugh filled her head. She closed her eyes, truly wondering how much longer she could do this. Sanity felt like it was slipping further away with each passing day.

She frowned down at the layout, narrowing her eyes, determined to get her work done so she could be through yet another day.

The summer fashions were bright and cheery this coming season. She tried to focus on the job she'd once loved. Adored. Been brilliant at. She'd built *HOT!* magazine into the fashion industry powerhouse it now was.

Finola White was taking the credit.

But Liza had been the editor-in-chief who had put the magazine on the top, and now it was her job to keep it there. Or Finola would make sure Liza was no longer on top, but deep, deep below. In Hell.

Of course, Liza was already in hell.

You and me both, sister.

Liza ignored the comment and continued with her task, glad that work did seem to quiet down the demon who resided inside her. Only after several more minutes did the man who'd been with Elton creep back into her thoughts. Something had been different about him. Something that made him even more attractive than the day before.

His clothes were better, she realized. They actually fit. But that wasn't the only thing. She considered what she remembered about him, which she would have thought was basically everything. After all, he really had made a big impression on her.

She thought about him standing outside the elevator, and all she could recall was that he'd been gorgeous. And he was just as gorgeous today.

Gorgeous, huh? Even in ill-fitting clothes. I have got to see this guy.

Liza let out a low growl and reached under her desk for her purse.

Oh no, you don't. You are not going to do this to me again. I've already warned you that I will tell Finola.

It was Liza's turn to laugh.

"You, my dear, can tell her. All she cares about is that I stay at this job and get this magazine out at a standard that will keep her on top."

I control you, bitch.

"No, you don't. Finola controls us both. We are just stuck with each other. We're both Finola's puppets."

Her demon was silent. For a moment.

Finola will always take my side.

"No, you have been commanded to possess me to make sure I keep this magazine on top. And to make sure I will continue doing it, because that's the only way to get rid of you. As long as Finola has that control and gets what she wants, she doesn't care what I do. Or what happens to you."

Silence again, and then a low growl of frustration.

"Exactly."

This time she grabbed her purse and stood up.

"Time to really let you get some rest."

Bitch.

"The demon's lair," Elton whispered, leading Michael down yet another hallway where recessed lighting illuminated the red walls. *HOT!* really did look the way Michael imagined Hell might—at least the corporate sections of the magazine.

As he approached the small reception area, he noticed the woman who had been chasing Finola down the hallway. She sat at a desk, a phone to her ear, her fingers flying over her computer keyboard, unless she stopped to jot down notes on a clipboard beside her. Now that she wasn't racing after her demanding and purely evil boss, Michael could see her better. With her multicolored hair, which Michael thought had once been blond, and her overdone makeup, heavy black eyeliner, deep green eye shadow, and deep purplish-red lipstick, she looked more like someone who should be working at a tattoo parlor or vintage store than a high-end fashion magazine.

She certainly didn't look like the type of woman Finola White would hire for her personal assistant.

Elton approached the desk with a large bundle of mail. Michael lingered back, taking in the whole area. The receptionist was so busy she was oblivious to anything but her work.

It appeared this woman was one of the naïve humans who'd been lured in by Finola's irresistible promises and now found herself working to keep her mortal soul.

Possibly she was a demon, but he doubted it. He didn't think a demon would take that particular form. Demons were notoriously vain, and while the girl wasn't exactly unattractive, she wasn't a knockout. A demon would be nothing less than gorgeous.

Liza popped into his mind. She was the type of human a demon would emulate. But Elton's reaction to her made it clear she was also one of the unfortunates who'd gotten taken in by a demon's pretty promises. False promises.

Suddenly Michael was glad things had changed, that the DIA was working on saving lost souls. Like Elton, he still didn't understand not taking out the demons—or the possessed for that matter. But saving the people lured in—that would be a wonderful thing.

Michael watched the receptionist again, and from her intensity, he guessed she had to be working on something important for the demanding Ms. White. He stepped a little closer so that he could peer through the glass walls that kept the rest of the world away from Finola and her minions.

Elton wasn't exaggerating when he said it was like a beehive back there, a honeycomb of glassed-in boardrooms and offices.

In one of the boardrooms off to the side, Michael noticed a movement, then realized that someone sat in one of the high-back, red velvet chairs at the board-room table. The person's head was ducked as if he appeared to be writing something down. He also appeared to be occasionally talking to someone beside him, although Michael couldn't see anyone there.

Michael stepped even closer, scrutinizing the man more intently. What was the guy doing?

"That's Finola White's assistant editor and right-hand man, Tristan McIntyre," Elton whispered from beside him. "He's just as bad as she is. In fact, I think he could be worse, if given the chance."

Michael glanced at Elton. "So why are we giving him that chance?"

Michael's fingers twitched involuntarily like they always did in the presence of a demon. Itching to be curled around his sword, blade poised to strike. He was so close. It wouldn't be difficult at all to go in there and behead the bastard. A perfect opportunity to rid the world of one filthy, vile minion of Satan himself.

They watched as the demon turned to speak to someone again. What was he doing? Michael still didn't see anyone. But the demon was definitely talking to someone. Who?

Liza had been doing the same thing in the elevator. Although he'd decided she was probably using one of those headset things. Shit, why couldn't he remember what were they called? Blue . . . teeth. Something like that.

"He's talking to something," Elton said, and again Michael stopped watching the demon and looked back at the old man. Elton's eyes were narrowed as if he were seeing something. Of course, he was seeing something.

"Can you tell what it is?" Michael asked quietly.

Elton shook his head. "It's small and evil. But I can't tell what it is. A demonic presence of some sort."

The old man again surprised Michael with another sudden movement. "I have to go tell Eugene about this right away. This is something I have not seen before. This is an interesting change."

Elton hurried out of the reception area, moving like a spry young man. Amazing.

Michael looked back through the window, trying to see what Elton had seen. He had to admit seers did have an amazing ability. One he'd never fully appreciated, he guessed.

Just then, Tristan McIntyre stopped in what appeared to be midsentence and peered out through the glass walls, his eerie gaze landing directly on Michael as if he'd suddenly sensed he was there.

For a moment, their eyes met, but then Michael managed to rally and head toward the receptionist's desk. The receptionist still hadn't noticed him and he'd been only a few feet away. And Michael hadn't even been using his warrior stealth.

This woman was definitely human.

"Hey," he said quietly to the assistant, not glancing back at Tristan McIntyre again.

The woman behind the desk started, blinking up at him.

"Sorry to interrupt you," he said. "I'm just here to pick up any late outgoing mail you might have."

The woman, whose nameplate read Georgia Sullivan, cast a look around her cluttered desk, clearly having some trouble shifting gears from what she had been working on to his question.

"Umm, here you go," she said, snatching up a couple of letter-sized envelopes and handing them to him.

"Thanks," he said, glad she actually had something. It made his reason for being there look legitimate. But even though his cover was still intact, he didn't linger. He didn't want to draw attention on his very first patrol.

He added the letters to the cart, then headed back toward the offices and cubicles in the center of the *HOT!* floor, making sure to look busy with the cart and mail as he went.

Once he was back down the red hallway and out of view of the receptionist area, he stopped, wondering what McIntyre had been up to in that boardroom. And what he'd been talking to. Was Satan bringing in some other form of demons? And did that mean this demonic warfare was about to take another twist?

Maybe The Brethren would be needed after all.

Michael considered going back and trying to see if he could get closer and discover what exactly the demon was doing, but then decided that wasn't a good plan. Not now. Not on his first night up here.

Still he didn't move, fighting the urge to go back and see what else was happening. Fighting that inherent urge within him to see McIntyre and whatever other demon he was dealing with dead.

"Damn it!"

Michael slowly turned his head, listening. Who had just sworn? He couldn't see anyone, and for a fraction of a second he wondered if something demonic was near him now. But then he heard the other noises. The thump of a paper towel dispenser being pumped. A rattling like that of something in a plastic container, followed by the glugging, bubbling noise of water. Recognizable noises, not demonic.

"Damn it," came the voice again. Female and frustrated.

Silently, he moved away from the mail cart and toward the noises.

Reaching the same alcove where he and Elton had paused to talk, he realized it housed the restrooms. He paused outside the ladies' room, wondering if he should really open the door and peek in. After all, it didn't sound like the person inside was in any severe distress.

Just then something hit the wall and bounced on the floor, followed by, "You aren't going to stop me. Damn it."

The voice was louder and more agitated.

Michael didn't hesitate any longer. He pushed the door open and peered inside. The brightness of the fluorescent lighting and blinding white tiles made it hard to focus after the red lighting of the hallway. But his eyes did adjust, and he saw a woman standing at the sink.

Even though he couldn't see her face, only her stat-uesque build and long, wavy black hair, he knew ex-actly who stood there. Involuntarily, his gaze dropped to the delightful curve of her derriere. Yes, definitely Liza.

"Enough!" she muttered then, and Michael wasn't sure if she was talking to him. "I've had enough. I can't take any more."

She turned slightly, showing him enough of her profile that he could see her perfectly shaped lips and nose. She looked down, her hair falling forward to hide even those features from him.

Then he realized she was looking down at some-thing clutched in her hand. With her other hand, she fumbled with it, her movements jerky and awkward. Like she didn't quite have control of herself. But de-spite her strange movements, he saw what she held. A pill bottle.

She finally got the childproof cap off the bottle and dumped over a dozen of the small pink pills into her palm. She immediately clutched her fingers around them as if they were precious jewels that might slip through her fingers.

Before he realized what she planned to do, she lifted her palm up to her lips and tilted her head back, cramming the pills into her mouth like a handful of M&M's or peanuts. But instead of chewing, she leaned over the sink and scooped a handful of water to her mouth from the already running faucet.

Michael only watched a split second longer, realiz-ing what she'd done. And what she intended those pills to do.

She was committing suicide.

She was still in the middle of ladling more water to her lips, when Michael grabbed her around the waist.

She screamed then, and with amazing agility and more strength than he would have guessed she could have, she shoved herself free of him.

He let her go and she crossed the bathroom before spinning to see who her attacker had been. Though he didn't think of himself as her attacker, but as her rescuer.

She gaped at him. "What are you doing in here?"

"What did you just take?" he demanded, his eyes roaming her stunned features, searching for any ill effects. She looked alert and scared. Of course, it would be too soon to see any consequences yet anyway.

"What did you take?" he repeated, his voice harder.

Instead of answering him, she stated sternly, "You can't be in here. This is the ladies' room."

Chapter Six

Liza wanted to scream. Just her luck. It would be Mr. Hunky who caught her downing a handful of allergy meds. And she knew exactly what he thought he was witnessing.

Her OD'ing.

And he looked surprisingly unhappy about it. He glowered at her, and she also noted his harsh expression did very little to mar his handsome features. Intelligent dark eyes; full, almost sultry lips; and chiseled jawline.

Leave it to you to finally be alone with a hot man when you are about to be hopped up on allergy medicine.

"Shut up," Liza hissed under her breath, but unfortunately the giant in front of her didn't miss the softly muttered comment.

He frowned, his dark brows coming together in sudden confusion. "Excuse me?"

Come on, touch him. Give me a little peek before I pass out.

"Hell, no."

The man's glower turned to a look of real concern. He took a step toward her.

Liza raised a hand to stop him. "Stay right there."

Damn it, let him touch you. A little sex-shhual arous-shu-al could be fun mixed with this high.

Liza ignored the demon, although she was relieved to hear his words were already growing slurred. Thank God his metabolism worked faster than hers.

"Don't touch me," she warned, wanting to be sure the demon was truly out. The drugs were already starting to hit her too, and she was worried how she herself might react to this man's touch, never mind damned Boris.

Bartoris, my damned name is . . .

Liza laughed, pleased that he was unconscious already.

"Liza, you need to go to the hospital."

She laughed at that. "No doctor can help me. Apparently no one can."

Were her words slurring now too? She giggled.

Michael stared at this woman, unsure what exactly to do. She was clearly being affected by the drugs and quickly. She weaved, then fell heavily against the wall.

She giggled again. "Maybe it wasn't a good idea to do that here. But I just couldn't deal anymore." She laughed again. The sound would have been adorable, if she wasn't overdosing. Which she was, and he needed to do something.

Without a second thought, he rushed to her and scooped her up. Despite her height, she was surprisingly light in his arms.

"Put me down," she gasped, even as she put her arm around his neck to steady herself.

"We have to get you to a hospital."

She shook her head, then winced as if the gesture

wasn't agreeing with her. "I'm feeling extra-woozy. Maybe I took too many."

He raised an eyebrow at that. "Yeah, I'm pretty sure you definitely took too many, sweetheart."

She smiled, her eyes closed, the gesture yet again adorable. "I like being called sweetheart."

"Okay, sweetheart, let's get you to a hospital."

She rested her head heavily against his chest and sighed. "I like your chest too."

He smiled at that, even as knew he had to hurry out of there. Maybe he should call an ambulance, but he wasn't sure how to go about that without drawing a lot of attention to the situation. As it was, carrying her out would attract a lot of notice too.

Oh well, he didn't know what else to do. She needed help. Now. He'd reached the bathroom doorway, when Liza stiffened in his arms, almost sitting up in his hold. Her hand shot out and she caught the door frame, stopping him from exiting the restroom.

"You can't touch me," she told him, her eyes meeting his and for a moment, she looked almost lucid.

"I know," he reassured her softly, deciding it was best to humor her as much as possible. "But I don't see how else to get you out of here. I will put you down soon."

She glanced around as if she didn't remember where she was, then gave a slight nod. But when he tried to step through the door again, she held fast to the door frame.

"I can walk," she said, her words still slurred, but determined.

"Sweetheart, I don't think you can."

She smiled, just briefly, then her eyes grew hard and focused again. "I can. I can't be seen like this. I can't."

Michael realized that was probably true. She was in a soul contract, and it was clear to him, even as a newly returned DIA agent, that Finola would use anything as a breach of contract. Attempted suicide included.

"Okay," he agreed, although he really wasn't sure she could stand. But slowly he slid her down his body and onto her feet. She wobbled, but managed to gain some balance.

"You are going to have to hold on to me." He slipped an arm around her back.

She nodded, allowing him to help. "I guess it's okay. He won't see anything now."

Michael wasn't exactly sure whom she was referring to, but he suspected it had to be that demon he'd seen in the boardroom. Tristan McIntyre.

"No," Michael told her, beginning to walk her through the door. "No one will see anything. I will make sure of that."

She made a noise, although he wasn't sure whether it was in agreement or not. But she did allow herself to be walked out of the bathroom. And he didn't plan to let Finola or the diva demon's flunkies see Liza this way.

"Who was the man who was here earlier?" Tristan McIntyre asked, surprising Finola White's newest personal assistant, Georgia Sullivan, from her flurry of work.

Georgia frowned, looking around as if she expected to find the man Tristan was referring to still there.

"Who?" she finally asked.

"The man who was here just a little while ago. Tall,

dark, presumably someone you might find hand-some."

Georgia's gaze involuntarily moved over Tristan, before she caught herself. She frowned, whether trying to recall who Tristan was asking about or just a gesture of irritation with herself . . . and her attraction to Tristan, he wasn't sure.

Finally she seemed to gather herself, and a dawning knowledge widened her green eyes behind her jeweled cat's-eye glasses and heavily made-up lashes. "Oh, the man from the mailroom?"

Tristan nodded with a wry smile. "He was from the mailroom?"

"Yes, just coming around for the last mail pickup."

Tristan considered that for a moment, then nodded.

"Thanks, Peaches," he said, unable to stop himself from using the ridiculous nickname he'd given her on the day she'd started here.

Her reaction to his little endearment filled the air instantly. A sweet, ripe scent that seemed to mimic the fruit he'd just called her drifted all around him.

Tristan smiled to himself. Oh, she was ripe for him all right, and as a demon of lust, he savored her attraction like a particularly delicious indulgence. Quirky and chubby wasn't usually his type, but her desire was so strong, it was hard not to admire it and play with her. Just a little.

But he only had a moment to tease and torment her, because he was in the middle of something bigger than even his own libido.

"Don't stay too late," Tristan called back to the assistant, breathing in her reaction one last time before he headed back to his meeting.

"So who was he?"

Tristan stepped back into the boardroom and took a seat before answering. "Just someone from the mailroom. No one of any consequence. Although I don't recall ever seeing him before. It is good, however, to see they are finally following Finola's demands and only hiring attractive people."

"Well, soon they will be following *our* demands."

Tristan smiled in agreement, reaching for his computer tablet. He tapped the now black screen, then typed in his password. His notes from earlier appeared.

"Finola only needs to make a few more mistakes, and Satan will step in and banish her back to Hell himself."

Tristan nodded. "And all we need to do is make sure she slips up. The best way to do that is to get her to cast a couple more souls to Hell by breaking their contracts unfairly."

"That won't be hard. We could probably just sit back and let her do that all on her own. But if we pick the targets for her, it will make things go quicker and easier."

"I agree. So who?" Tristan sighed. "Maybe attractive mailroom staff isn't such a good thing after all. I'm sure we could easily get her to dispose of a few souls there."

"What about her new personal assistant? She seems like an obvious choice. Finola is unrealistic and brutally hard on them. It would take very little maneuvering to get Finola annoyed with that girl. And voilà, one contract broken. Plus, her looks are bound to get on Finola's nerves."

Tristan's hand paused in his note-making. Peaches. He hated to admit it, but he would miss the luscious scent of her. And he did kind of enjoy her quirkiness, but he supposed she was the most obvious choice. And she was expendable.

He nodded, jotting down her name.

"But," he found himself adding, "we should have several others, just in case. Finola isn't always as predictable as we'd like."

"True."

As if to prove that very point, the boardroom door opened and Finola White herself sashayed into the room.

"Darling, what are you still doing here?"

Tristan automatically pulled up another application to hide the notes he'd made, then shifted in his seat to greet his superior. His superior for the time being.

"I'm just finishing up some work for the new Greta Shields layout."

Finola raised an eyebrow, but Tristan wasn't sure whether the gesture indicated she was impressed or in doubt.

"That is very industrious of you," she said, stepping over to the table and leaning in to look at his tablet. Apparently the eyebrow arch had been one of doubt.

Fortunately the application he'd pulled up was indeed the layout of an up-and-coming designer's spread for *HOT!*

Finola touched a finger to the screen, dragging the pages so she could see them all.

Finola nodded, her expression definitely impressed now. "It looks wonderful, Tristan. Truly wonderful. I'm almost wondering now why we keep that dreadful Liza McLane around. You are learning the fashion magazine ropes quite well."

Tristan thanked her, and silently thanked Satan himself that he'd actually opened the correct application in his rush.

"If I didn't know you so well, and know how much you love your creature comforts and personal time, I'd start to think you were becoming a workaholic."

Tristan chuckled. "Hardly. You know I'm too self-indulgent to work too hard. And that's why we have to keep that dreadful Liza McLane working here. I just happened to have a couple ideas and decided I should get them down before I forgot. I'm actually finished."

He rose. Reaching for his briefcase on the chair beside him, he placed his tablet inside.

"Speaking of working late, what are you doing back here?" Tristan asked, keeping his voice casual as he zipped up his case. Was Finola more aware of the changes in Tristan than he'd believed? Sometimes Finola was surprisingly perceptive. "Aren't you supposed to be at a gala hosted by Stella McCartney? I heard even Paul was going to be there."

"Yes," Finola said and Tristan noticed for the first time she was dressed in a white and crystal-encrusted evening gown. The gown was beautiful, but Finola was always wearing something extravagant and white, so truthfully they all blended together in his mind.

"I just came back here to get my sweet little puppy," she explained. "And there my baby is!"

She sashayed over to the chair next to Tristan to pick up her maltipoo, Dippy. "You know the McCartneys—totally animal crazy. And I forgot that my precious boy was on the invitation too."

Tristan nodded, shooting her dog a covertly regretful look.

"So I came back here, but I couldn't find him," she crooned with a little pout. "That awful new assistant of mine was supposed to be taking care of him tonight, but she claimed she hadn't seen him. I should have known you would look after him for me."

Exactly on cue, the little white dog yipped.

"Oh my lovely baby," she cooed, cuddling the squirming ball of fluff to her cheek. She snuggled him for a moment, then glanced back at Tristan.

"I should have guessed my precious would be with you. He's been spending a lot of time with you these days." Finola looked almost peevish, but the expression quickly disappeared. She didn't like emotions that might make her perfect features look less than flawless.

Tristan shrugged and waved a dismissive hand in the air. "I just think that beast is half-cat. He lives to pester the one person who doesn't adore him."

Dippy growled.

Finola laughed at that and nuzzled her pet again. "That is probably true." She then headed to the door. "Well, I must go."

Tristan, now alone, watched Finola leave the offices through the glass walls. He finished gathering his stuff and headed out of the boardroom.

Finola didn't have any idea what a short time she had left to be in charge of *HOT!* magazine and the demon rebellion. She also didn't realize that right at this moment she had Tristan's coconspirator tucked under her arm.

You are in for some surprises, Finola, my dear.

Chapter Seven

Hailing a cab didn't seem like the most efficient way to get an overdose victim to the ER, but Liza was a surprisingly stubborn patient, even in her less than coherent state.

Fortunately, getting a cab wasn't too difficult, and within only a few minutes he had her maneuvered into the backseat and had ordered the cabbie to get them to the closest hospital.

"I don't need a doctor," she insisted again for at least the fifteenth time.

Her head lolled against his shoulder as she said it. But her words were a little less slurred. He prayed that was a good sign.

"You probably don't," Michael lied, discovering very quickly it was easier to get her to cooperate if he humored her. "But just tell me one thing, what did you take?"

She nuzzled her cheek against his shoulder. "Just allergy medicine."

Okay, he didn't know anything about allergy medicines or how much it would take to overdose on them. But he did know having her cuddled up against him felt good, which was a highly inappropriate thought given that she was possibly headed toward coma or heart failure.

"How many do you think you took?" he asked, ignoring the fact that she now had a hand on his chest, almost . . . caressing him.

Focus, man. What the hell was wrong with him?

He felt her shrug. "I'm not sure. Maybe twenty. Maybe thirty. Just a few." She held her thumb and forefinger slightly apart to indicate just a tiny amount.

Twenty or thirty? That was not "just a few." He leaned forward, which caused Liza's head to slip off his shoulder and wedge between his back and the taxi seat.

"Put the pedal to the metal," Michael urged loudly.

The cabdriver gave him a strange look in the rearview mirror, but did speed up. Behind Michael, Liza giggled, the sound muffled against his back.

"Breaker, breaker, good buddy," she said, giggling again as she managed to lever herself upright on her own before he could help her.

He didn't understand her reaction; clearly she was getting delusional or something.

"This is fun," she suddenly announced, her head falling back against his shoulder.

"I'm glad you are enjoying yourself," he said wryly.

"It was just enough," Liza then murmured. "Enough to quiet that damned voice. God, that annoying voice."

Michael wasn't sure what exactly she meant by "that damned voice," but he suspected it was Liza's own guilt. She had to have realized the huge mistake she'd made signing a deal with Finola. People who sold their souls always realized very quickly the error of their decision. But now, from what Elton had said, maybe her soul could be broken from the bonds of the contract. She had to hold on and find out. She couldn't give up when help was, hopefully, right around the corner.

And thank God, the hospital was right around the next corner quite literally. Michael threw the driver a twenty, not sure if that was too much or not enough. He really didn't care. He had to get this woman to a doctor. Frankly, it was amazing she was still conscious at all.

This time, she didn't argue when he scooped her up in his arms.

"You really do have a nice chest," she murmured, her hands curling almost affectionately around his neck. "And really nice shoulders."

He thanked her, although his attention wasn't on her words or her roaming hands, miraculously. He remained focused on finding someone to help her. It turned out overdoses got a person to the head of the line, which in this ER was very long; the waiting room was packed with miserable-looking people. But the triage nurse only had to look at Liza, limp in his arms, and she directed them to a large room lined with hospital beds and only separated by curtains.

"Place her on the bed."

Michael did and stood back as the woman began taking her vitals.

"I'm fine," Liza tried to assure her with one of her cute giggles. And while the nurse agreed, clearly knowing that people in Liza's state dealt better with compliance, her frown as she took Liza's blood pressure and pulse didn't reassure Michael.

"Can you fill out the top of this form?" the nurse asked. "I will have a doctor in here as soon as possible."

Michael nodded, looking down at a white form on

a clipboard. He really didn't know enough about Liza to fill in much, but he at least wrote down her first name.

"I can do that."

Michael looked up from the clipboard to find Liza sitting up in bed. She held out a hand, and aside from blinking a little more than natural, almost like she was waking up from a sleeping state, she appeared relatively fine.

"I think you should rest and wait for the doctor, sweetheart."

She gave him a stern look and again gestured to the clipboard. "You don't even know me, so I highly doubt you can fill that out."

He stared at her for a moment, amazed that she suddenly seemed almost totally lucid. Actually more than lucid; completely in control like she was back at her job, rather than in a hospital bed.

He handed her the board.

She pulled the pen out from under the clip and started to fill in the paperwork.

"Are you feeling better?" he asked, almost hesitantly. She looked a hundred times better, but how could that be?

"I told you I'd be fine," she said, her voice clipped almost as if she was annoyed with him.

Before he could say anything else, the doctor pushed back the curtain, rushing into the small cubicle, clearly expecting to find a patient in serious distress. She immediately halted as soon as she saw Liza sitting up in bed, filling out her own forms.

"I'm sorry." The doctor frowned. "I think I must have the wrong cubicle." She double-checked the chart the nurse had filled out earlier. "Are you Liza McLane?"

* * *

Liza looked up from the form she did not want to be filling out, seeing this as her opportunity to get out of there, but that hope was quickly dashed when she realized her would-be rescuer was bound to correct her if she tried to deny being Liza McLane. "Yes, I am, but I think we've just had a small misunderstanding. Nothing major is wrong with me. I was just experiencing a little light-headedness, but now I feel—"

But the man, the mailroom clerk and hunk, interrupted, "She took at least twenty allergy pills."

She just knew he wasn't going to let her get out of here. Not easily anyway.

The doctor looked from Liza to the man, then back to her.

"You look surprisingly alert for someone who took that many pills."

Liza smiled, giving both the doctor and the man an indulgent look. "I'm sorry. I fear he misunderstood. I said I took too many allergy pills. I took four, which I know is too many, but honestly my allergies are just making me crazy." She rubbed her nose for good measure. "I knew it was too much and it did make me a little loopy. And my friend here overreacted. Believe me, nothing like this will ever happen again."

That much was true. She knew better than to medicate her demon at work. She'd just been so tired of Boris and his constant running commentary. And it had been the end of the day. She'd intended to take the pills, go back to her office, wait out the side effects, and enjoy a quiet evening at home.

But here she was in the hospital. What a waste of her quiet time.

She forced another smile at the doctor, trying to ignore the baffled expression of the man beside her.

The doctor looked at the chart in her hands again. "What did you take?"

"Just Benadryl."

The doctor nodded as if that confirmed what she had written down there.

"And you say you only took four?" she asked, looking up from the chart.

Crap, she wasn't buying Liza's explanation either, but Liza nodded.

"Well, the nurse recorded here that your blood pressure and pulse were very highly elevated. Both of which would be a symptom of antihistamine overdose."

"Maybe I should stop taking them then," Liza said, trying to sound duly concerned. "Wouldn't that be something if I was allergic to allergy medicine?" She forced a laugh.

The doctor nodded. "That is actually a possibility. And I would definitely recommend not taking this type any longer. I would also recommend we do some blood work as well. Just to see exactly how high the levels of the drug are in your system."

No. No, Liza couldn't risk that. She had no idea how the high dosage of allergy medicine would appear in her bloodstream. All she knew was that high doses knocked out the damned demon possessing her, and aside from a few minutes of wooziness and confusion herself, she always felt fine. And she had a blessed six to eight hours of peace.

She couldn't risk that the antihistamine would show up as an unusually high dose. If the doctor thought she really had tried to kill herself, she'd be admitted, and that she absolutely couldn't risk. She dared to drug the demon, but she sure as hell didn't dare to miss work. Finola White would really make her pay then.

Liza shook her head. "I don't want to do that."

From behind the doctor, the man looked like he was going to argue, but when Liza shot him a warning look, he remained silent.

"Well, you do seem fine now," the doctor admitted. "I am worried about how high your blood pressure and heart rate are, and I'd like to see them lowered before you discharge yourself. But again I can't make you stay. Only recommend it. I will, however, give you a list of allergy meds that won't affect your blood pressure."

Liza pretended to listen as the doctor discussed further reasons why maybe she'd had such an adverse reaction to the Benadryl and other ways to combat severe allergies. Mostly her attention was on her rescuer, who listened with his arms folded across his massive chest and an expression of disbelief on his handsome face.

He knew what he'd seen, and he didn't understand what was happening now. Liza understood that, and even felt a twinge of guilt. After all, he'd only been trying to help her. But she needed to stick to her story. She'd only taken a double dose, despite what he thought he'd seen.

Finally the doctor finished her exam, still concerned that Liza's heart rate was elevated, but since Liza wouldn't agree to any further treatment, and the physician clearly needed the bed in this busy ER, she had little recourse but to let Liza leave.

"I would feel better, at the very least, knowing you have someone to stay with you tonight." The doctor looked at her rescuer.

He nodded. "I will stay with her."

Liza appreciated the man's lie. At least that would help get her out of here. Finally.

Liza sighed as she stepped outside the hospital, breathing in the cool spring air. That had been close. And she still had her would-be savior to deal with.

He walked beside her, not saying anything, but she could feel his gaze on her. He had to be completely confused and she did feel bad about that.

"I'm sorry for getting you caught up in this mess," she said.

He shrugged. "I was just concerned."

His comment made her chest tighten and fill with an unfamiliar warmth. He had been concerned and he'd done something she hadn't seen in a long time. He'd gone out of his way to help another person.

How could she not admire that? And appreciate it? Suddenly she felt ashamed for not being more grateful. He'd been doing the right thing, and that was so nice to see.

"I'm Liza McLane," she said, not immediately offering him her hand, out of habit. But then she remembered old Boris was knocked out and she reached toward him.

He accepted her hand, his own huge and roughened and warm, encompassing hers wholly.

"Michael Archer."

His gaze roamed her face, suspicion still clear in his eyes. She supposed she didn't blame him.

"Nice to meet you, Michael. Sorry it was in such a strange way."

He nodded, his expression stating that he found the circumstances very weird indeed.

"I have never had that happen before," she said, giving him what she hoped was a believably baffled shrug. "I guess I will have to try some of the other allergy medications the doctor suggested."

He nodded again, his expression still skeptical.

"Thanks for getting me there and staying with me," she added, not sure how to bring this situation to an end. Especially before he started to ask the questions she could see he wanted to ask.

"Well, I guess I should head home and get some rest," she said, looking around, realizing she wasn't totally sure where she was. But she wasn't going to admit that fact. That would reveal that she had truly been totally out of it when he'd brought her here. Fortunately it only took her a moment to get her bearings, and she was pleased to see she was just a few blocks from her apartment.

She gestured in the direction she needed to go. "I live right up this way. So I can walk." She started to step away from him, but Michael's hand on her upper arm stopped her.

"Were you trying to kill yourself?"

She'd known he had questions, but for some reason, she hadn't expected that one.

Fortunately, it was one she could answer with all honesty.

"No, I wasn't."

His eyes roamed over her face. Beautiful eyes somewhere between green and brown. And she felt her body react to him. Again. She might have been loopy on the way here, but she still knew she'd been attracted to him. She'd wanted to touch his hard muscles and feel his wonderful warm body against hers.

And even now, she was very aware of his hand on her arm. A very strong, warm hand. She felt her cheeks burn with a combination of embarrassment and longing.

She had to go. These feelings could lead her to yet another awkward situation.

He finally nodded, apparently finding the answer he wanted on her face. Or maybe he saw her discomfort. But still he didn't remove his hand from her arm.

Heat curled through her belly and lower. Why did this man have such a powerful effect on her?

Because he was handsome, and she was so unfamiliar with the touch of another human being these days, she reminded herself. It had been years since she'd really allowed anyone to touch her. Of course she would react. But gosh, she couldn't believe how good even this simple contact felt. How would his touch feel on her bare skin?

No, no, she warned herself. Her thoughts could not go there. Even with Boris unconscious for the moment.

"Well, I should head home," she said, shifting away from his hand. He let it fall away.

"Yes, that probably is a good idea," he agreed.

She smiled, thanking him again, realizing she actually meant it. She felt better knowing there were people like this man out there in the world. It was easy to forget that, living around evil as she had been for so long.

She turned, her movement almost reluctant, even though she knew leaving was the best thing to do for both of them. Okay, she was attracted to the man, but where could this really go? She only had room for one male in her life at the moment, and that was a bitchy, annoying demon who resided inside her body. There was no place for a real, live, human male in her world. Not now, and she didn't know when.

She closed her eyes briefly, and gritted her teeth. But God, she wanted one. She wanted Michael, she realized. She'd wanted him from the first moment she'd seen him.

She groaned slightly and then opened her eyes.

"Are you okay?"

She jumped, a hand flying up to her chest at the voice coming from so close to her side. An almost comical reaction, since she heard voices all the time.

Then she saw it was Michael. He'd fallen into step beside her.

"I'm fine. You just startled me."

"Sorry," he said, giving her a genuinely contrite look.

Her heart skipped. He was so good-looking.

"Do you live in this direction too?" she managed to ask.

He shook his head. "No, but you can't really believe that I'm going to let you walk home alone after everything you've been through already."

It was on the tip of her tongue to tell him that she really would be fine, but she suddenly discovered she didn't want to say that. She was free for a few hours to be a normal woman. And she was attracted to this man. What could it hurt to simply enjoy his company for a little while? It had been so long since she'd enjoyed any company, really.

"I guess you are right," she said with a wide smile, feeling almost carefree, which seemed strange given what this man had seen tonight. But he wasn't questioning her about any of that. He was just being a nice guy. A gentleman. A hero.

"I think it would be a good idea if you walk me home."

Chapter Eight

Michael was surprised that Liza allowed him to walk her home. And he was even more surprised when she stopped on the brick steps of her apartment building and said, "Would you like to come up for a drink?"

He raised an eyebrow, but smiled. "Do you really think you need a drink along with your allergy medicine?"

She smiled, taking the comment as it was intended, as a joke.

"No, definitely not. I was thinking you could have a drink and I would stick with some herbal tea."

"Good plan," he agreed. "And yes, I would love a drink."

She nodded, the gesture almost one of determination. As if she wasn't sure whether she should be doing this, but wanted to anyway.

Michael was feeling the same way. He knew as an employee of the DIA, he shouldn't be allowing himself to become attracted to a *HOT!* employee. It was an obvious security risk, as well as a conflict of interest, but he found himself not worrying about it. Not tonight anyway. He wanted to stay with Liza, for just a while.

After all, he should be sure she was truly okay, he reasoned.

He still didn't understand how it was possible. He was positive she'd taken more drugs than she'd admitted to the doctor, but he'd also decided it must have been less than he'd thought. And the loopiness and odd comments must have been because she was allergic to that type of medication. It was the only explanation that made sense. Although she had said things that did make him think she wanted to take her life, to just end her struggles.

All the more reason to stay with her for a while. To be really sure she was okay. Her situation was a tough one, and though he couldn't reveal that he knew what she'd done, the bargain she'd made, he could be supportive in other ways.

She smiled at him again, a truly beautiful, radiant smile. Then she turned and walked up the stairs, her rear end swaying back and forth with each step.

And damn, it had been thirty-three years since he'd been near such a beautiful woman. He pulled in a deep breath, telling his long-starved libido to stay calm. This was just a drink.

Liza's fingers trembled as she fumbled with her apartment key, taking three tries to actually get it into the lock. Fortunately Michael was kind enough to act as if he didn't notice, surveying the hallway, rather than her ineptness.

"Here we go," she said, with a slight laugh, opening the door and reaching inside to flip on the light. They stepped into her small eat-in kitchen. And she was glad to see that she'd actually done her dishes this morning.

Dealing with demonic possession and an evil boss often outweighed mundane things like housekeeping. But she couldn't exactly explain that to Michael.

"Well, this is my kitchen," she said, her voice sounding a little shaky. She hoped he didn't notice. He nodded, looking around at the stainless steel appliances and wood floor.

"Very nice."

"Have a seat," she said, pointing to the café-style table and chairs. "I'll see what I have for drinks."

Behind her, she heard him pull out a chair, while she busied herself looking in her cabinets and then her refrigerator. All the while telling herself not to be nervous, to just enjoy his company and the novelty of her attraction to him.

After all, she didn't even know if he was attracted to her in return. He probably wasn't, which meant she really had nothing to be nervous about.

"Well, it looks like all I have is coffee, Sam Adams, and tea. Oh, and some orange juice." She turned, expecting him to be across the room at the table, only to discover he hadn't sat down, but leaned against the counter, only inches away from her.

She made a surprised noise, and he gave her an apologetic smile.

"I'm sorry I keep managing to startle you. Right from the very first time we met." He reached forward and brushed a strand of her always disheveled hair away from her cheek. His fingers brushed her skin, just lightly, just a fleeting touch, but with that simple brush of skin against skin, her knees felt weak.

"You cut your hair," she said, suddenly realizing that was what had changed about him.

"Yes, I did." The hand that had just touched her hair moved to his own, running through the shorter locks. "So you recognized me from the other day?"

"Yes," she said, then reached out to touch it, just as he had, ruffling the soft locks against her palm. "I like it."

She started to pull her hand away, suddenly realizing she probably shouldn't have touched him that way.

But instead, he caught her hand and pulled her closer to him. She could smell his soap and shampoo, and a spicy scent all his own, and her head swirled with a light-headedness far more intoxicating than the dizziness caused by Benadryl, or wine or any drug imaginable.

She stared up at him, not sure what to do now. It had been so long. For a moment, she just raised her face toward his and waited. And just when she was certain he would lean in and kiss her, he released her.

She swayed, unsteady and a little confused. Did he not find her attractive after all? She thought she'd seen something smoldering in his green-flecked eyes, but maybe not. She certainly hadn't had enough experience with men of late to even remember, honestly.

Taking a breath, she willed her body to calm down. Then she managed a smile. "So? What can I get you?"

She could have sworn she saw his eyes flick over her body, but then he straightened, gripping the edge of the counter, the change in position putting a little more distance between them.

"What is a Sam Adams?"

His question actually managed to distract her from her confused and desirous thoughts. Who didn't know what Sam Adams was? "It's a type of beer."

"Oh," he said, then made a face. "That was a silly question. Of course it's a beer."

She smiled.

"So the Sam Adams?"

"Sure."

She opened the fridge and leaned in to grab one from the bottom shelf. When she turned to hand it to him, she could have sworn his eyes were snapping up to meet hers as if they had been focused somewhere lower.

"Were you just checking out my butt?" she asked, then nearly groaned. What was she doing asking such a ridiculous and forward question? Did she really expect him to admit—

"Yep." He smiled, attractive creases appearing on either side of his mouth like parenthesis highlighting his beautifully sculpted lips.

Wow, she hadn't expected that. His straightforward answer and that very distracting smile. A shivery thrill tingled throughout her body. Was he really attracted to her?

"And what did you think?" My God, was she being this forward herself? Apparently she was.

"I think it's stellar."

Liza laughed at that. "Stellar, huh? I'm pretty sure no one has ever said that about my behind."

Before she realized what he intended to do, he reached forward and caught her arms, pulling her toward him until her breasts brushed against the hard wall of his chest.

This time, he did exactly what she'd thought he was going to do earlier. His head came down and his lips brushed against hers.

She moaned, stunned at how wonderful a kiss could feel. How perfect. His lips continued to move, shaping hers, controlling her.

She moaned again, and he used that moment to

deepen the kiss, his tongue seeking out hers, hot and exciting.

She wasn't sure how long the kiss lasted. Time didn't seem to exist in that moment, but all too quickly Michael pulled away.

"I'm sorry," he said, although she couldn't fathom why. What was there to be sorry about? That was perfect.

When she only stared at him in lust-hazed confusion, he added, "I didn't come up here with the intention of making a play for you."

He waited for her to react again, and when she still didn't formulate any words, he said, "I just wanted to make sure you were really okay and spend a little time with you."

She continued to stare up at him, trying to get control of her desire, but failing miserably.

"I hope you aren't offen—"

Liza cut him off, doing the only thing she could think of, the only thing she wanted to do. She pressed her lips hard to his.

She didn't want to hear any more of his explanation. She just wanted to feel his hands all over her body. Then she wanted his lips to touch every place his hands had. And she wasn't going to think about whether that was wrong, or a bad idea.

She hadn't had anything she wanted in a very long time, and she so wanted this. Michael's touch. She wasn't going to worry about the consequences right now. She was taking this.

Michael hadn't expected Liza to kiss him again. He'd had the feeling that she was nervous around him, unsure, and that was why he'd ended his kiss. He didn't want to pressure her into something she wasn't positive she wanted. But with her lips clinging to his, silently begging him, he realized he'd misread her. She wanted him in the same way he wanted her, and his long-denied libido roared to life, desire ripping through him like raging waters breaking down a flimsy dam.

Shit, it had been so long since he'd touched a woman, tasted one. He wanted to make love to Liza right here, and before he thought better of it, he spun them around so she was against the counter and he was pinning her there.

She made a low, hungry noise deep in her throat and her kisses grew more aggressive, telling him with her body that she liked his dominance. That made his desire surge even stronger.

Not breaking the kiss, he lifted her onto the countertop. The beer bottle she'd somehow managed to hold on to until now clattered loudly on the granite countertop, although neither of them stopped their frenzied embrace to see where it ended up.

Instead, with her now fully freed hands, Liza tugged at his shirt, pulling at it roughly until her hands made contact with the skin of his back.

She groaned then, her hands roaming all over him. His own hands worked the buttons of her shirt, until frustration got the better of him and he tore at the garment. Buttons popped off, clattering onto the hard work floor.

"Sorry," he breathed against her lips. "I will replace it."

"I don't care," she said, her teeth capturing his bottom lip in a desperate moment of her own. He groaned and shoved the ruined blouse off her shoulders. Under her expensive shirt, she wore a simple white bra, but Michael couldn't recall seeing anything sexier.

"Damn, you are beautiful."

She smiled and stole his breath away. Her dark hair was loose around her shoulders and face, her skin pale and flawless. The hint of perfect breasts swelled above the cups of her bra.

He tugged a strap down over her shoulder, until one breast was bared, a pale pink nipple puckering up at him.

He bent forward and licked it. Liza gasped loudly, shoving her swollen nipple harder against his mouth, silently begging him to suckle her.

He obliged, pulling the hardened bud deep into his mouth. She cried out, her nails digging into the flesh of his back.

"So sensitive," he murmured, sucking her again.

"Yes," she cried. "Yes."

He toyed with her one nipple until she was writhing and panting. Only then did he stop and pull down the other strap of her bra. With her arms effectively trapped at her sides, he took his time lapping and nipping her other nipple until she was pleading with him almost incoherently.

"Please, Michael, please."

"Please what?" He smiled against her breast, loving her responsiveness, her hunger.

"I want to kiss you," she demanded, but he didn't stop swirling a leisurely tongue around her left nipple.

"I want to kiss you too," he murmured and he finally straightened.

She lifted her face to him, her eagerness adorable.

But he had other plans. He placed his hands on both her legs, and he slowly slid her fitted skirt upward over her thighs. She made a small noise, a frustrated little groan, but shimmied her hips to allow the material farther up until it was banded around her waist like a wide belt, her small white bikini underpants exposed.

Michael spread her legs.

"I want to kiss you too," he repeated, leaning forward so his head was between her parted thighs. He ran a finger lightly over the crotch of her panties. He could feel the moisture dampening the cotton, steamy, hot.

His cock pulsed and hardened even more at the feel, at the idea of feeling that heated wetness around his rock-hard erection. She was so wet, so ready for him. And he wanted to be inside her, but not before he had a little taste of her.

"I want to kiss you there," he said, his voice low and husky with need.

He nudged aside the moist cloth and licked her. Her mons and labia were smooth, bare, a fact that surprised and excited him. He licked her again, loving how sweet and soft her bare flesh felt against his tongue.

"You are so sexy, baby," he said, delving his tongue deeper into her.

She cried out, her arms still trapped at her sides, her fingers digging into the edge of the counter. He licked her again and again, until her hips were rising off the countertop to meet each stroke, mimicking the way he wanted to thrust into her.

He raised his head, his lips wet with her arousal. She looked down at him, her eyes heavy with desire. Her own lips were deep red from their kisses and from her teeth worrying her lower lip with each orgasm he'd given her.

"I want to be inside you," he told her, and she nodded without hesitation.

"But not here," he said. "I want us both naked."

"Yes. God, yes."

He lifted her off the counter, holding her waist until she was steady; then he waited for her to lead the way.

She caught his hand and led him through the doorway into the living room. Michael had a vague impression of comfy furniture and nice big windows, but he was more intent on Liza. The sway of her hips, the way her skirt was still up around her waist. Her panties clinging to her perfectly curved ass.

Liza guided him through another doorway into another room. Her bedroom.

He could make out the queen-size bed in the waning light of dusk.

She stopped at the foot of the bed, turning back to him. He reached for her, unfastening her bra and tossing it to the floor. Quickly, her skirt, shoes and panties followed until she stood before him, gorgeous and naked.

He then turned to his own clothing, making short work of it.

Liza's eyes roamed over his body, appreciation evident under her desire-laden lids. But when her gaze moved back to meet his, for the first time since they'd started, Michael could see a hint of uncertainty in her aquamarine eyes.

"I should tell you it's been a long time for me," she admitted, her voice soft and unsteady.

He smiled. Oh, if she had any idea how long it had been for him.

"Believe me," he told her. "I think we are going to do just fine."

She hesitated for only a moment longer, then nodded. Given how hard his body was and how fiercely his blood pounded through it, that was all the encouragement he needed.

Chapter Nine

Liza was glad when Michael pulled her back into his arms, and his lips found hers. Somehow it was so easy to just relax and let go when he was touching her. Standing there naked was too overwhelming, too lonely. His hands on her gave her strength and conviction.

It gave her the daring to do this. To not worry about anything past this moment. She wanted nothing more than to be lost in this very instant. In fact, she hadn't even noticed that he'd walked her backward toward the bed, until he was easing her down onto it.

With the weight of his hard, muscular body pressed against her, his smooth, hot skin gliding over hers, it was easy to just give in. To just enjoy.

She groaned, and God, she did enjoy it. He felt wonderful. Perfect.

"I love the little noises you make," he whispered against her lips.

"Do you?"

"Mmmhmm."

He kissed her deeply.

She moaned for him and he laughed, the sound

wonderful, the vibration of it in his chest even more amazing. She groaned for real. He laughed again.

He lifted his head and looked down at her, brushing her tangled hair from her cheeks, his eyes roaming over her features.

"You are amazing," he told her, and while she wasn't sure he could make that assessment yet, she accepted the compliment.

And she wanted to touch him more. Touching. What a wonderful, wonderful thing. She slid her hands over his back, shaping the sinew under his velvety skin, her fingers dipping into the indentation of his spine, traveling down to the hard muscles of his buttocks. His own hands wandered over her body, her shoulders, her waist, the curve of her hips.

As wild and impulsive as their lovemaking had been in the kitchen, this round was more leisurely, more methodic. A learning of each other through their bodies. And both ways were amazing to Liza, heady and thrilling in their own right.

But by the time her roaming hands reached the thick, heavy girth of his erection, she was panting again. Both from touching him and from his touches.

Michael's breathing was uneven too, his touch growing a little more desperate. A little more demanding.

And when his finger parted her sex and began to stroke her wet flesh, she was nearly begging for him to be inside her.

She did manage to rouse herself from her desire long enough to reach into her nightstand. Michael watched, confused by what she was doing.

She fished blindly around in the drawer until she located what she was looking for. She waved the gold packet in triumph.

"What is that?"

She grinned at him, sure he was teasing. "A con-dom."

Michael frowned, but then nodded. "Okay."

She found his reaction a tad odd, but given how desperately she wanted him to be deep inside her, she wasn't going to question it now.

She ripped the packet open. "I hope this is still okay. I've had them for a while."

She never had an opportunity, or reason, to use them. But she was glad she'd still thought it wise to have some.

She sat up, sliding the condom down the length of him, which wasn't easy, given his girth.

"Is it uncomfortable?"

Michael looked down at it dubiously. "It's—okay."

She smiled sympathetically. "You are a big guy."

He looked up from his latex-squeezed penis. "Am I now?"

She nodded. "Very."

He gently pushed her back down against the pil-lows.

"Hmm, I wonder if I will fit."

Liza giggled, enjoying the teasing as much as she did everything else about this man.

"I think we should check and see."

"I agree," he said, positioning himself between her parted knees.

Slowly he eased himself inside her, and she was ac-tually surprised that he had to go slow. She hadn't done this for a long time, and the tightness of her body was proof of that. But when he was fully inside her and she was stretched and full and he started to move, his size felt . . .

"Oh my God. Amazing."

He groaned this time, a deep, pleasured sound.

Soon they were both lost in the rhythm and over-whelming sensation of their lovemaking.

And when Liza's orgasm tore through her, power-ful, breath-stealing, and perfect, she realized that in all her life she'd never been touched like this.

Michael looked down at Liza, her body curled against his side, her head on his chest. She'd been asleep now for thirty minutes or so. In fact, she'd had the quintessential "guy moment," having promptly fallen into a deep sleep almost as soon as her orgasm was finished.

Hell, he'd barely had time to ease himself off of her limp, sated body and settle in beside her, before she let out a cute little snore.

He smiled when, as if on cue, she made that sound again, a sound somewhere between a small snore and a sigh. She then nestled her cheek against his chest, and fell back into soft, even breaths.

Man—Michael stretched as much as the constraint of having Liza's body across his would allow—*that was amazing sex.*

"Dyn-o-mite," he murmured to himself, then winced. Even though that saying was out these days, damn, it had been that good, the best sex he'd ever had. And he didn't think it was the fact he hadn't had an orgasm in over three decades talking.

His reaction to Liza was unlike his feelings for any woman he could recall. He adored everything about her. Her body. Her smile. Her smell. He lifted his head to nuzzle his nose amidst her tumble of raven waves. He liked the way she could flip between being a little shy, to suddenly outspoken. He loved the sweet little noises she made.

Another snore/sigh answered his thought.

He smiled, then raised his head and breathed in her flowery, sunny scent again. He closed his eyes, savoring it.

He sighed. Again she seemed to answer him with another snore/sigh.

His whole body hummed with satisfaction. He felt content for the first time since he'd returned. Damn, that felt good.

And this woman felt good beside him. He sighed again, letting sleep drift peacefully over him.

Liza roused, coming out of a lovely, tranquil sleep. Her body warm, her limbs feeling heavy in a pleasant, relaxed way.

She stretched, her legs twining with longer legs, her fingers stroking smooth skin over hard muscles, and only then did she realize she wasn't alone in bed, and the man beside her was the reason for her satiated, deliciously weak feeling.

Michael.

She lifted her head to look up at him, his face serene and beautiful in sleep. His new haircut, mussed and adorable. His bare skin and chiseled muscles cast in the mellow golden glow of the faint light shining in from the other room.

Wow, she admired him further. Wow. This man was truly a perfect specimen of masculinity. And he'd made love to her.

She smiled, pressing a light kiss to his chest.

Amazing.

A low growl filled her head. In her bliss and contentment, she didn't even register the irritated sound for a moment.

Then another growl echoed through her head. This time a little louder. A sound she knew well and couldn't believe she had managed to ignore, even for a few seconds.

Oh God, he was waking up.

She sat upright, her heart beating wildly in her chest.

He was waking up.

She scrambled away from Michael, her movements awkward, panicked. The bed bounced under her frantic effort to move away from him.

Michael woke immediately, sitting upright too. He peered around him, surprisingly alert, considering that she had just jostled him out of a deep sleep. Or she assumed she had.

"Liza? What's wrong?"

"You—" She rushed over to her bureau and pulled out an oversized T-shirt, tugging the garment over her head. "You have to go."

"What?"

She turned toward him. Michael watched her, confusion clear on his face, his brow furrowed, his hair still adorably mussed.

So gorgeous.

Another groggy, irritated sound ricocheted through her head.

"You have to go," she repeated, almost shouting her command this time.

Michael still didn't move. But he had to. He had to go before the demon woke up. She wouldn't be able to hide her reaction to the damned thing, who would, without a doubt, be ranting in her head.

She couldn't act normal with that going on. Plus, this had been her night, her stolen moment, and she wasn't going to let a bigmouthed, interfering demon try to be a part of it. This was hers and hers alone.

But mainly, she did not want Boris to know whom exactly she'd been with. As it was, the demon knew too much. He knew she was attracted to someone, but she couldn't risk his knowing too much. She had to keep Michael away from the craziness of the demon world she was stuck in. Michael worked at *HOT!*, but he didn't need to know exactly what that meant.

"Liza? What is wrong?"

She hated that look on Michael's face, but her abruptness couldn't be helped. Maybe she could explain herself to him later, when the demon was drugged again, but right now, he just had to go.

"I told you," she said, keeping her tone hard and adamant. "I want you to leave. Now."

Michael stared at her for a moment, and when she didn't look away, didn't soften her determined glare, he finally threw his long legs over the edge of the bed and stood.

He started to move around the room, gathering his clothing, and Liza couldn't take her eyes off of him. His long, muscular legs, his broad back and shoulders, the strength rippling under that golden skin of his. He was breathtakingly beautiful and utterly masculine, like some gladiator from ancient times.

He stopped, his shirt and boxers held in his hands.

"There has to be some reason for this," he said, his tone almost pleading—or at least as close to pleading as she imagined this man ever got.

Her heart twisted in her chest, wishing she could tell him why she was acting this way. Or even better, she wished she could still be in bed with him, cradled in those strong arms.

Fuck.

And there was the reminder of why she couldn't handle this any differently—and how un-freaking-fair it was.

"I—I don't let anyone stay the night," she stated.

Again he stared at her, his eyes stony, unreadable. But then he nodded and began to pull on his clothes without any other comment.

She watched, feeling heartbroken. She should have guessed this evening would end this way. But she hadn't thought that far ahead. Hadn't that been her whole plan? To just live in the moment, with no thoughts of later.

Well, that sort of thing never really worked out, did it? Only in books and movies, where impulsive actions somehow turned into happy endings.

Another groan filled her head. The demon was close to waking up completely. She'd heard him struggle to consciousness enough times to know his pattern.

"Okay," Michael finally said, dressed. "Well, I guess I will be going."

She nodded, not daring to speak.

He nodded too, his expression one of lingering confusion and something else. Something that tore at her already aching heart even more. Disappointment.

"Maybe I'll see you around," he said.

She didn't reply, really struggling to keep her own expression passive, indifferent.

He nodded again as if he couldn't believe she wasn't saying anything more, wasn't giving him an explanation.

"Keep on keepin' on," he said wryly, then headed out of her bedroom.

She didn't move. Keep on keepin' on. An odd good-bye, but not any weirder than her suddenly ordering him to leave. And keeping on was all she ever did, so she supposed it was an apropos farewell after all.

She didn't move as she heard her apartment door open and close. He was gone.

You bitch.

Liza closed her eyes at the sound of the demon's voice, clear and alert.

And that was appropriate to how she felt too.

Chapter Ten

"So what's eatin' at you today?" Elton asked, not looking up from bundling a bunch of envelopes with a rubber band.

Michael paused in his sorting, however, glancing at the older man. "Nothing. Why do you ask?"

He shot Michael a sidelong look, and a knowing smile split his leathery face. "I'm a seer, son. I don't miss much."

Michael smiled too, although the gesture felt forced, difficult. "I'm beginning to realize that."

Elton nodded, then returned to his work.

They both continued on silently for a few moments before Elton spoke again. "Are you finding it any easier to be back?"

Michael nodded, automatically. "This way of working is definitely different. I'm used to a more hands-on approach, but if DIA can save more humans in the end, then we have to try."

"I wasn't talking about the business. It's got to be hard to come back to a world you don't know or fully understand."

"Oh." Michael shrugged. His first instinct was to

simply gloss over his feelings. He felt lost. Confused. Not sure how anything worked in this new era. Especially after last night. But the burden of acting as if everything was fine was too much for him this morning.

"Yeah, I am finding things a little confusing. And overwhelming."

"That's understandable. And to be expected."

Michael nodded. He silently sorted more mail.

"I'm not always sure how to understand the changes I'm seeing," he said after a moment. "Or how to find the answers that would help me understand."

Elton glanced at him, then shrugged himself. "I would imagine you just ask."

He'd tried to ask last night. He'd tried to get Liza to explain her abrupt shift. Her sudden demand that he leave. But she hadn't told him a thing. It was as if the incredibly responsive lover he'd been with all night had disappeared, replaced by a cold, distant woman he didn't recognize. Someone who was as shut down as the Liza he'd made love to was open.

But maybe Elton could help him understand. After all, he had said Michael should just ask if he was confused. And damn, he was confused.

"Last night, I—um—hooked up?" Was that still a phrase that was used now?

Elton stopped sorting and waited, one eyebrow cocked.

"I hooked up with a woman."

Elton gave him an impressed look. "Well, I suppose it's good you aren't waiting too long to get back in the saddle. But then, after thirty-three years . . ."

"Exactly," Michael agreed.

"So what's confusing?" Elton asked. "I can't imagine anything has changed much in that department."

"No," Michael agreed slowly, trying to explain exactly what had him confused. It definitely hadn't been the act itself.

"The hookup went fine, better than fine. It was amazing."

Elton nodded approvingly, another wide smile spreading across his face. "Very good. Very good."

"It was what happened afterward. She—she just kicked me out."

Elton's smile withered.

"No explanation. No warning that something was bothering her. Just literally—get out."

Elton studied him for a minute, then gave a helpless shrug. "You know, maybe I'm not the one to talk to. After all, I've been with my Dolores for nearly fifty years. I can't even remember my hooking-up days."

Michael chuckled, although he was a little disappointed. "That's okay. Maybe there just isn't an answer." But even as he said that, he knew it wasn't true. There had to be a reason Liza's demeanor had changed like that, and so suddenly.

He returned to his mailroom work, although his thoughts were still on what had happened with Liza.

"Maybe she was honestly just looking for a one-night stand," Elton said, giving Michael a regretful look.

Michael didn't think so. And even if that were the case, he didn't think Liza would react the way she had. He could see her apologetically telling him she couldn't get involved. Maybe even making a joke of it, but she'd been emphatic, almost desperate, for him to leave right away.

"Or maybe she was hiding something. Something she didn't know how to tell you about."

Of course! She'd woken and remembered her soul contract. She'd made a pact with the devil. That was a pretty heavy burden, and certainly something she couldn't share with an average guy. Hell, an average guy wouldn't even believe her.

That had to be it.

"Like maybe she's seeing someone else," Elton added. "Or she wasn't that into you."

Michael frowned at the old man.

Yeah, he liked his theory better.

Liza let her head fall back against the back of her office chair, closing her eyes, exhausted. Her temples pounded, and she just wanted to close her eyes and sleep, but she couldn't do that without another massive dose of Benadryl. And she was growing more concerned about taking so many of the allergy meds. She had been noticing her heart racing more and more lately, and she knew the drugs were affecting her heart rate and blood pressure.

Although a massive heart attack might be preferable to this.

Rah, rah, ah, ah, ah
Roma, roma, ma
Gaga, ooh, la, la

Liza gritted her teeth, determined not to scream. But Boris had been singing at the top of his lungs since he'd fully come to last night, both furious that he'd been drugged yet again, but also that he'd missed sex.

And Lady Gaga had been his preferred torture of choice. Over and over. And off-key to boot.

"Stop it!" she cried out. Not for the first time, but

apparently even Boris was getting tired of it, because he trailed off just as he got to the part of the song where he wanted her psycho, her vertical stick.

When are you going to learn, darling? Drug me, and you will pay.

Liza was tempted to tell him it was well worth hours and hours of awful singing, but when she thought about how tired she was and how badly her head hurt, she wasn't sure anymore.

Then she thought of Michael. No, that had definitely been worth it. Unfortunately it really had been just a stolen moment.

And I missed it.

Liza closed her eyes again, frustrated that she was so tired, she couldn't keep her thoughts hidden from him. Sometimes she could, but masking her thoughts took a lot of energy and concentration, neither of which she had much of today.

Finally, I could have gotten a little action. And you deny me. P-p-poker face. P-p-poker face.

Liza groaned. Great, Boris was angry enough to begin his Lady Gaga torture again—although at least he was doing a medley. Still she was going to have to resort to the Benadryl again. Obviously.

Don't you dare.

"Then just stop singing. Please." She didn't even care that she was begging. She was so tired. And so upset.

"Ms. McLane."

Liza spun in her desk chair to find Finola's newest personal assistant at the door. Sadly, Liza didn't even know her name, because frankly most of them didn't make it long enough to bother with names.

"Ms. White would like to see you in her office," the goth/rockabilly-looking woman said, pushing up her funky cat's-eye glasses. Liza absently wondered if the woman had always fidgeted with her glasses like that, or if it was a nervous habit from dealing with the demanding, and oh so evil, Finola White.

"Tell her I will be right there."

The assistant looked like she'd rather do anything else. Poor woman. But she simply nodded and disappeared out of the doorway, rushing away on a pair of chunky-heeled, red patent-leather dolly shoes that Finola was guaranteed to despise.

Poor woman, she thought again, then sighed. Poor me.

Her day was already the pits, and now she had to have a meeting with Finola.

I just want to point out that she's a bigger bitch than me.

Liza snorted. "I think that one is debatable."

Boris snorted back, but then actually fell blessedly silent.

Liza gathered up some of the articles and layouts she'd been working on for the July issue of *HOT!* and tried to brace herself for the next trial of her day.

"What took you so long?" Finola asked as soon as Liza stepped into her office, which was decorated in a sort of the-arctic-meets-the-future motif. Everything was white and ultra-modern—and somehow inherently pretentious.

"Forgive me," Liza said, not bothering to keep the hint of sarcasm out of her voice. "I've had a rather distracting morning dealing with the little friend you've cursed me with."

Finola raised a perfectly arched eyebrow, whether at what she'd said, or how she'd said it, Liza wasn't sure. Then Finola gestured to her lackey, Tristan McIntyre.

Tristan crossed the room and pulled an oval mirror out from behind a dressing screen that stood in the corner of the office. He positioned it at an angle so that Liza was reflected and Finola could look into it as well.

Behind Liza stood Boris in all his flaming glory. And not the flames of Hell way, but rather the kitschy, over-the-top way of a very flamboyant gay man.

"What are you doing now?" Finola said into the mirror, which was the demonic equivalent of a video chat.

Boris pouted. "She drugged me again."

"I don't know that I can blame her," Tristan murmured from where he stood beside the mirror.

Boris made a face at the other demon. Liza probably would have found the interaction amusing if she didn't have to be a part of it.

Finola clearly didn't find any of it amusing. Instead her pale, icy gaze moved over each of them.

"I'm not concerned with your petty dramas," she finally said.

"She is drugging me, Finola. That is hardly a petty drama," Boris said, placing a hand on his hip, his expression somewhere between irritated and wounded.

"I'm possessed," Liza stated. "I wouldn't call that a petty drama either."

Tristan suppressed a chuckle.

"And," Boris added, "the prude finally got laid last night, and where was I? Out cold. I finally had a chance for a little carnal fun, and nothing. Nuh-thing."

He cocked his head and raised an eyebrow, waiting for Finola's sympathy.

Finola's usually beautiful and flawless expression tightened, appearing hard, frustrated.

She narrowed her eyes at Boris. "Do you really think I care about her love life or about you missing it? Your only concern is making sure Ms. McLane is doing her job." She sighed. "I am starting to truly believe you are not the demon for this task."

Boris immediately dropped his indignant stance and looked contrite. "I am the right demon. I'm sorry, mistress."

Finola stared at him in the mirror for several seconds, then nodded. "So Ms. McLane, amid your adventures in drugging your possessor and seeking carnal gratification, did you find time to get the July issue together?"

Liza didn't answer, but instead rose and placed her work in front of Finola. Again, Finola's eyebrow rose at Liza's lack of verbal response or cowering respect or maybe both, probably both, but Liza was at her wits' end and frankly, nothing could scare her at the moment.

Finola didn't say a word, however. Instead she focused on the newest magazine submissions.

After several moments, she looked up. "These are good. I like most of them. Although I think you could liven up the cover articles. Some of these are old and overdone."

It was on the tip of Liza's tongue to ask her what she really knew about running a magazine, or about what would inspire the consumer to pick up a copy of *HOT!*, but she caught herself.

She might be tired and frustrated and angry that she was in this wretched situation. Basically an indentured slave, chained to Finola by the fact that she was possessed and Finola was the only one who could ever free her of the demon in her body and mind. But Liza was smart enough to know Finola White, despite looking like a pale, elegant ice queen, was the evilest of all demons. And Liza had to show her some respect, if she wanted to survive this possession. If there was a way to survive it.

"I will work on finding more intriguing articles," Liza said passively.

Finola nodded, appearing to be somewhat mollified. "Good. Otherwise, it would appear the issue is nicely on track. I will let you two go and get back to work. And remember, Bartoris, you are never to interfere with Ms. McLane's work."

Boris nodded.

"But," Finola added, "what you choose to do when she is away from work is your choice."

Liza gritted her teeth. That was as good as giving him a microphone and a Lady Gaga CD.

"Now leave," Finola said, waving a hand toward the door. "I have important things to do, like meeting Donald Trump for lunch."

Liza retrieved the mock-ups of her work, recalling a time when she'd gone to lunches like that. When she'd run this magazine. Of course, she still did. Finola just took all the credit.

More frustration filled her.

See, I told you she was a bigger bitch than I am.

For once, Liza was inclined to agree with Boris.

It's Bartoris.

Chapter Eleven

Finola didn't speak until the heavy glass door of her office closed behind Liza McLane.

"I don't like how she is acting."

Tristan wheeled the mirror back behind the screen, then strode across the room to lean against the edge of Finola's desk.

"She is getting a little rebellious."

Finola nodded, her gaze distant as she thought. "I actually think Bartoris has become a detriment."

Tristan had always thought the relatively weak trickster demon was annoying. He could only imagine what it would be like to be possessed by him. His voice alone would be enough to drive anyone insane.

He started to say exactly that, but thought better of it. Having Finola irritated with Liza McLane and Bartoris could be a good thing.

"Well, we need some way to keep McLane in check and working for the magazine. She wasn't willing to sell her soul, so possession was the only way to keep her here."

He waited, allowing Finola's thoughts to head in the very direction he wanted them to.

"I'm not sure we need her as much as we once did," Finola said. "After all, I know fashion, and you are becoming quite proficient at many of the things Liza does. The layouts, the articles. Your work is very, very good."

Tristan bowed his head, offering the meekness Finola so loved. He found it easier to do that these days, knowing he wouldn't have to do it much longer.

"Perhaps you are right," Tristan agreed. "Maybe both McLane and Bartoris are more work than they are worth."

Finola nodded. "It is something to think about, but right now I need to run. The Donald is flying us to Maine for lobster."

Tristan made an impressed face, although he was barely listening to her.

"Will you watch Dippy while I'm away? I would bring him, but the precious boy doesn't care for air travel."

Tristan feigned a mild look of disgust, but nodded. "You know I will. Even though I will never fathom why you love that mangy creature so much."

The mangy creature in question lifted his head from his jewel-encrusted bed, blinking his small, sleepy eyes.

"Oh, my little poopsie is not mangy," Finola cooed at the beast. "He's my perfect little boy."

Tristan made another face, then told Finola to have a wonderful time as she gathered her purse and coat and rushed out of the office on a wave of white and gardenias.

He walked over to the door, watching her departure through the glass. Once she was gone from sight, he turned back to look for Dippy. The hellhound was no longer in his dog bed, but sitting in Finola's desk chair, regarding Tristan with his small but intelligent eyes.

"So we have a potentially perfect target for Finola's last victim," Tristan said with a smug smile.

"McLane could be perfect, but we just have to be sure that when Finola takes her soul, it is over something that will make Satan truly furious. An indisputable breach of Hell's laws."

Tristan nodded. "Yes. We definitely have to make sure it is the final straw for Satan. McLane is getting rebellious, which can only work in our favor. But it will take a little planning."

It would take some planning and a bit more time, but Tristan did like the option of McLane best. That way not only would Finola be out of the way, but so would the real editor-in-chief of *HOT!* That would leave him and Dippy to rule the demon rebellion and make Tristan the sole editor of *HOT!* He liked the idea of being completely in charge of both.

Yes, Liza McLane was the best candidate to lose her soul.

Michael was starting to wonder if being in a state of suspended animation for over thirty years had done something to his brain.

But he couldn't stop wondering why Liza had reacted that way last night. Part of him could believe it was just a one-night stand. Hell, the seventies had been all about one-night stands. But he just didn't think that was the kind of woman Liza McLane was. She also wasn't the kind of woman who would just coldly kick a man out. His gut told him that. And he always followed his gut.

So why? That was what he couldn't stop thinking

about. Why had she reacted like that? He had to know. It was going to eat at him until he talked to her.

"Shit."

Elton slowed down pushing the mail cart to look back at Michael.

"What's wrong?"

"I just realized I forgot my—my phone, you know, cell phone, down in the mailroom."

Elton regarded him for a moment, then said, "Well, you better go back and get it."

Michael smiled, knowing the old seer didn't believe him in the slightest, and Michael liked him all the more for accepting his lame excuse.

"I'll be right back."

"Take your time," Elton said.

Michael smiled to himself as he strode off, not back to the mailroom, but toward the elevators to go to the fifteenth floor.

Once up there, Michael realized that the reception-ist in the front lobby might not allow him into the main offices. But that was where the awful blue mail-room coat and his mailroom ID badge came in very helpful.

"Hi," he said, greeting the attractive blond recep-tionist, "I need to go back to pick up a package from Liza McLane."

The blonde smiled warmly at him. "Sure."

Well, it was true; no one found the mailroom staff suspicious.

Michael thanked her and headed through the huge double doors that led into the glowing red maze of of-fices, cubicles, and frantically busy employees.

He paused once inside, trying to remember exactly where he'd seen Liza yesterday. He wasn't sure where her office was, but it had to be near the spot where she'd come racing toward them with the envelope to be mailed.

He moved to the offices on the right. Carefully, not wanting to draw any more attention to himself than necessary, he began searching. Even though he was large and hard to miss, his warrior training had taught him how to blend in, to move stealthily.

He peeked into first one office, then another. No sign of her. For a moment, he debated if this was such a good idea. Was there really any point in trying to talk to Liza? She had categorically told him to leave. Maybe that was all she had to say and he was just going to make a fool of himself.

But still he found himself looking in yet another office, and this time it was as if destiny answered him. There, sitting at a cluttered desk, her eyes closed, her head resting against the back of her office chair, was Liza.

He remained in the doorway, simply taking in the sight of her. She had such a strong effect on him, he innately knew this was the woman he needed to be with. He simply knew it, and he also knew deep in his heart, she wanted to be with him too.

So whether she liked it or not, they were going to discuss what had happened last night.

He took a deep breath, because he, a member of The Brethren, a demon slayer, was actually nervous. He straightened to his full height and raised his hand to knock, but before his knuckles could connect, he noticed she was speaking, her voice muffled, but clearly agitated.

Talking to herself again.

He also noticed she looked wan and tired. He wanted to take that weariness away from her. He wanted to shoulder her burden. If she would just let him.

Then he watched as she blurted something out, real anger and frustration evident on her face.

She needed him.

You should be working.

Liza ignored Boris, too tired, too stressed, and too depressed to care about work. She couldn't handle this anymore. And all she wanted was to go back to last night and when she was safe and content in Michael's arms.

Mmm, I'd like that too.

"Please just shut up. Please."

Tears blurred her eyes, and she willed herself to hold them back. Her chest tightened and she struggled to pull in a calming breath. She wouldn't fall apart, afraid if she did, she'd never get herself back together.

But dear God, she felt as if she'd finally hit her breaking point. After years of living this way, just one night had showed her the one thing that could make this existence truly unbearable.

Having to let Michael go. That was it. Not being able to see where a relationship with a man like that could go. She wanted to scream with frustration.

"It's so stupid. So stupid. It was just one night." Why had Michael had such an effect on her?

Because you never get laid.

"Just shut up!"

"Liza?"

Liza started, looking toward the door, seeing Michael there. Great, now not only did she have voices in her head, but she was seeing things as well.

But then logic kicked in. She wasn't seeing things, Michael was really there, in the doorway of her office.

She shouldn't be that surprised to see the man; they did work for the same company. She just didn't think after her harsh dismissal, he'd actually seek her out. Honestly, she'd expected him to avoid her like the plague.

But he was there, watching her have a breakdown, if his concerned expression was any indication.

"Are you okay?"

Oh yeah, he'd seen.

She pulled in a deep breath and swiped her fingers over her eyes, praying he couldn't see that she'd been dangerously close to crying. Hopefully he would just think she was tired. She *was* tired, so, so tired.

"I'm fine," she managed, although not as believably as she would have liked.

Why was he here? Then she noted his mailroom smock. He was working, and she was probably being arrogant to believe he was actually here to see her.

"I don't have any mail to go out at the moment," she said, busying herself with the papers on her desk. She didn't even know what she was doing with them; she just needed to have something to do. Something to focus on, besides the man she couldn't have. Anything to keep from melting down completely.

Oh dear God, please do hold it together. The only drama I enjoy is my own.

She ignored Boris, shuffling her papers more determinedly.

But after a moment she realized her office was silent. Had he simply left when he saw she had no letters to be mailed? She looked up, both relieved and troubled to find he was still there. In fact, he now stood a foot or so from her desk, watching her with those gorgeous green and golden-brown eyes of his.

"Liza, we need to talk."

She took another deep breath. "About?"

"About last night," he said as if she were a complete dolt.

She began shuffling her piles of paper again, suspecting that she looked like she didn't know what she was doing. Which she didn't.

"I'm not really sure what happened," he said, "but I do think you owe me some sort of explanation."

God, how could he sound so rational when she felt as if she was losing more of her sanity with each passing second?

"Liza, please, talk to me."

Out of her peripheral vision, she saw Michael's hand reaching out to still her agitated shuffling.

She couldn't let him touch her. Boris wasn't going to have any part of this.

Before his fingers reached her, she jerked her chair backward, so hard the back hit the wall behind her.

"Please, don't touch me."

Party pooper. Let me sneak a peek.

Shut up, she hissed mentally. She focused on Michael, who gaped at her, clearly shocked by her violent, erratic reaction.

"What the hell is wrong?" Michael asked, and she could tell he was finally seeing her behavior as disturbing. Who could blame him?

"Michael. I'm sorry," she said, her voice quavering. "I know I'm acting crazy, but you have to believe me, I can't do this."

"Can't do what?" He stared at her, clearly feeling helpless.

"This." She gestured back and forth between the two of them. "You and me. I'm sorry about last night.

I never should have invited you home with me. I thought I could handle it, but I realize now I can't. I'm just not in a position to be with any man."

But especially one I could potentially fall in love with, she told herself.

Really? You are talking about love? Already? Leave it to you to turn a perfectly good one-night stand into a grand love affair. Damn, you are so provincial.

Liza gritted her teeth.

"Liza," Michael said, stepping closer. "I think you'd be surprised how much I could understand if you would just talk to me."

Why was he so nice?

He is nice. I'm already bored with this one.

Michael stepped closer. Liza scrambled out of her chair, pushing it between herself and him, knowing again her reaction must seem extreme to him.

"I'm not trying to pressure you," Michael said calmly, holding up his hands in a sign of surrender. "I just wanted to be sure you were okay. And to find out what happened last night."

"Nothing happened," she told him, desperate for this conversation to end, before she said something stupid. "I just—just realized I'm not the type to have a fling. I thought I could, but—"

"Who said I was looking for a fling?"

Liza gaped at him, her mouth still open, even though she was now speechless. Was he saying what she thought he was saying?

Oh for Satan's sake, is he as provincial as you? Never mind, I don't want to see him. He's probably wearing a golf shirt and khakis, isn't he?

Liza didn't acknowledge Boris's comment. Nor did she care to go into what the man was wearing, but suffice it to say Michael could even make a royal-blue mailroom smock look sexy.

Besides, she was too amazed at what he seemed to be implying.

"What—what exactly are you looking for?"

Chapter Twelve

"I'm looking for a woman like you," Michael said, vaguely surprised that he was speaking the truth. "And I wanted to see where this thing between us could go."

Liza stared at him, her eyes wide, filled with that combination of uncertainty and longing he'd seen before.

But that uncertainty only made Michael more sure that he'd been right thinking she had decided to pull away because of her situation with Finola White and her soul contract. She didn't know how to get close to someone, because there was the risk that she could be damned for all time.

But he knew otherwise. He knew the DIA was working on freeing those with soul contracts and even getting back the souls that had already been lost. He still had his doubts about the DIA's work, but he wanted to believe they could save the soulless.

He wanted to believe they could save Liza.

But while they worked on that, he could protect her himself. He would slay any demon for her. Real or imagined.

That realization stunned him, just for a moment. But then he shrugged it off. He'd always been a man who knew what he wanted and went for it. At least he had been before.

Hell, if anything, this conviction, this confidence, was a good sign that he was back. And he knew he wanted this woman.

The longing in her aquamarine eyes told him that she felt the same way about him. But he knew it was going to take some convincing to get her to trust him. To let go of her fears.

"I just moved here," Michael said suddenly, hoping that if he revealed something he was unsure about, she might feel better. Might realize she wasn't alone in her uncertainty. "Just moved back actually."

She frowned, her previous emotions replaced by confusion. She clearly didn't understand the sudden shift in conversation.

"I was gone a long time, and I'm finding everything so different. Really different. It's like starting my whole life all over, honestly. And I would love to have someone show me around. Reintroduce me to this place."

Her brow furrowed, some of her misgivings returning.

"Liza, I'm not asking you to make some huge commitment to me. I'm just talking about dating each other."

She looked down at her hands, still gripping the back of her office chair like it was the only thing keeping her safe. The only thing stopping her.

When she met his gaze again, he could see that longing outweighed her doubts.

"I—I would like that too," she admitted, but he

didn't get the feeling from her tone that she was conceding.

But at least he knew he wasn't completely off the mark about how things had been last night. She had been into him.

Ha, Elton!

"So let's just date," he said. "Go out. Dinner. A movie. That would be okay, wouldn't it?"

He took a step closer.

She didn't move away, which he took as a good sign, although the chair was still there. Her not-so-metaphorical wall.

"I would like that," she repeated, but her tone still didn't say she was agreeing. Her eyes met his, the yearning there undeniable.

But then she winced, closing her eyes for a moment, almost as if a sharp pain had shot through her head.

Michael reached for her hand. "Are you okay?"

Just as his fingers were about to touch the back of hers, her eyes snapped open and she jerked backward, this time nearly falling with her desperation to get away from him. Only the chair saved her from landing hard on her perfect little rear end.

But why? Why the hell was she telling him in one breath she wanted to date him, and then in the next she was practically injuring herself to get away from him? Her reaction seemed too extreme, even for someone hiding a secret like hers.

"What are you so afraid of?" he asked, realizing his tone sounded harsh. But damn it, having her jumping like a scared rabbit wasn't doing much for his ego. It sure as hell didn't jive with his memory of the woman who had made love to him on her kitchen counter, demanding more of his touches with her writing body and wanton whimpers.

"It—it's not you," she said, her expression pleading.

He stared at her. Well, that was something that hadn't changed in the years since he'd been gone. The classic rejection.

It's not you. It's me.

Oh yeah, his ego was really stinging now. Maybe he'd jumped the gun feeling smug that Elton's theory was wrong. But he tried to keep his voice even, unaffected, as he said, "I know something is holding you back, and you probably think it's something I couldn't possibly understand or accept, but you'd be surprised. Whatever is making you so scared probably wouldn't shock me in the least."

She stared at him, the desire to believe him burning in her glittering eyes. But then she shook her head, her doubts too much for her.

"I'm sorry," she said, her gaze dropping back to her hands again. Her fingers squeezed the chair back until her knuckles turned pure white.

Michael studied her for a moment, then shook his head in defeat. He wanted this woman, but he couldn't railroad her into a relationship.

"You can trust me," he said, feeling the need to say something before he walked away. Then he simply turned and left her office.

What else could he do? Damn it, wasn't that what he'd been saying about every part of his "new" life? What could he do but resign himself to each change, each outcome?

At least his frustration with his changed role in the DIA and within The Brethren made sense. He was having to change his whole belief system there. But what difference did it really make if he couldn't have a relationship with a woman he barely knew?

Yet for some strange reason, it didn't feel like he barely knew her. As strange as that was, it was true.

"So," Elton said when Michael returned to the mailroom. "Did you find it?"

Michael knew they both realized they weren't talking about his damned cell phone.

"Yeah. I did."

Elton's gaze roamed his face, those damned seer eyes of his reading far too much.

But all he did was nod and return to his work.

Watching Michael leave was one of the hardest things Liza had ever done.

So why did you? We could share him. Even though he does seem a little—intense. Then again, intense can be fun. Maybe.

And there was the reason she'd made the right choice. She couldn't get involved with someone when she was living like this. How would that ever work?

It wouldn't.

It would work fine. We'd be like swingers.

Liza closed her eyes, wishing she had the energy to block her thoughts. She couldn't block Boris totally, but when she was rested and feeling emotionally stronger, she could at least cancel out some of his running commentary on *her* every thought. As well as keep a few things private. But she was too stressed to have that kind of focus now.

So she'd been right to let Michael walk away. He might be the most understanding man in the world, but there was still no way he was going to be fine with having a girlfriend who was possessed.

Who knows, maybe he'd like it. Maybe he's freaky that way.

Her head was silent.

Yeah, probably not.

For once, Liza agreed.

She had no other choice. And really, she barely knew Michael anyway.

So why did she feel like crying again?

Because it's always a sad, sad thing to lose good sex.

Liza sighed, not even bothering to react to Boris's comment. Instead she pushed her chair back to her desk and sat down.

She began sorting through her work. What was she supposed to be doing? That's right, new articles. New articles for the July issue.

She turned to her computer, willing herself to think about something other than Michael Archer.

Michael Archer? Michael Archer. Now I swear I've heard that name before.

Articles for the summer, Liza thought, refusing to listen to Boris. Swimsuit reviews were always a hit, but July was too late for that idea. Secret and sexy vacation spots. That might be a good one, and Liza didn't think they'd done anything like that since doing hot holiday rendezvous in the November 2010 edition.

She made a note to have one of the assistant editors work on that.

Now what else?

I suppose Michael Archer is a common name, though.

What about something to do with beating the summer heat? Liza considered. Cocktails to beat the holiday heat maybe?

I could use a cocktail.

Liza didn't know quite what to make of this. She never agreed with Boris.

Bartoris.

She ignored him.

I could also use some cock. But I guess I missed that. And Satan knows, it will be another six years before you see any action.

"Probably," she said, wishing that idea didn't make her feel like crying again.

I want to cry too.

Liza closed her eyes and breathed in deeply, both to keep from crying and from screaming. She'd let an amazing man go, and she might very well have Boris stuck inside her for another six years. She couldn't do this. She just couldn't.

Believe me, sugar, this ain't no picnic for me either.

Liza rubbed her eyes. Then refocused on her work. The only thing that would make this day suck worse was pissing off Finola and ending up in Hell.

Oh wait, she was already there.

Chapter Thirteen

"These are your best ideas?"

Liza watched as Finola riffled through the dozens of article suggestions Liza had struggled to assemble, giving them nothing more than a quick once-over.

"Cocktails? The best fashions to beat the heat? Exercises that can be done at the beach?" Finola pushed the pages away from her as if they were a particularly unappetizing plate of food.

"I expect more," Finola said, arching a pale eyebrow at her.

As if Liza didn't know that. Finola White always expected more. And more. And more.

"I think several of those ideas are perfect for the July issue. Our readers have always loved articles like these," Liza stated, as unconcerned about Finola's wrath as she'd been before. She was tired, she was harried, and she just didn't care.

Dangerous attitude there, missy.

Liza didn't react to the ever-present voice in her head. Instead she held Finola's gaze, another thing

Liza knew would irritate the great Finola. She liked submission.

But Liza had submitted enough for one day. And it was late.

Out of the corner of her eye, she noticed Tristan, who shifted slightly beside Finola's desk. Liza noticed that even Finola's yippy little dog picked up its head as if watching what was going on, like they both knew this was going to be ugly.

"I just told you that I am not pleased," Finola said, clearly stunned that Liza would be so audacious, although she still sounded melodic, unaffected.

"And these are the best ideas I have."

What the hell are you doing? You are so playing with fire.

Liza rolled her eyes. She sure as hell didn't need Boris to tell her that.

Bartoris.

Finola regarded Liza silently, her calm expression not wavering, which surprised Liza. She'd expected something more. Again, Tristan shifted, moving closer to Finola, as if he expected something to happen too.

The little dog jumped up from its bed, moving closer to Finola as well.

This is going to be bad.

Okay, so everyone agreed that Liza was making a colossal mistake talking back, but again, she felt as if she had nothing to lose. She'd lost everything already. And letting go of Michael today had been the last straw.

Liza didn't want to lose her immortal soul, but she just couldn't go on like this. She had to make Finola understand that something had to change.

"I cannot believe you are standing here before me, telling me these are the best ideas you have, when you once ran this magazine yourself," Finola stated, that usually melodic quality of her voice changing, taking on almost a sibilance. Still the only sign the great demon was angry.

Liza frowned, having never heard her speak like that before. The sound was eerie, almost inhuman. The hairs on the back of Liza's neck stood up and a chill prickled her skin.

Then again, Finola was inhuman.

Tristan moved again, and the dog followed suit. Liza almost got the impression that they were moving closer to have a better view of the carnage that might follow. They appeared almost eager for a full-fledged confrontation.

Why are you doing this? You are courting big trouble with this behavior. The bitch is going to blow.

"You are right," Liza said in response to Finola's comment. "I did run it."

She still did, but she wasn't going to say that.

Finally. A wise choice.

"Not only did I run this magazine myself, but I ran it by myself."

Finola regarded her for a moment, her expression now totally unreadable.

"Explain yourself," Finola said after a moment.

"I ran this magazine without a demon in my head," Liza said simply. "And now when I try to work I have constant yammering. Constant complaining. It makes it hard to create a brilliant, best-selling magazine. That's for sure."

Traitor.

Liza wasn't sure how she was a traitor, when she'd never once pretended to be on his side.

Fine. Bitch.

"I could do far superior work for you if you would just cast this demon out of me and back to Hell."

She will not agree to this. I'm the very thing that keeps you chained to her. Her slave. She knows you won't sign a soul contract.

Liza knew it was a long shot, but she thought it was worth a try. And she could tell by Boris's voice he wasn't as positive as he'd like to be. Finola had already voiced her displeasure with him.

"I would be so much more productive for you if I simply had silence," Liza said.

Finola regarded her for a moment, then shook her head, her loose, white-blond locks appearing even more perfect with the motion.

"You know I can't allow you to go without supervision," she said, her tone regretful, even though Liza was pretty sure that Finola had never had a regret in her life. Regret implied sympathy, and Liza was sure Finola didn't even know the meaning of that word.

Liza was disappointed, but not surprised, by Finola's response. She hadn't believed Finola would actually cast Boris out, but she had nothing to lose by trying.

"You are needed," Finola added, and this time Liza could tell she struggled to say those words. Ha, that had to be a bitter pill to swallow.

"Bring me the mirror," Finola said suddenly to Tristan, who seemed to have been startled away from sharing what appeared to be a significant look with—Finola's dog.

Liza glanced between the demon and dog, telling herself she had to have imagined the look. See what stress did to a person?

It doesn't do good things to a demon either. And if I end

up being cast out of you, I will be back. And then you will know what it feels like to be truly possessed.

Would Finola be pleased by such threats, Liza wondered, feeling almost smug even though nothing had really changed for her. It felt good to speak her mind for a change. And it felt great to hear Boris worrying.

Before Liza had a chance to speak out some more, Finola changed her mind. "Forget the mirror. I don't need to deal with yet another annoyance today."

The head demon turned her attention back to Liza, although this time she spoke to Boris.

"This is truly my last warning. To both of you. This magazine and the success of it is all that should concern either of you. *HOT!*'s success is what is keeping both of you safe. So Bartoris, you'd better make sure Liza succeeds. Period."

A low, frustrated growl echoed through Liza's head.

"He says he understands," Liza said, repressing a smile. It wasn't a win, but anything that could irritate or upset the demon inside her made Liza feel better. Just a little anyway.

"Now leave," Finola said with a sigh. "This meeting has been disappointing and exhausting."

Liza wondered if Finola really thought any of them cared about her displeasure or fatigue. She glanced at Tristan, who Liza could swear again was sharing a look with the dog.

But before she could ponder that, Finola lifted a hand and waved toward her door. "I said leave. I need some time to think."

Liza didn't know what Finola had to think about. She didn't actually run the magazine. Nor did she seem the type to second-guess her decisions, but Liza supposed it didn't really matter.

And she didn't want to be here any longer anyway.

So without further comment or even a look, Liza turned and exited the office. Winding her way through the glass maze, she considered what other ways she might free herself of this demonic noose.

Demonic noose. I kinda like that.

"Be quiet," Liza hissed, only to receive a confused look from Finola's assistant as Liza walked past.

Are you working? Hmm, no, I don't believe you are, so I don't need to be quiet. In fact, I can be a whole hell of a lot more annoying than I have been. I do not appreciate your trying to get me in trouble.

Liza didn't respond, not surprised by Boris's reaction. She'd known he was going to be furious, but she didn't care. She was finding it exceedingly difficult to care about anything.

I can make your life much worse than I have. You have seen The Exorcist, *haven't you? Do you need a few spewing-pea-soup moments to recognize who is really in control here?*

But instead of feeling threatened or intimidated, Liza laughed. She stepped inside her office and closed the door before she spoke.

"You won't do that, because you can't. You aren't that powerful. You are just an annoying little mosquito of a demon, buzzing in my ear but not effectual enough to do much else. You can tattle to Finola and irritate me. That's it, but you aren't going to get to annoy me much longer."

What do you mean?

But before he could even get the question out, Liza was reaching for her purse and pulling out exactly what she needed to silence him.

Damn you. I will tell Finola about this.

"Feel free. I'll just tell her I was working, and you

wouldn't be silent," she said calmly as she poured a handful of Benadryl into the palm of her hand. She set down the bottle and reached for her cold coffee on her desk.

She won't believe you.

"It's a risk I'm willing to take."

Without further comment, she scooped the pills into her mouth, willing her throat to relax as she swallowed them. The cold coffee and the pills were bitter on her tongue.

I hope you choke.

Liza did struggle for a moment with some of the pills, but managed to work them down.

Yep, she thought, swigging down the rest of her coffee. This was a bitter pill for them both, but she wasn't living this way any longer.

She would do whatever she had to do to gain some freedom, some happiness.

Within twenty minutes of taking the pills, soft, even breathing echoed quietly through her head, but Liza didn't find that annoying. She actually found it comforting. Listening to Boris's sleeping breaths must be like the sounds of a baby sleeping, finally, after a long, sleepless night.

Liza yawned too. Tired, very tired. But despite the sleepiness she felt, her mind soon returned to the biggest distraction of her day.

Michael.

She hadn't been able to get rid of her demons. Neither her literal one, nor the haunting demon of Michael's words and frustrated departure.

Suddenly she stood, her body seeming to know the plan before her brain did.

She couldn't have her freedom, but she sure as hell wasn't going to give up her one chance at happiness. Even if it had to be stolen.

She grabbed her purse, only to realize she didn't know where she was planning to go. She didn't know where Michael lived—or really anything about the man. Was it possible to be this interested in someone she barely knew? Her heart told her yes—even if her head told her what she was doing was pretty much totally nuts. But her heart was winning this argument. After all, what had using her head done for her over the past few years? A whole lot of nada.

He worked in the mailroom. She could look for him there, but it was after-hours now. She doubted he would still be at work. But maybe someone else would be. Someone who might know how to contact him.

A long shot at best, but she didn't want to wait until tomorrow, and actually tomorrow was Saturday. He might not even be back in until Monday. She wanted to see him now. She wanted to tell him that she wanted to date too, desperately. It would be tricky, but she was going to make it work. Not that she was going to reveal any of that to him. But she needed something to keep her going. Someone to believe in.

Grabbing her purse, she stood. She only swayed slightly as she did, the effects of the massive dose of allergy medicine mostly gone.

Her heart raced in her chest, skipping and fluttering in a faint erratic way that made her feel breathless, but she wasn't going to worry about the sensation.

You are just nervous, she told herself. She'd rejected Michael, and now she was changing her mind. That was nerve-wracking. What if she'd missed her chance with him? She wouldn't know unless she tried.

So she ignored the strange beating of her heart and

told herself to buck up. She could do this. If she wasn't going to let a demon stop her, she sure wasn't going to let her own nerves.

She headed into the main hallway of the *HOT!* offices. Many employees still sat at their cubicles, heads down, diligently working, and would do so until late. The magazine ran on deadlines, of course, which often required long hours, but since Finola White had taken over, long hours took on a different meaning. She expected every one of her employees to be available to her at any time. Liza knew she wasn't the only one exhausted, burnt out, and dangerously close to a breakdown.

She just happened to be one who planned to do something about it.

But looking at the depressed, stressed faces, she wondered why any of them would ever be afraid of Hell.

She'd once been scared of it too. But not anymore.

Well, not totally anyway.

She walked out to the reception area and toward the elevators. A receptionist still sat at the front desk. She was the typical blond beauty that Finola seemed to favor for the job. The woman nodded, but otherwise didn't speak.

Liza was glad. She didn't feel like chatting, and she also didn't want the woman to notice where she was heading. It was better to be as careful as she could. Liza knew what happened around here. The expendable disappeared on a regular basis. Or had until the NYPD started to take notice. Now the MIAs had dwindled greatly, but Liza didn't trust it would stay that way.

She knew the only reason she wasn't expendable

was because none of the demons actually knew how to run a magazine. Demons were good posers, but not so great at getting the actual job done.

She stepped into the elevator, relieved when no one else joined her. She pressed the button marked LL. Lower level. That was where the mailroom was, housed deep in the bottom of the building. Subterranean.

She shivered, her thoughts going to where she might end up if she wasn't careful. Was Hell underground like it was depicted? Or was it in another dimension? She really didn't want to find out. But she was willing to take this risk anyway.

The elevator shuddered and vibrated as it approached the lowest level, a place she'd never been. After a couple of bobs, the elevator stopped, but the doors didn't open right away.

Her heart fluttered again in her chest, stealing her breath. Nerves, more silly nerves. And for what reason? It was just the mailroom, and frankly she didn't even know if she'd get the answer she wanted here.

Approaching Michael after having rejected him was a valid reason to be anxious. Though just asking about him was hardly reason to be this stressed. But still her heart pounded.

She waited, taking a couple of deep breaths, then finally pushed the OPEN DOOR button. She waited, then pushed it again.

Finally the doors parted, opening into one huge room. Wow. If she'd thought the *HOT!* offices were busy, they had nothing on the mailroom. It was well after office closing hours, after postal hours too, yet the vast room still bustled with employees.

Liza's first impression was worker bees in a large hive, but then she amended that analogy to ants. Ants working away in an underground nest.

"Can I help you?"

Chapter Fourteen

Liza blinked, turning to find a man standing beside her. She hadn't even noticed him approaching, but she supposed that wasn't so weird given how distracted she was by the number of people still working down here.

"Yes, I'm looking for Michael Archer."

The man, a very average, innocuous guy wearing a royal-blue smock and a name tag with *Dave* printed on it, frowned slightly.

"And this is in reference to what?"

Liza returned a frown. Why did this man care? She supposed they couldn't very well let random strangers into the mailroom, but she was a *HOT!* employee too. Surely she could come down here looking for one of their staff without reporting her purpose.

But this guy, despite his average Joe appearance, didn't look like he was fooling around. He looked very serious.

"Umm, I was—hoping to get back a—um, an envelope I gave him earlier today. I—need to add another document to it."

She hoped that sounded believable. Her heart fluttered again. Dave didn't look terribly convinced.

"Do you recall about what time he picked this package up?"

She didn't answer him, instead glancing around the room, trying to spot a tall, muscular man with dark hair and golden-brown eyes. She didn't see him.

"Is he still here?" she asked. "I can just take a quick look around."

"I'm afraid we can't allow just anyone to wander around the mailroom," he said. "Postal theft is a federal offense."

"Well, I'm not just anyone. I'm the editorial director of *HOT!* Surely that gives me access to the mailroom too. I can also assure you I have no intention of stealing anything. I'm just looking for Michael Archer."

Dave started to shake his head, when his action was interrupted by a voice that Liza knew well.

"Liza, what brings you down here?"

Liza turned, relieved to see Elton approaching them in his slow, uneven gait. The older man smiled, and some of her anxiety dissipated.

"Elton, hi. I'm looking for Michael Archer. Do you know where he is?"

"Oh, Michael," he said as if he'd expected as much. Liza suspected it was to calm the uptight man beside her. "I believe he's left already. I think he actually left a couple hours ago. So I would imagine he's home now."

"Would you happen to know how I could reach him?" she asked, glancing quickly at Dave and wishing he would just go away. But this time the man's attention wasn't on her; instead he regarded Elton closely. His eyes were narrowed as if in warning, although Elton didn't seem to pick up on the silent gesture.

"No," Elton said, "but maybe I can help you."

She started to shake her head, but Dave answered for her.

"She claims she is looking for an envelope that she gave to Michael earlier today. She says she needs to add something to it."

Liza gave the man an irritated look. Claims? Says? Could he be any more obvious that he didn't believe her story? Okay, it was a story, but still he could at least give her the benefit of the doubt. She didn't care for Dave. At all.

"Well, I would be happy to look for the envelope for you," Elton said, shooting Dave a look that made it clear he thought the other man's behavior was rude too.

"It probably went out already," Liza said, hating to send the sweet old man on a wild goose chase. Dave made a face as if to say, "See, she's lying."

"Well, it can't hurt to look, now can it?"

"Elton," Dave said, his voice low and not pleased.

"Dave, it's fine. It will only take a second." Elton placed a hand lightly on the small of Liza's back. Her first reaction, as always, was to pull away, but then she realized Boris was out. Ah, what a lovely thing.

She let Elton lead her away from the other man.

"He's very uptight," she whispered to Elton.

"You have no idea."

Liza smiled and followed him through the sea of machinery, sorting stations, desks, and computers. Only after a few seconds did she notice that many of the employees were watching her quizzically. Then she noticed some were not just quizzical, but almost suspicious.

"The people down here really aren't used to strangers, are they?"

"It comes from working underground," Elton said with a smile. "Makes you a little off."

Liza smiled, although she did glance warily around her again.

"Well, this is Michael's station."

They stopped in front of a tidy stainless steel table.

She stared at it, seeing nothing that would give her any hint of the real information she wanted. So after a moment, she decided to just come clean.

"You know I'm not actually looking for an envelope, right?"

"Yes, so what can I really do for you?"

She smiled gratefully at the old man. "I was hoping to get his address."

He studied her for a moment, his gaze roaming over her, until she felt almost awkward under his perusal. Then when she would have said something, anything, to get him to stop looking at her that way—as if he could look deep into her soul—he nodded, almost as if he was satisfied with what he'd seen.

"I will get it for you. But you can't ever tell where you got it from."

"I won't."

He studied her a moment longer, then nodded again. He started away from her, then stopped.

"You finally feel like yourself, don't you, sweetie?"

Liza frowned, shaking her head, not really understanding what he meant.

"It's all good," the old man said with another smile. "I will get you that information."

Liza watched him amble away, then looked around herself again, feeling decidedly uncomfortable. Apparently the mailroom was just as odd as the rest of *HOT!* She'd had hopes that somewhere in this building normalcy survived.

She glanced at a rather geeky-looking man wearing black-rimmed glasses that were exact replicas of the type the fathers always wore in fifties sitcoms. The man watched her over his computer screen, only to look away when he realized she'd noticed.

Beside him a large woman who could pass as a Russian fitness instructor also stared in her direction. She didn't look away when Liza met her eyes. Liza did.

Yeah, definitely strange. Liza decided to busy herself with finding a pen and paper in her purse, so she could write down Michael's address, if Elton did actually manage to get it.

Somehow she didn't think that was going to be an easy feat. This place felt a little like Fort Knox. At the very least, Big Brother was watching.

"Hello."

Liza looked up from rooting around in her handbag to find another man of average height and looks standing in front of her. The only thing that stood out about the man was the vivid blueness of his eyes. Pale blue. A strange blue.

Dave appeared at his side.

"Um, hi," she said, not sure what was going on now.

"I'm Eugene, the manager of the mailroom."

"I'm Liza. I work at *HOT!* as the editorial director."

"I know who you are, Ms. McLane."

Liza gave him a bewildered look. How could he know who she was when she'd never been down here before?

"Working in the mailroom, we get familiar with the *HOT!* staff via their mail," he answered as if she'd actually asked her question aloud. "I'm sure that must seem odd since you usually don't see us."

She nodded, not sure what to make of this new

member of the mailroom staff. What did these men want? She really couldn't imagine that they made this much of a to-do about every *HOT!* employee who set foot down here.

"Well, it's nice to meet you all. I'm just trying to retrieve an envelope that I sent out prematurely."

"Ah," Eugene said and Liza got the feeling he didn't believe her. "Well, I certainly hope it hasn't already left the building."

Liza just hoped that Elton returned soon. She was distinctly uncomfortable down here. And disheartened that there really was no normal place in the whole company.

After a moment, when she realized Eugene and Dave didn't intend to leave, she gathered herself to agree with Eugene's comment.

"Yes, I definitely hope it didn't get mailed yet."

Eugene nodded. Dave just watched her. Damn, this place was weird.

"You know," she finally said, feeling the need to just get away from here. "I think I should probably head back up to my office. I guess if Elton finds it, he can run it up to me."

"That's a good idea," Eugene agreed.

Liza edged around the two men, giving them a wide berth, but she didn't make it too far before Elton called out to her.

She stopped, scanning the mailroom to locate him. He headed toward her, waving a manila envelope in the air.

"I found it," he said, with a small smile.

She frowned, staring at the golden envelope as he held it out to her. Had Elton misunderstood? Did he truly not know she wasn't looking for an envelope?

Or was he just offering her an easy way out, so she

wouldn't have to suffer any more of the weird mail-room staff's odd questions and even weirder stares. That had to be it.

"Thanks, Elton," she said, giving him a brief know-ing smile as she accepted the envelope.

"I'm just glad to have been able to help you."

She nodded, her gaze moving from him to where the other men stood, still watching them. The fifties geek and Russian fitness instructor watched as well.

She glanced down at the missive in her hands, then nodded again, ready to leave. She had no idea what had just happened down here.

She thanked Elton once more and hurried for the elevator. A distinct wave of relief washed over her as soon as the doors closed.

Once the elevator started moving upward, she looked down at the envelope. It was addressed to a name she didn't recognize. A Mrs. B. Silver. Liza wasn't familiar with the mailing address either.

She frowned, wondering if Elton really had misun-derstood.

But then she noticed the return address. Not the usual *HOT!* magazine stamped return address. This one was handwritten.

M. Archer
432 West 65th Street, Apt. 3B
New York, NY

So Elton had understood after all. And he'd also understood those two guys down there weren't going to allow Elton to just give her Michael's address.

She supposed that could be because it broke some confidentiality rule, but Liza didn't feel that was the whole reason. The mailroom was a strange place.

Maybe Elton was right, working underground had made them all a little socially inept. Or maybe only the socially inept were willing to work there.

No, that wasn't it. Michael hadn't been socially awkward. Nor was Elton. But then there were always exceptions to most rules.

Whatever. It didn't really matter. She'd gotten the information she'd wanted, and she also knew to avoid the lower level from now on, which should be easy enough. She'd already avoided it for nearly six years. It shouldn't be that hard to avoid it for the rest of the time she was stuck working for Finola. Even if she did start dating Michael.

In fact, especially if she started dating Michael. She didn't get the feeling the rest of the mailroom staff would approve. Although she couldn't imagine why they would care.

But it didn't really matter at the moment. She wasn't even sure she could get Michael to take a chance on her again after her crazy reaction to him today.

Wait, maybe that was why those men had reacted so strangely to her. Maybe Michael had gone down there and told them that Liza McLane, the editorial director of *HOT!* was a wackadoo. A certified nuttyhead.

And if he had told them about her reaction, she couldn't really blame him. Her behavior had been over the top. She'd literally jumped away from his every touch. Although he'd reacted pretty well to her strange behavior. He certainly hadn't treated her like she was crazy.

But then he worked with those guys down there. He might just be used to odd behavior. Really, there was no point speculating. She should just go to him and find out what he thought directly from him.

She reread the address, then waited for the elevator to come to a stop. Fortunately, yet again, no one joined her on the elevator, and she hit the button to take her right back down to the building's first floor lobby.

She really wished she had time to go home and freshen up. She knew she must look a mess, between stress and being tired and taking all those meds. But she only had another few hours before the Benadryl wore off. So she had to talk to Michael now.

She hoped she could find him quickly and that she wouldn't be disappointed in his reaction at seeing her.

Tristan set down his highball glass with more force than necessary, but he was pissed, and the aged scotch he'd just consumed wasn't helping his irritation.

"I thought for sure Finola would react. That she would banish Liza and Bartoris with her."

Dippy stopped licking and said, "I thought so too." He continued licking—in an area that Tristan didn't like to consider.

He grimaced and poured himself another glass of whiskey.

"Why didn't she? Why would she show restraint now? Satan knows she never has before."

"She's still scared of Satan," Dippy said. "And she knows Satan will not be pleased to lose the real editor-in-chief of *HOT!*"

Tristan knew the dog was right. Maybe they had to choose a new person, someone Finola would see as expendable. That always made her more cavalier.

"I say we go back to her personal assistant. That should be easy enough to make happen, and will still get us the reaction from Satan we want." Dippy stretched a furry leg up in the air and licked more, making a snuffling noise as he did so.

Tristan made another face. "Do you really have to do that now?"

Dippy didn't respond, or stop.

Tristan took another swig of his liquor. "I still think getting rid of Liza is perfect. It will absolutely tick off Satan, and her departure would leave me in the position to run the magazine as well as the takeover.

"With your help, of course," Tristan added.

Dippy stopped his self-grooming and regarded him over his still cocked leg. "But maybe we should just go with easy for now. Get Finola gone and proceed from there."

Tristan nodded, although he didn't agree. He didn't think Peaches was the best target. Of course, Dippy was right. It would be easy enough to set up a situation where Finola would lose her temper with Peaches, and bam, the assistant would be gone. Soul cast to Hell, her body an empty shell.

Tristan downed the remainder of his drink. He didn't like the idea.

"I still say we try for Liza," he finally said.

"Fine," Dippy said, "but I don't think we should wait around too long."

Tristan nodded. He didn't want to wait too long. He wanted to be the head demon of this takeover now. But he could wait a little longer, especially if it meant he got everything.

Chapter Fifteen

"You seem different today," Gabriel said over the top of his draft beer.

Michael frowned, then shrugged. "Well, I'm trying to fit in. I'm trying to learn and accept what the mail-room does. That is different, I guess."

Gabriel nodded, then took another sip of his beer. But even though he appeared to agree, Michael didn't get the feeling he really did.

"I guess that's it, but something else feels different to me."

Michael shrugged. "Maybe I am a little off. It's been a crazy couple of days. And I'm still trying to accept all the differences. I'm just going to keep on truckin', and it will all work out."

Gabriel made another face that stated he didn't really buy Michael's excuse.

"Don't worry," Michael said wryly, "just because I'm having an off day doesn't mean I'll go get my sword and start hacking my way through the *HOT!* offices."

"Well, that's an improvement anyway," Gabriel said with a smile, toasting him.

"I'm not so sure," Simon said, sliding onto the bar stool on the other side of Michael. He took a sip of the beer he'd left there while he'd been playing pool. "Gabe here thinks that DIA has the right idea, but I'm still not convinced."

Michael gave Simon a curious look. "Really? I thought The Brethren were in agreement about the changes."

Simon shrugged, taking another large chug of his beer. "I guess I am, if it works. But I don't totally believe it will."

Michael glanced at Gabriel, who didn't look pleased about the turn the conversation was taking, but he didn't speak.

Michael turned back to Simon. "What don't you agree with?"

"I don't know if we can really save everyone. Especially the two most dangerous categories."

Michael didn't have to ask who those two were. He knew Simon referred to the demons and the possessed. They had always been and would be the most dangerous. Michael had a hard time believing they could be saved too.

"I so kicked your ass, Simon," taunted John, another member of The Brethren, as he rejoined the others. He frowned as he sat down. "What's got all of you looking so damned serious?"

"We're talking about the DIA—and if they can really make good on all these big promises of saving everyone," Simon said.

"Ah," John said as if they often talked about this.

Funny, ever since Michael had returned to The Brethren, Gabriel had made it sound like all the brothers were in agreement with the DIA's new policies and strategies.

Apparently, they weren't. At least they didn't accept the changes as blindly as Gabriel appeared to.

"What about the lost?" Michael asked, moving forward on his stool, keen to hear what the others thought.

Just because he was interested, he told himself. Not because he was interested in anyone in particular.

"That's the one area where I really do hope they are right," John said. "The lost are truly the hapless victims of the demon takeover."

"Even though they willingly agreed to the contracts they signed?" Gabriel asked.

"They were conned," Simon stated. "It's not like the phrase 'silver-tongued devil' exists for no reason."

Gabriel made a face that said he couldn't disagree. "But don't you think the possessed are equally hapless victims? Maybe more so, because they have no choice. They are simply taken over."

"Absolutely," Simon said.

John nodded. "But that doesn't mean they are going to be savable. We've seen over and over what possession does to a person."

"It makes them crazy," Simon said matter-of-factly.

Michael nodded too. That was exactly what happened and often worse. Possession made them violent, without morals, often evil themselves. Sometimes exorcism did work, but not always, and less often than the human world would like to believe.

"But we might be able to rescue some of them," Gabriel said.

"Maybe," John said, but he sounded doubtful.

Michael was doubtful too.

"Shit," Simon said suddenly. "I'm not here to talk about the DIA or work. Michael, wanna play a game?" He gestured to the pool tables.

Michael shook his head. He knew he wouldn't be able to focus on the game. Not when his thoughts were stuck on all this heavy stuff—and other things. Even though he'd repeatedly told himself to let the "other thing" go.

Simon turned to Gabriel, who also shook his head.

"Looks like you get to lose to me again, Simon," John said, downing the rest of his beer, then standing.

"I don't think so, Johnny," Simon said, also polishing off the rest of his beer. He then swaggered away toward the pool tables.

John followed, shaking his head.

"Well, some things never change," Michael said with a chuckle.

"Not between those two, that's for sure," Gabriel agreed.

They both were silent for a moment, each sipping his drink, thinking.

"Elton doesn't agree that they all can be saved either," Michael finally said.

Gabriel nodded, staring into his glass of beer. Some kind of beer called a microbrew. Michael was good with his plain old Pabst. He studied his friend, wondering why Gabriel had changed so much. He'd been the most vigilant of The Brethren, fully dedicated to ridding the world of evil. He'd always used his sword first, asked questions later.

Now he seemed so hesitant. So unwilling to do the job he'd been created to do.

"Don't you have your doubts?" Michael asked.

"I'm not saying what the DIA is planning and working toward is foolproof," Gabriel finally said, still not looking up from his beer. "But I think if we could save humans rather than just avenge them, that would be a great thing."

Michael couldn't argue with that. "But demons still need to die. That is our job, our calling, our purpose for existing."

Gabriel nodded again, although this time, he looked almost saddened.

They both remained silent. Over at the pool tables, Simon swore as John landed a tricky shot.

"I'm not sure I can totally accept that everyone can be saved," Michael said. "But I would like to see the soul contracts ended."

"Me too," Gabriel agreed.

Michael stared into his own beer, not seeing the pale gold liquid, but a pale face and black hair. He really did want to believe Liza could be saved. She didn't want him, but he wanted to know she would be fine. Safe.

Michael did not live in the nicest part of the city, Liza thought as she looked up at the dilapidated building. She walked slowly up the steps, looking for some sign of an intercom system, where she could ring his apartment to be let in. But there didn't seem to be one.

Fortunately, or unfortunately if she were some undesirable trying to get into the building, she only had to wait for a few moments before an ancient old man exited the building, and she entered, slipping inside behind him. The old man didn't seem to notice, not that she thought he'd care anyway.

She paused in the run-down lobby, which was more like a dingy foyer that housed beaten-up mailboxes and an elevator. She double-checked the envelope. He lived on the third floor. She walked over to the elevator, but then rethought getting on the rickety-looking thing. Instead she opted for the stairs.

The stairwell was dim and dirty and not much more inviting than the elevator, but it appeared to be empty and silent. She decided it was safe enough.

But she didn't dawdle, hurrying up the steps as quickly as her high heels and pencil skirt would allow. She really wished she'd had time to change before coming here. Especially now that she realized she might have to make a rushed escape from some shifty character—or charging vermin.

She glanced over her shoulder, feeling as if someone might be following her, but then she decided it was the echo of her own shoes on the stairs.

At least she hoped.

She reached the third floor without incident and was again pleased to see, once she pushed open the metal stairwell door, that the hallway was empty.

She stepped out, looking both ways, making a random guess that Michael's place must be to the right.

Fortunately her guess was correct. Apartment 3B was at the end of the hall. She hesitated only a second, her apprehension about the building overcoming her nervousness about seeing him.

She rapped twice, then waited. She heard no sound from within the apartment. Great, was he out?

She knocked again. Still no hint of anyone being inside. The door on the other end of the hallway opened, however. A beefy man in a dirty undershirt and what Liza thought were boxers, but she really hoped were shorts, leaned out to see who was in the hall.

Just little ole me, she thought nervously, now please go away. But he didn't. In fact, he stepped farther out to see her better.

She didn't know what to do. Wave? Smile? She really didn't want to offend the rather frightening-looking man, but she also didn't want to encourage any interaction.

So she returned her attention to Michael's apartment door. She knocked again, trying to appear casual. Please just let him be asleep in there and hear her now. Please.

"He ain't home."

Liza jumped, realizing the man had left his apartment and now only stood a few feet away from her. But she quickly tried to conceal her startled reaction, hiding it behind a look of mild aggravation.

"I hate when he's late," she said, then looked at her watch, only to wonder if that had been a bad move too. The timepiece wasn't a Rolex or anything, but it wasn't cheap either.

"Well, he should be here any minute," she said, offering the man another exasperated look. She didn't know if her tactic would work. She felt that being too friendly and smiley might make this man think she was an easy mark.

Acting nonchalant and as if she was focused on Michael's tardiness seemed like her best strategy.

The man's bloodshot gaze roamed over her, but she couldn't decide what he was trying to assess. He took a step closer and she could smell the sour stench of old liquor laced with cigarette smoke.

"You can wait at my place, if you like."

"Oh no, that's not necessary. Michael should be here any minute."

Okay, now she knew panic tinged her voice, making her talk a little too fast, and a little too breathy.

"I know it's not necessary," he said, seeming to find her response funny, "but it could be nice."

The man stepped closer again and Liza couldn't stop herself from backing away. She was definitely not

pulling off cool and unaffected, but this man's near-
ness was overwhelming.

He smelled awful, and she didn't like the almost
hungry look in his puffy, red eyes. She also didn't like
the fact that despite his lack of hygiene and weight
problem, he still looked fit enough to subdue her. She
could see muscles under his thick girth. If he wanted
to grab her, she would be hard pressed to struggle out
of his grasp.

Her heart raced again in that fluttery, breath-
stealing way.

Stop, she told herself. Panicking or growing light-
headed wasn't going to help the situation; that was for
sure.

"Come have a drink," the man said, holding out a
hand. The skin of his fingers was yellowed from nico-
tine, and his nails were a little too long and caked with
dirt.

More panic rose in Liza's chest. She tried not to be
obvious as she considered an escape route.

The man wiggled his fingers. "Come on, pretty girl.
We can have a little fun while you wait."

He touched her then, his dirty, calloused fingers
curling around her thin wrist.

She wanted to scream, but told herself that wouldn't
help in a place like this. Likely no one would even
bother to see what the commotion was about, and if
they did, they'd probably turn a blind eye anyway. Or
worse, want a piece of the action.

Liza told herself to remain calm, but still she
couldn't stop herself from trying to jerk her arm from
his grasp. But he held fast, his hold strong.

"You'd better let me go," she managed to say evenly
after a moment. "Because I wouldn't want to be you
when Michael arrives. He's very possessive."

The man smiled, revealing that his nail care wasn't the only thing he'd been slacking on. His teeth were yellowed, too, except for the ones that actually looked brown from decay.

"I bet he can. But I don't think he'll be back as soon as you think."

She didn't know how he knew that, but the idea that he was right sent a new wave of alarm through her. She had to think of some plan to get away.

But then the man's grip tightened more, verging on painful. It definitely told Liza this guy was a real threat. He planned to do something with her, and he had a lot more than coming in for a drink in mind.

She met his gaze, telling herself not to flinch, not to react in any way.

"You are a pretty girl," the man repeated, his bleary gaze moving over her again. And this time there was no denying the hunger there—and it was menacing.

This man intended to do something awful to her. And she had to get away.

She struggled again, but that only made the man wrench her closer. His hulking girth pinned her to the wall, and he leaned in, his foul breath panting excitedly in her face.

"I like a little fight in a lady."

He ducked in closer and she turned her head, trying to get as far away from his mouth as her trapped position would allow.

She made a noise, struggling again, as she felt his breath, damp and fetid, on the skin of her cheek and neck.

Then it was gone. She slapped her hands against the wall, almost falling as his heavy weight was abruptly removed, disorienting her for a moment.

But then her all her focus was on the scene before

her. Two men grappling. Actually, not exactly. One man beating the crap out of another.

It took her a moment to realize it was Michael. Michael twisted quickly, somehow jerking the other man's bulky weight around so Michael had him pinned to the wall. The jerk's face smashed against the wall, his arm wrenched behind his back. The whole thing was done so quickly and easily that Liza could only blink, stunned. And Michael did it with very little effort. In fact he didn't even seem to be out of breath.

The other guy wasn't as fortunate. He gasped for air as if Michael's shove had knocked the breath from his lungs.

"What the fuck, man," the hulk sputtered after a second.

"I think I should be the one asking that," Michael said, his voice low and ominous.

Chapter Sixteen

"This is just a stupid misunderstanding," the man said, but Michael clearly didn't buy it. Michael shoved the man's arms upward at a painful angle.

The man cried out, and remained totally still.

"Do you have a—cell phone?"

Liza blinked, realizing Michael was speaking to her. She nodded, but didn't move to find it. She was still too stunned by what she'd seen, too amazed that a mailroom clerk would have the moves of a seasoned law enforcement or military man.

"Liza? Do you have a cell phone?"

She blinked again, but managed to respond to his gentle tone. A tone so different from the one he'd used with the jerk.

"I—um, yeah." She began to fumble in her purse, her hands still shaking from the whole event.

"Call the police," he said, his voice still quiet, yet threatening again. Not to her, she knew, but the sound still gave her chills.

She finally found her cell, but her fingers were numb and she couldn't seem to make the touch screen work.

"Don't call the cops, man," the big man pleaded, not sounding nearly so menacing now. "I'm on probation, man."

"You should have thought about that before you tried to attack a lady. My lady."

Liza stopped her efforts to get her phone to work, startled by Michael's words. She supposed he was being possessive to make this slimy guy feel extra intimidated, but even as shaken as she was, a warm feeling permeated her fear-chilled limbs.

The man made another attempt to yank free of Michael's hold, but Michael subdued him with an efficiency that made Liza think he'd done this sort of thing before. That he was trained in combat. And he was good.

"Did you find it?" Michael asked over his shoulder.

She nodded, her hands still shaking as she tried to bring up the call screen.

"Seriously, dude, I won't come near you two again. You won't even see me," the scumbag pleaded.

Michael wrenched his arms again, hard. "And why should I trust you?"

"I'm serious, man," the jerk insisted. "I will stay the hell away from you."

Michael glanced over his shoulder at Liza. "Should I trust him?"

Liza didn't know. The man sure as heck looked and sounded scared, but given the hold Michael had him in, she was pretty sure the guy knew Michael could really hurt him.

Liza knew they should report him, since he could do this to someone else. But she really just wanted the situation to be over. He hadn't actually hurt her—although she wasn't sure he wouldn't have if Michael hadn't stopped him.

Then there was the added issue of the return of Boris. She didn't think she could handle giving a police report with Michael *and* Boris there. Boris would be asking questions nonstop about this situation, and she couldn't act normal with that going on. And she really did want to have a few moments with Michael to tell him she'd changed her mind about dating him. Maybe that was selfish—and not socially conscious—but it was the truth.

"I think he's learned his lesson," she said.

She saw the man slump with relief, but then Michael jerked his arms again and the man moaned.

"I'm not sure."

"Dude," the guy pleaded, but quieted again at another tug of his arms.

They all fell silent. Then Michael glanced over his shoulder at her again.

"Why are you here, Liza?"

Her gaze moved to the hulk still pressed against the wall, surprised at the sudden shift in conversation and also feeling a little awkward discussing this in front of the jerk.

"I—" She looked at the man again. "I wanted to see you and tell you I'm sorry about how I acted today."

Michael frowned. "Well, you certainly didn't have to come here to tell me that. It could have waited until Monday at work."

Liza supposed that was true, if that was all she'd wanted to tell him. But now she wasn't sure what to say.

"I—I guess you are right."

The man shifted, and Michael pushed him harder against the wall, yanking his arm up higher.

"Fuck," the man groaned. "I'm not trying to do anything. Shit."

"Just hold still and I won't have to pop your shoulders right out of the sockets," Michael warned, that quietly threatening tone back in his voice. "I haven't made up my mind what to do with you yet."

The man moaned again, but remained still.

"So how did you get my address?" Michael asked, looking back at Liza, his manner conversational again.

"I thought you were a couple," the jerk said, and Liza wondered if he was just that clueless. Michael had told him not to move and she was pretty sure that included his mouth too.

As if to validate Liza's thoughts, Michael ordered him to be quiet. "This conversation is none of your business." His attention returned to Liza, and he raised an eyebrow quizzically.

"I got it from Elton. I—I hope that is okay."

"It's fine. It's just not the best area to be wandering around alone."

"Yeah, I noticed," Liza said, looking pointedly at his neighbor.

Michael jerked the man's arm just slightly, and the man moaned again.

"So you came here just to apologize," Michael said, that gentle, kind tone returning.

Liza shook her head, but then didn't say anything more.

"Well, go on," Michael urged, his voice soft, but coaxing rather than harsh. She liked that tone. It was sexy and somehow exciting.

"I—I wanted to see you tonight, because—" She couldn't admit this now, in front of the man who'd had nefarious plans for her.

"Because?"

She looked sheepishly at the man, silently trying to

tell Michael she wasn't willing to talk in front of this stranger.

Michael frowned, but she wasn't sure he understood what her look meant.

"I would rather talk to you alone," she explained.

"Oh please," the jerk said, "don't let me interrupt your private moment. Hell, I'd be very happy to leave you two alone."

His words ended with a groan, as Michael shoved him harder against the wall.

"This is your lucky day." Michael leaned in to whisper to the man. "I'm going to let you go, but if I see you anywhere near my apartment. Or if I hear of you bothering any other person, anyone at all, then we are going to have a very real issue. Do you understand?"

The man made a grunting noise, but nodded his head.

"Good," Michael said, his voice still holding that menacing quality that sent chills down her spine. She could only imagine what it would feel like to have it directed at her.

She hoped she never would.

Again, she wondered how Michael knew the moves he'd used to pin this large man in place. It didn't seem like a skill a man would need to work in the mailroom, but then again, she didn't know how long he'd been with the mailroom and she didn't know what he'd done before that.

"I hope you realize that I'm not kidding around," Michael stated.

"I totally get it," the man assured him.

Michael held him a moment longer, then released him with a shove toward his own place.

The man stumbled, but caught himself before he

fell to his knees. He then walked away, rotating his shoulders as he went. He didn't even glance at them as he disappeared into his apartment.

"Do you really think he'll behave himself?" Liza asked once the jerk was in his apartment with the door closed.

"I think he will if he's smart."

Liza couldn't disagree with that. She wouldn't want to tangle with Michael. Not when he was in attack mode, that was for sure.

He turned his full attention to her. "You want to talk?"

She nodded, feeling apprehensive again. What if he had decided his offer no longer stood, and he didn't want to date?

She watched nervously as he stepped forward and unlocked his apartment door.

"Come on in," he said, pushing the door open, so she could slip past him and step inside.

Chapter Seventeen

"It's not great, but it's okay for now."

Michael didn't like Liza seeing how he was living. A run-down, dingy apartment and scary, ex-con neighbors. Yeah, this wasn't a way to make a positive impression.

Her expression didn't exactly hide the fact that she did find his apartment a bit squalid. She wandered into the center of the room, her eyes roaming over the worn furniture and lack of décor.

"How long have you been here?" she asked.

"Just a few weeks or so," he said. "A friend actually located this for me, but I don't plan on staying here long. Especially after tonight."

Liza nodded, and he could see her face was still pale. She clutched the strap of her purse as if it was a lifeline or something. Slowly she walked over to the threadbare sofa. She seemed shaky as she sat down on the edge.

"Are you okay?" he asked.

She nodded too quickly. "I'm fine. Just very glad you showed up when you did."

He was glad too. Things could have gone very differently, and the idea of the man touching Liza, possibly hurting her, made him furious.

So mad, it actually shocked him. He'd managed to keep his anger in check, but the idea of someone hurting Liza made him want to lash out. He couldn't understand his possessiveness, and at this moment, he didn't care to analyze it. He was just glad she was safe.

"So you said you wanted to talk to me."

She still clutched her purse, and her color didn't look much better, but she nodded, though she didn't speak for a few moments. When she did, he didn't immediately understand what she was asking.

"Have you had some formal training?"

"Training?"

"Combat training, or something like that?" she said. "It's just that you subdued that man so quickly, and you clearly knew the best position to keep him in, so he couldn't fight."

"Oh." He was kind of surprised she'd noticed that. The move wasn't anything too advanced, just a common enough restraint. But maybe she didn't expect a mailroom clerk to have fighting skills. Wasn't that exactly why the mailroom was a good cover? No one expected mailroom staff to be out of the ordinary in any way.

Suddenly he didn't want her considering his behavior too closely. Nor did he want her to mention this to anyone in the mailroom. He'd already brought enough attention to himself.

"Yes, a little," he said, then changed the subject. "Can I get you a drink? You look like you could use it."

She hesitated, then nodded. "That would be nice."

He nodded too and walked over to the kitchenette that took up one small corner of the room.

"All I have is beer." He opened a dorm room–sized fridge and pulled out two beers.

"That's fine," she said. He crossed over to her, unscrewed the cap on one, and handed it to her.

"Thank you." She glanced at the bottle, making a slight face. Probably another who didn't drink Pabst either, but then she took a sip. Then another.

"So what kind of training?" she asked.

Boy, she didn't want to let that one go, did she?

"I've done several martial arts," he said, which was true. "Karate, kung fu."

"Because everybody was kung fu fighting," Liza said with a slight smile.

Michael smiled back, glad to see some humor on her face. "Exactly."

After a short pause he asked, "Are you really okay?"

"I'm fine," she said with a shaky smile. "A little stunned, but glad things didn't go any worse."

He studied her for a moment. "Me too. It's lucky I decided to make an early night of it."

She nodded, then took another sip of her beer.

"So you said you came here to talk about something," he said, when it appeared as if she wasn't going to say anything more.

She glanced up from her beer bottle, which seemed to be infinitely fascinating.

"Yes." She sounded uncertain again, but then when he thought he was going to have to prompt her to talk, she just blurted out, "I want to date you too."

He stared at her for a second, not sure exactly what that meant. Had she changed her mind?

But before he could ask, she added, "I mean, I realize I probably blew my chance with the way I acted in the office, but I wasn't prepared for what you said. And now that I've had time to think—with a somewhat clearer head—I know I want to date you too."

"Are you sure? Because honestly, you seemed pretty set against—well, anything to do with me."

"I know. I was worried that it might be hard for us to see each other. Finola White doesn't approve of inter-office dating, so we'd have to be very careful about it."

"Okay," Michael said without hesitation. After all, it was unlikely Eugene or The Brethren would approve of a slayer dating someone who worked directly for Finola White and *HOT!* That could be dangerous.

And that was exactly why he shouldn't be agreeing to keep this relationship a secret. He should not be agreeing to the relationship period.

But again, he ignored what was sensible, because the drive to be with this woman was so strong. Even now, realizing she wouldn't pull away from him, he wanted to cross the room and kiss her. He'd wanted to hold her from the moment they'd walked into the apartment. He'd wanted to hold her after that creep's attempted attack. He knew he'd probably agree to whatever way she wanted to date.

"You—you are okay with that?" she asked, and he couldn't tell if she was pleased or nervous about his agreement.

"I think it's wise. And in truth, it isn't anyone's business but ours." It definitely wasn't Eugene's business.

She nodded, then looked back at her beer bottle as if she still wasn't sure.

"Liza, this can work." He crossed over to her. He set down his untouched beer and reached for her, pulling her up. He wrapped her in his arms, the way he'd wanted to since he'd spotted her standing in his hallway, relieved that she didn't pull away. In fact she curled around him as if she'd wanted him to hold her this whole time too.

He tightened his embrace, resting his cheek on the top of her head. He didn't know how this would work. Or if it would work, but he was going for it.

Liza sighed, sinking against his warm, broad chest. She'd wanted to feel him against her again, from the moment she'd left him after they'd made love. She nestled her head against him, feeling safe. A false sense she knew. But he'd rescued her tonight, and although he couldn't ultimately save her from her fate, her possession, for a little while she wanted to pretend he could.

She didn't know how they were going to pull this off. But she couldn't stay away. She knew that.

"It's so strange, but I just can't seem to stay away from you. I knew this would be complicated and dangerous"—she paused, realizing he might find "dangerous" an odd way to term it—"I mean dangerous because we could lose our jobs."

"I have no fear of Finola White," he assured her, his hand caressing down her back. She shivered, losing herself to the feeling of his hands moving over her. But his wording did eventually seep past the haze of contentment his delicious touch created.

Did he realize Finola White was a creature to fear? Did he know what Finola actually was?

She doubted it. He was new to Finola White Enterprises. And as far as she knew, no one would sell their soul to work in the mailroom. Nor would demons lower themselves to work down there.

He was probably just stating his feelings. And while Liza knew the situation was very dangerous, and what the real danger could be, she wasn't afraid of Finola either.

At least not here.

She lifted her head and he did too. Their eyes held, and then they were kissing. An intense, passionate kiss as if both of them had longed for this. Liza knew she had.

"I'm so glad you changed your mind," he murmured against her lips.

She nodded slightly, unable to speak, just wanting to kiss him some more. He readily obliged her, his lips moving over hers, kissing her senseless.

Only when she nearly dropped the bottle, forgotten in her hand, did she break off the kiss. Michael smiled, taking the beer from her and placing it beside his on the rickety coffee table. Then he reached for her again, this time taking her hand.

She didn't hesitate as he led her toward his bed, a full-sized mattress and box spring on a metal frame. Truthfully it could have been a blanket on the bare floor for all Liza cared, or the bare floor itself for that matter. She just wanted to be in his arms, feeling his hands moving over her skin, his lips against hers, against her bare flesh.

He stopped at the edge of the bed and kissed her again.

"I know I said we should date," he murmured after a moment, his forehead resting against hers as if he didn't want to break their touch.

Liza understood what he was saying. They both knew they were headed back to bed, but he wanted to make sure it was okay with her first.

"We can have dinner or a movie next time," she said, her fingers moving to the buttons of his shirt.

He smiled at that, a crooked, pleased, breathtaking smile.

"Definitely next time," he agreed.

"Definitely," she said, smiling back. Then she parted his shirt and kissed his bare chest. She pushed the garment off his shoulders, letting it fall to the ground.

He gasped as her tongue lapped his nipple. She licked him more as her fingers moved to his belt, working the buckle open. She felt very forward, undressing him so aggressively, but it also felt wonderfully liberating.

And maybe the adrenaline left over from being attacked in the hallway was making her bold. Or maybe she simply wanted this man more than she had ever wanted anyone.

Maybe it was all of it. But whatever the reason, she did feel more daring, more wanton, than she ever had before in her life.

She pushed down his jeans and boxers, and he toed off his boots and kicked the crumpled jeans aside. Standing before her naked, he really was the vision of perfection. Muscles, smooth skin, a face that would make most male models jealous. Other powerful, perfect parts of him . . .

"You are like Michael," she suddenly realized.

He smiled. "I'm not like Michael. I am Michael."

She laughed. "I know. I mean, you look like the paintings of the archangel Michael. Strong, powerful, and yet almost achingly beautiful."

Michael gazed at her for a moment, then offered her another crooked smile, although this one seemed almost embarrassed. "I'm definitely not an archangel. Or an angel of any sort. But I'm pleased you see me that way. Because like Michael, I will always act as your protector."

She stepped forward to touch him, his skin warm and smooth under her fingers. Golden and heavenly. She didn't know if he could truly be her protector, but he had saved her tonight. And more than that, he'd saved her from the misery she'd been living in.

That alone made him an angel to her.

She reached up and kissed him sweetly, a kiss of gratitude, but he quickly shifted that touch, deepening the kiss.

Soon he had her clothing off and pooled around her on the ground.

They stood naked in each other's arms, again kissing and touching, their exploration somehow slow and desperate all at once. Almost like they had to memorize each other's bodies.

"This is torture," Michael finally groaned against the sensitive flesh just below her ear. The vibration of his voice, the heat of his breath, the brush of his lips sent shock waves straight through her body. Desire, warm and tingly, pooled deep in her belly, moving lower and lower.

She nodded her agreement. It was torture. Delicious torture.

"I have to feel you under me," he whispered and again she nodded.

Yes, she needed that too.

He scooped her up and placed her on the bed. Liza was always one of the tallest women in a room, but in Michael's arms she felt petite. Tiny. Fragile.

He followed her down on the bed, stroking his hands over her arms, across her chest and belly to her long legs. Even that touch made her feel delicate, treasured.

"I think you are the angel," he said and Liza immediately laughed, a harsher sound than he would have expected.

Michael frowned, surprised that her laughter sounded almost bitter.

"I'm hardly that," she said, her troubled gaze reminding him of her precarious situation.

But she was wrong. Making a mistake, signing that soul contract didn't make her a less good and pure woman.

"You are perfect," he assured her, pressing a kiss to her lips.

She kissed him back, but he could still feel her reserve, her doubts.

She was ashamed of what she'd done. He understood that, but her soul would remain safe. He would protect her.

That thought spurred him on, his touch becoming more insistent, more dominant. She was his woman and he'd defend her, love her, keep her out of harm's way.

She moaned, responding instantly to his possessive touch, writhing at each stroke. She liked his possession, her breath speeding up to short little pants. Her body moved against his, demanding more of his forceful touches.

He obliged, parting her legs to stroke the hot flesh between them. His finger penetrated her, filled her, and she arched to take more. She was so giving, so ready for him. It was hard not to just take her right then.

But he wanted his possession to be one of ultimate pleasure. He wanted her to orgasm over and over for him, until she was weak from his lovemaking.

So he continued to stroke her, his fingers soon replaced by his tongue. Her legs were anchored to his shoulders, her hips lifting up to grind against his mouth, her desire as wild as his.

"Michael," she moaned, her head twisting back and forth. "Michael."

"Yes, baby," he whispered against her wet flesh.

She moaned again, before answering. "Please. I need you inside me. Please."

He didn't leave her right away, continuing to lick her, feeling another orgasm pulse under his lips and tongue. Only when she collapsed back against the mattress did he slide up her body.

She watched him from underneath sleepy eyelids. Her arms above her head, her posture open to him, willing, ready.

He kissed her as he slowly slid into her tight heat. She was slick and hot and it took every ounce of his willpower not to lose control.

"You feel amazing," he muttered, gritting his teeth in determination not to come too quickly. But damn, she felt so perfect around him. Like her body was made solely for him.

"You do too," she breathed, wiggling her hips.

He answered her movement, thrusting in and out of her. Quickly they were both gasping, both grinding together, both demanding that the other submit. Give in to the fever that burned in them both.

Liza cried out as her orgasm tore through her, her release violent and overwhelming. He barely got to feel that wild pulsing before he joined her, his own orgasm powerful, mind-blowing.

He collapsed on her, making sure his full weight didn't crush her.

"Mine," he murmured.

She stroked his back, and whispered, "Mine," back to him.

Then they both fell into an exhausted, blissful oblivion.

Chapter Eighteen

Liza gasped. She pressed her hand to her chest, where she could feel her heart pounding against her palm, rapid, erratic. She stared up at the dingy drop ceiling, trying to focus on the yellowed panels, the chips, the water stains. Anything but her racing heart, which threatened to thump right out of her chest.

She couldn't ignore this, or say this reaction was nerves. She'd been sound asleep after making love to the gorgeous man beside her. She'd been content, sated, sleepy.

This reaction was the medication. That was the only answer, and it was scaring her. She pushed harder on her chest, willing the thumping organ to calm down.

She also breathed in slowly and deeply, then released her breath just as gradually. She could get control of her heart rate.

She lay there for several minutes, determined to get this episode under control. Finally, when she thought she'd gotten her racing pulse and heartbeat quieted down, she pushed upright, moving carefully, concerned as much with waking Michael as she was about how her change in position might affect her.

Once sitting, she remained still. Her heart had seemed to calm down. She still felt an irregular flutter, and her breath felt like it hitched in her lungs occasionally, but overall, she felt much better.

Nothing to worry about, she told herself. So the meds had a slight side effect, and it was a little scary when it was happening, but the racing heart didn't last long, and it was certainly a manageable side effect, when compared to dealing with Boris.

Bartoris.

Liza froze. Oh my God, he was awake.

But then she heard that soft snore of his. Had that just been one of those random moments in sleep when he became aware for just a second? Or was he groggily waking up?

She couldn't risk staying here any longer, and she hadn't had the forethought to bring extra allergy meds with her. She also didn't want to risk waking Michael. He would ask too many questions, and she needed to get out of here as quickly as possible.

Moving inch by inch, she shimmied her way toward the end of the bed until her feet touched the floor. Then she cautiously stood. She glanced back toward Michael. Only his silhouette was visible in the bed, but he didn't appear to have moved. In the faint light, she could see his arms were still flung up over his head.

She allowed herself half a second to admire his bare chest, the muscles emphasized by the shadows. Then she quietly gathered her clothes. Once dressed, aside from her panties, which she couldn't find, she crept to her purse.

Finding a pen and paper wasn't as easy as she

hoped, and twice she almost dropped her purse, which would have made a heavy thud on the floor. But finally she did find a pen and what she thought was a receipt from Starbucks. She wasn't quite sure in the darkness.

She tiptoed to the window.

A grumbling yawn echoed through her head, and she quickly jotted down a note to Michael. Then she debated, also as quickly as possible, where she should place the note. She wanted to be sure he'd find it.

She decided her pillow was the best bet. Carefully leaning over him, she placed the note in the indentation in the pillow where her head had been. Hopefully he'd find it.

Again, a groggy grumble ricocheted through her skull, making her wince and rush her actions.

She hurried to the door, twisting the lock and handle as quietly as she could. When she opened the door, it creaked and the fixture from the hallway cast a shaft of light across the room and right onto the bed over Michael's face.

She paused for a minute, her breath held. But Michael remained still.

She released her pent-up breath and quickly stepped out of the door, pulling it shut behind her, wincing, this time at the loud click the door made as it closed.

But then her head filled with that voice she so dreaded.

You bitch. I'm telling.

Even though she hated hearing Boris, his words made her chuckle. "Go ahead and tell."

Bitch.

She chuckled again, but then cast a wary look first at the creepy neighbor's door, then back at Michael's. She didn't want either man to hear her.

She debated taking the elevator, but opted for the stairs. She suspected they would be quicker as well as safer. Well, as long as no other creepy apartment dwellers were around this time of night.

She slipped through the door and dashed down the stairs.

Michael opened his eyes as soon as Liza slipped out of his apartment. He crept over to the door, listening. He heard the faint sound of Liza's voice, then what he thought was a laugh.

What was she doing? He reached for the doorknob, turning it very, very slowly. Then he cracked the door slightly, just in time to see Liza disappear into the stairwell.

Why was she leaving? Again, making a break for it after they'd made love.

Talk about commitment issues.

He debated whether he should follow her. This building had proven to not be the safest place, and the outside neighborhood wasn't much better. Besides, he'd really like to catch her and ask her what the hell was going on.

But instead he went back into his apartment, crossing to the window where he could see the street. In just a few seconds, Liza appeared on the sidewalk below. She waited only a second before a cab came by and she flagged it down. Once she was safely on her way to wherever, Michael turned back to his bed, knowing she'd reached over him while she thought he slept to place something there.

He switched on a light and found a small rectangle of paper. Written in uneven, hurried handwriting was a note apologizing for leaving so abruptly, and explaining that she remembered she had to meet an important deadline back at work. She finished by asking him to please text her when he woke up, and inquiring whether he'd like to meet her for dinner tomorrow night.

A real date, she wrote, followed by a winking smiley face.

He glanced at the clock on his nightstand. It was after midnight on a Friday night and Liza was rushing back to work.

He wondered if the deadline could be true, but then he remembered who her boss was. She probably was headed back to work. Although that didn't explain what he'd heard in the hallway. He doubted Liza would be laughing about returning to the magazine. But since he had no idea, he was going to have to believe that was what she was doing. At least she did want to see him again. A real date. That was a better ending than their first time together.

He lay back down on the bed, rereading the note. And he had her phone number. That was good too.

Now if he could just figure out what the hell texting was.

"Do you think Liza McLane is becoming a problem?"

Tristan stopped pouring vodka into a martini glass to glance at his boss—"mistress" was really her title, but he couldn't bring himself to call her that at the moment. He was getting far too hungry to finally be the one in charge.

And at last she appeared to be giving him his chance to make a move. A few properly planted seeds of doubt and paranoia, and he could have Finola doing something rash to their real editor-in-chief, probably within the next couple days. Then Dippy could go report the incident to Satan, Satan would finally see that Finola was a loose cannon, and *ta-da,* Tristan would be in charge.

It could be that simple.

He set down the vodka bottle, staring at it for a moment, gathering his thoughts, debating how to play this conversation.

Part of him still thought Liza McLane might be a risky choice, because she could still be needed. Not to mention she was possessed by that weasel of a demon, Bartoris. If he caught wind of a takeover, he'd spill the whole plan to Satan in a heartbeat. And then Tristan and Dippy would be on the chopping block. Satan didn't tolerate disloyalty, and for whatever reason, their boss still backed and believed in Finola. Tristan knew even a rumor of rebellion would end any chance of Tristan becoming the leader of this demon invasion. It would, in fact, end his stay here in the human world. Something he really didn't want either. He liked the human realm very, very much.

Just then, there was a tap on Finola's office door. Georgia stood on the other side, with Dippy held awkwardly in her arms as if she was holding a scaly lizard rather than a fuzzy, white pooch.

Of course, Dippy was a hellhound. For all Tristan knew, his demon form might be scaly.

Finola waved to her, clearly irritated to be interrupted before Tristan had answered her.

"Ms. White, your dog is all groomed."

Tristan could tell by Dippy's disgruntled expression, he hadn't enjoyed his evening of pampering.

"Did you buff and paint his nails?" Finola demanded, holding out her arms for her beloved pet.

"Yes, and I used the white polish and then did silver tips like you requested," Georgia replied, quickly relinquishing the dog to its owner.

Tristan noticed that Peaches rubbed her forearm as soon as the dog was gone, as if it was hurting, although he couldn't see any injury because the sleeves of her black, vintage-looking dress covered the area.

"I believe I said I wanted the silver polish on the nails with white tips," Finola said, inspecting Dippy's claws with a dubious frown. Then she blinked up at her assistant. "You have seen a French manicure, haven't you?"

Peaches nodded, but Tristan could almost hear the woman's thoughts—*not on a dog*.

Finola sighed, clearly not satisfied, even as she said, "Well, I suppose this will have to do." Then Finola's expression softened to one of complete adoration, "You look beautiful, my little sweetie."

Finola nuzzled Dippy to her cheek.

Tristan could almost hear the dog's thoughts too. He'd love to bite his doting mistress.

Tristan didn't blame him.

Peaches waited as Finola fawned over her pet for several moments. When Finola stopped long enough to wave the overworked woman away, Georgia didn't hesitate, turning toward the door, but not before she shot Tristan a look.

Tristan saw lust in her wide eyes, behind her funky glasses—that usual desire he always saw and felt when he was near her. And his body reacted, his usual response too.

But he was a demon of lust, so that was to be expected. But even her desire for him didn't slow her steps as the personal assistant left the room without looking back again. He couldn't blame her. Grooming her boss's dog long after her workday should be done probably wasn't high on Peaches's list of fun things to do on a Friday night.

"I swear my assistants get worse and worse with each consecutive one."

Tristan didn't respond, but rather returned to mixing his drink.

But before he could even pour the vodka into the martini glass, Finola asked again, "So you didn't answer me. What do you think about Liza's recent behavior?"

He looked at the vodka bottle he held. *Diva Vodka.* Of course, Finola would have Diva Vodka. Only because it was $1,060,000 a bottle, and not because it was the best damned vodka in the world. No, it cost that much because it had actual diamonds and rubies in the bottle.

He finished making his dirty martini, then took a sip. Shit, he was more of a Stoli man himself.

Another reason he was a better demon for this job. He could be just as decadent and over the top as Finola, but he could be practical too.

"Tristan?"

He knew he had to say something, but he wasn't sure what was the right answer. On one hand, if Finola got rid of Liza McLane, it would definitely get Satan's attention. Tristan had little doubt that the big man downstairs would take action immediately if Finola cast Liza's soul to Hell without a legal and binding soul contract, which Finola did not have. Liza hadn't agreed to sign one. Hence the need for possession to keep her under control.

But there was still the fact that he—and Dippy, of course—might need Liza; and that Bartoris could potentially discover something and tattle. Someone like

Liza's personal assistant would be a safer choice, and would probably get the reaction they wanted without as much of the risk. After all, Satan already knew about Finola's rash behavior toward past assistants, and the illegally broken soul contracts that she'd left in her tyrannical wake.

But he did also think Peaches, with her barely contained desire for him, could be useful too. He'd need a devoted assistant when he took Finola's place at the head of *HOT!* magazine and the demon takeover.

This wasn't an easy decision.

He took one more sip, then turned to the person who'd gone from boss and lover to nemesis, his decision made.

She arched an eyebrow at him, her impatience clear in her pale, pale eyes.

"I think she might be a problem," he said. "Even with Bartoris possessing her, she's getting more rebellious, and I do think she could get worse."

Finola nodded, but didn't speak. Instead she seemed lost in thought, absently stroking Dippy's curly fur.

Dippy shot Tristan a look. A look somewhere between annoyed, at what Finola was doing to him, and pleased.

Tristan still found it weird that a dog could have that much expression. But then again, he was a dog who could also talk. Tristan wondered if he had been in the human world too long.

Oh well. He planned to stay.

"I do think action might need to be taken," he said to Finola. "And soon."

Finola nodded, but continued to rub Dippy, who now just looked like he wanted to get away from her as fast as his white- and silver-manicured paws would let him. He wiggled, but Finola didn't seem to notice, still lost in thought.

Leave it to Finola to now suddenly think things through rather than just react. Maybe Satan's warnings had finally sunk in. At the worst possible time.

"I think you should keep a close eye on her," she said after a moment. "I agree with you, but we need a really good reason to take any drastic action."

Tristan hid his frustration by taking a sip of his drink. Then after letting the liquor—which he still wished was Stoli—burn the back of his throat, he said, "Of course." But then he added, "Still, I don't think we should let her get too out of control."

"I'm well aware of that," Finola said, her voice sharp. She didn't care for being told how to handle her business, even when she'd asked for advice. She stroked Dippy one last time, and then set him on the floor. Dippy scampered away, clearly glad to be released. He positioned himself in his bejeweled dog bed so he could watch both Tristan and Finola, much as if he was about to watch a tennis match . . . or a boxing match.

And this could get ugly, but it would also be a good time to push Finola a little, get her a little more agitated about Liza. An irritated and agitated Finola was more impulsive. He just hoped if he pushed her, she would not simply become irritated with him. Or Peaches—since he'd now made up his mind that Liza should be the target. And Tristan might also be able to get rid of Bartoris too—if he played his cards right.

"I think Liza has a point, though," he said.

Finola frowned, then let her face relax, appearing almost serene, even though her eyes flashed with impatience.

"What point is that?"

Tristan pretended to ponder the contents of his martini glass, then when Finola was almost ready to snap, he looked back at her.

"Perhaps she would be more productive and compliant if Bartoris was gone." He lifted his eyebrow. "After all, he is one annoying demon."

Finola didn't say anything, although Tristan could see the wheels turning in her head again.

Dippy made a small noise somewhere between a growl and a whine, and Tristan glanced at the dog. Dippy nodded his head slightly, and Tristan knew his canine conspirator agreed with what he was trying to do.

Damn, was it a little worrisome that he understood the barks, growls, and expressions of a dog?

"Maybe you should just exorcise him and send him back to Hell," Tristan continued, telling himself it wasn't odd that he rather appreciated the moral support of a dog.

Finola still remained silent for a moment, then shook her head. "I think we should wait. Satan specifically assigned Bartoris to her, and I'm not willing to do anything that might upset the Prince of Darkness. I know he's still watching me."

Tristan frowned, surprised at how rational she was being. Finola was many things, but rational usually wasn't one of them. Again, leave it to her to pick this moment to be sensible and cautious.

"But I still want you to watch her. It's clear that Bartoris isn't doing his job, but we can't cast him out yet," Finola said, then picked up the glass of champagne he'd poured her earlier. She took a sip. "I don't want her getting out of hand, but we have to be certain there is really a problem before we take action."

Tristan stared at her. Who was this creature? Had Finola been replaced by a practical demon double?

"So," she said after taking another leisurely swallow of her bubbly, "I want you to focus on nothing but watching Liza McLane. That means here at work, when she leaves the building, when she's at home. You are going to follow her everywhere."

Okay, this sounded more like the wacky Finola he knew—and wanted to overthrow.

Tristan had no desire to traipse around after Liza McLane, spying on her. After all, he had a coup to stage, but he supposed this silly task could speed that up too. He'd follow Liza long enough to come up with something she'd done—real or not—that would provoke Finola's wrath. In fact, this little task might make the whole coup go much faster and smoother.

Finola sighed and stretched her back slightly as if this moment of reasonable—well, mostly reasonable—behavior had stressed her entire body.

"Where is that dreadful new assistant of mine?"

"I believe she's gone home." He glanced at his watch. "It is after midnight on a Friday night."

She sighed again. "I need a massage."

Tristan wanted to groan, knowing what was coming.

"Be a pet," she said, "and get the massage table so you can give me a massage. I need to relax. Being the leader of a demonic rebellion is exhausting."

Tristan polished off the rest of his martini, wishing it were his fourth rather than just his first, then left Finola's office to retrieve the massage table.

As he left, he heard Dippy make a noise, this one between a whine and a snicker. Yeah, this coup needed to happen soon.

Chapter Nineteen

"Wow, you are actually here."

Liza smiled as she saw Michael walking toward her. As always, she was struck by how handsome he was. Tall, muscular, brown hair, and those golden-brown eyes. She could hardly believe she was involved with this man. And frankly, she was just as surprised to see him as he sounded to see her.

She was actually sort of seeing two of him, because her allergy meds hadn't lost their effect on her completely. Figuring out the timing of taking the drugs so she was over the unpleasant initial side effects, but got as much Boris-free time as she could with Michael, was tricky.

"I'm kind of surprised too," she said, then quickly added, "Not that I'm here, but that you are. I was starting to think you might not be interested when you never texted."

She had been worried, and regretting that although he had her number, she didn't have his. But when a girl was making a hasty escape in the dark, after mindblowing sex, with a drugged demon swearing in her head, it wasn't the best time to exchange digits.

He gave her a sheepish look. "I have to admit I don't know how to text." He tapped his pants pocket, where his phone must be. "New phone. Cell phone, I mean."

Liza smiled, finding it amusing that he felt he needed to clarify that he was talking about his cell phone.

"But I'm glad you did finally call," she said.

"I'm glad that was your cell phone number too. I wasn't sure."

She smiled wider. "I don't know many people who have a separate text and phone line—or any really."

"Oh," he said with a shrug. "Well, we are both here. That's all that matters."

Liza couldn't agree more.

Then Michael slid into the booth, and all she could focus on was the size and heat of his body next to her. Honestly, she could not remember ever being so attracted to a man. He seemed to bring all her senses to heightened awareness.

But she was determined to actually have a date where they could get to know each other. She'd even asked for a table in a quiet, secluded corner just so they could talk with some privacy. She thought they should actually get to know each other, since thus far they'd spent most of their time together in bed. Or when Michael was rushing her to the emergency room, or manhandling would-be assaulters. Tonight, she hoped they would get a chance to learn more about each other.

But it was hard to remember that when he was close. Man, he really did send her body into overdrive.

"You look lovely," he said as soon as he was settled, his muscular thigh brushing against hers.

"Thank you," she said, feeling her cheeks heat from both the compliment and her body's reaction to his inadvertent touch. Her breasts instantly felt heavy and her nipples hard, and she didn't even want to consider what was going on between her crossed legs.

Good golly, this man affected her.

"So did you get your work done for Ms. White?" Michael asked, his tone even, calm.

Liza frowned, confused for a moment, first by the fact that he could sound so composed when her heart skipped and hopped like an Irish step dancer in her chest, and then because she didn't know what he was talking about.

Oh, she realized after a moment, the excuse she'd given him about why she'd had to disappear last night. Apparently he'd accepted it.

"Oh," she said, realizing her voice sounded breathless. "I did. Sorry to leave that way, but you have no idea how demanding and difficult she can be."

"Oh, I've heard," he said, his voice flat as if he was less than impressed with the woman. If fact, she would almost say there was an angry edge to his voice, but she wasn't sure.

"Yeah, she's hell to work for, actually." Which wasn't overstating the truth.

"I've definitely heard that too," he said, "and I'm sure all of it is true and more."

Again she got the feeling that he truly disliked Finola White, which didn't make much sense to her, since she knew he was new to the mailroom and probably hadn't even met the woman—or rather demon—not that he could possibly know what she really was. Unless he'd sold his soul to Finola. And again, who would sell their soul to work in the mailroom?

Either way, she would never know. It was a part of the soul contract that the deal would never be discussed with anyone other than the signee and Finola. So everyone, or just about everyone, who worked directly for *HOT!* magazine knew that Finola was a demon, but no one ever mentioned it. More torture, to know evil existed and was right beside you, but you couldn't say anything about it. More hell.

Still, Liza wondered if he could possibly know Finola, and the truth about her.

"How did you start working in the mailroom?" she asked.

He looked up from the menu that he'd idly opened. "Umm, I just kind of found myself with the job."

Liza frowned, not quite understanding that, even though she didn't imagine it was hard to get a position there. Weren't mailrooms considered starting at the bottom rung? Of course, she wasn't going to say that to him.

"So you've never worked in a mailroom before?"

"No. Never."

She supposed that wasn't so strange, although he didn't seem like the type of man who would work in a mailroom. It seemed like too inactive a job for such a strong, virile man. He had an energy about him that was more suited to an exciting, high-action job rather than just delivering and collecting mail.

"What did you do before this?"

He looked up from his menu again, and he seemed to hesitate.

"Law enforcement," he finally said, and this time his voice was laced with what she thought was both irritation and disappointment. She had asked him about his training after that creep attacked her the other night. But he hadn't mentioned working in law enforcement. Only martial arts training. Had he been forced out of law enforcement? Certainly working in a mailroom had to be a pay cut. Maybe that was the reason for his tone.

She hesitated now too, not wanting to bring up a sore subject, but her curiosity got the better of her.

"What part of law enforcement were you involved in?"

Again he paused, this time not looking up from his menu. "Special forces. But that was a long time ago."

Liza studied his profile for a moment, realizing he wasn't going to talk about it any further. Which, of course, piqued her interest even more, but she didn't ask anything else. Instead she opened her own menu.

"This place is supposed to be really good," she said, forcing herself to peruse the menu and let their previous line of conversation go. "I've never been here myself, but everyone raves about it."

Michael looked up from his menu, scanning the tasteful and expensive decor. "Last time I was here, this place was a dive pizza joint."

Liza immediately lifted her head to study him. "Last time you were here?"

Shit, why had he said that? He'd already said too much by telling her that his previous job had been in special forces. But he hated totally lying. Not to mention his own pride pushed him to say he'd been something else other than a mailroom worker. Mailroom—even though it wasn't exactly the job Liza thought it was, it was still lame.

But now he'd also said he'd been in this restaurant

before—when it was under different management. He needed to be careful.

"Well, I told you I lived in New York years ago, and I seem to recall this place being different. I think. Actually I'm not really sure," he lied.

"How long ago did you live here?" she asked, her gaze returning to her menu.

Shit, why hadn't he expected her to ask more about his past? He should have had these answers figured out and down pat. Not only for Liza, who was bound to ask things like this since they were involved, but for other people too. People were going to ask questions.

"I—um—" He pretended to consider. "It must have been 1990-ish."

Liza glanced up at him, surprised. "Oh, then you must have been young when you lived here before."

"Yes—yes, I was."

Liza studied him for a moment, then said, "I got the impression when you asked me to show you around that you'd lived here as an adult."

Shit. Well, he had lived here as an adult. An adult who was exactly the same age he was now. Shit.

"No," he said, forcing a smile that he hoped looked natural. "I was young. All the more reason I need someone to show me around."

She seemed to consider that, then nodded. "Yeah, I suppose you wouldn't know much about the city now."

Well, that much was true. Michael looked down at his menu, which he'd unconsciously closed while they were talking. He stared at it blankly for a moment. What had this place been called back in the seventies? Luigi's . . . or something like that. What were the chances they would even come to a place he remembered?

Then his eyes actually focused on the front of the menu he'd been staring at. Across the bottom of the menu in a loopy font was something that made his blood run cold.

Bardo's, established in 1982.

As soon as he read it, he noticed Liza looking in his direction, clearly curious about what had attracted his attention. She started to flip her menu closed as well, when he shot out a hand to press a finger down on her menu, so she couldn't close it.

"Look at this dish," he said, knowing his voice sounded a little desperate. "It sounds amazing."

Liza frowned at him, but looked at the description beside his finger.

"The Caesar salad?" she said, clearly confused about why he was so emphatically pointing out such a commonplace dish.

He opened his own menu without moving his finger from hers.

"Oh," he said, scanning the menu, searching for anything that sounded different and interesting. "I meant to point to this."

He lowered his finger several items. "The tuna tartare with seaweed salad. That sounds good."

Okay, he wasn't sure about that, but he'd committed, so he had to sound thoroughly intrigued by it.

Liza read the description, then nodded. "That does sound good. The beet salad with goat cheese and walnuts sounds yummy too."

"It does," Michael readily agreed, even though he really disliked beets, but he'd agree to just about anything to get her attention away from what he'd been looking at.

The distraction seemed to work, because she continued to read the menu. His luck continued as the waiter approached them to take their drink and appetizer orders.

"Why don't you get the tuna salad and I will get the beet. So we can try both of them," Liza suggested.

Michael nodded, not really keen about either choice. But since he had feigned such excitement about both, he didn't see any way around ordering them.

Maybe he should have stuck with being excited about the Caesar salad.

Once the waiter was gone, they both continued reading over the menu. He was going to get steak—that would make up for the rather disgusting-sounding salads.

Then beside him, he felt rather than saw Liza suddenly go tense, her posture taking on an almost frightened quality as if she was seeing a ghost.

"Are you okay?" he asked immediately and then followed her gaze. The bar area was crowded, the stools all filled and other people standing with drinks in their hands. Michael couldn't see what—or rather who—had captured her attention.

She didn't speak for a moment, then nodded, even as she continued to stare in that direction. "Yes—yes, I just thought I saw someone."

Michael looked away from her toward the bar again. He didn't see anyone who appeared out of the ordinary. To him, it just looked like a crowd of happy patrons out on a Saturday night.

But something had caused Liza to react powerfully.

"Are you sure?"

Liza tore her eyes away from the bar and offered him a small smile that was supposed to reassure him, but didn't.

"I just thought I saw someone, but I couldn't have."

But even as she said that, her gaze strayed back to the bar.

Michael looked again too. She had thought she'd seen something, and she still did.

Chapter Twenty

By the time the drinks arrived and Liza had taken a few sips of her chardonnay, she had convinced herself she'd just imagined that Finola's right-hand man, Tristan, had been standing at the bar, watching her and Michael.

And even if she had seen him, it could be coincidence. He could have just come here for a drink or dinner by chance. But even as she told herself that, she knew that nothing was coincidence with either Finola or Tristan.

She took another sip of her wine, and told herself to go with her original thought. She'd imagined him.

"How is the beet salad?" Michael asked, concern still in his golden eyes.

"It's delicious," she said, realizing it was true, even though she hadn't really noticed the first couple of bites. She'd been too troubled by the idea that Tristan might be there. But even if he had been, he wasn't now.

"Would you like to try some?" she asked, forcing herself to push aside the uneasy feeling that still made her chest tighten and her heart pound.

Michael glanced at her plate. "I'm good, but would you like to try this?"

Liza looked at his plate, noticing that he'd barely eaten any of his salad. She scooped up some of the pink tuna and bright green seaweed in her fork, then into her mouth.

"Mmm," she said, enjoying the tartness and texture of the salad. "This is delicious."

Michael nodded, but again, she didn't get the feeling he was thrilled with his food.

"Not what you expected, huh?"

Michael stopped poking at the small chunks of tuna with his fork and looked at her.

"Not really," he admitted with a rueful smile.

She smiled, more tension leaving her. That was until Michael asked, "Who did you think you saw over at the bar?"

She should have known he would notice her reaction earlier. She suspected he didn't miss much.

For a moment, she debated whether to tell him the truth, then decided there wasn't any reason not to tell him.

"I actually thought I saw Finola's assistant editor."

Michael nodded, glancing back in that direction.

"That seemed to have you upset," he said after a moment. "Why?"

She thought about lying. After all, Tristan didn't seem to be at the bar any longer, and she could be just blowing everything out of proportion anyway.

"Why would that have you so upset?"

Again she considered telling him it didn't, but then decided yet again, he had the right to know. And frankly, she wanted his opinion.

"I didn't want him to see us and tell Finola," she explained, which was true. But the question was, would

Tristan even know who Michael was and that he worked in the *HOT!* mailroom? Maybe or maybe not.

But surely Tristan wouldn't follow her for that reason? To see who she was dating? Liza doubted it. If Tristan McIntyre was following her, it was for far more nefarious reasons. At least that's what her gut told her.

But he isn't following you, she told herself. He was just an image created by her nervous and overworked mind. Her tired mind.

She reached over to take another bite of Michael's salad.

"I really like this," she told him with a smile, even as she fought the urge to shoot a glance back to the bar.

"It's all yours," Michael said with a rueful smile. "Thank God, I have a steak coming."

"A meat and potatoes kinda guy, huh?"

Michael smiled back, and again Liza's chest tightened and her heart pattered wildly.

This time because of that amazing smile of his, she assured herself. She was actually relieved when the waiter arrived with their main courses, because she needed a moment to collect herself—and get her heart back to a normal rhythm.

After they'd taken a taste or two of their meals, Michael said, "Do you think he might be checking up on you?"

For a moment, Liza didn't follow his line of thought, but then she realized he was referring to Tristan. "Oh, I—I doubt it."

But that was exactly what she'd wondered. After all, recently she hadn't been the good little worker bee she'd been for years. She was rebelling, and that could have Finola on her guard.

She already knew she had to be careful, and she intended to give Finola the work she always had—better even, just so she didn't have to reveal that she was keeping the damned demon inside her continually sedated. Nor did she want Finola to realize she was seeing Michael. She truly didn't believe he was involved, or even aware of who, or what, actually ran *HOT!* She wanted to keep it that way.

Maybe she had seen Tristan, maybe she was just being paranoid, but either way she had to play this all carefully until she figured out some way to finally free herself from her possession and ultimately from Finola White herself.

Liza believed she might be able to convince Finola she would be a better worker without Boris, but she had no idea how she would ever be free of Finola. Well, she'd just have to get rid of the first problem, then go from there.

"I think I just saw someone who looked like him. That's all," she said, waving her hand casually, then returning to her grilled salmon.

When she looked up again, Michael was regarding her closely, and she got the feeling he didn't believe her, although she couldn't understand why he wouldn't.

"How's your steak?" she asked, hoping to drop the whole subject.

Michael could see that Liza was uncomfortable with this topic of conversation.

"It's delicious," he told her, offering her a smile that he hoped would calm her. He got the feeling from her reaction that she actually had seen Tristan. Did that mean the demon was following her?

But why?

His protective slayer guard came up instantly. Did Finola and Tristan have plans for Liza? Were they looking for something that would break her soul contract and allow them to gain yet another soul?

He sure as hell wasn't going to let that happen. Not even if it meant going against all of DIA's new policies.

He glanced at the woman beside him. He realized that he hadn't known her long, but he felt a tremendous connection to her. Intense feelings of concern and caring and protectiveness.

She was his woman.

The thought seemed so strange, so premature, but it didn't matter. That was how he felt. Period.

And nothing was going to harm her, or change his feelings.

"I cannot believe within seconds of locating her, you allowed her to see you?"

Tristan glared down at Dippy, who was perched in the satchel he carried over his shoulder.

"You are supposed to blend in," Dippy stated with annoyance.

"I'm supposed to blend in while carrying a man purse with a fluffy white dog in it?" Tristan pointed out wryly. "I think this plan was doomed from the start."

Dippy rolled his doggy eyes and muttered, "Satan knows, you are metrosexual enough to pull off the look."

Tristan didn't acknowledge the comment, because he supposed it was rather true. "We just have to be more careful."

Dippy growled. Tristan didn't know if it was in agreement or not, and frankly he didn't care.

"Who do you think was that man with her?"

Tristan had been wondering the same thing. "I don't know. I have a vague feeling I've seen him before, but I'm not sure where."

"Well, I think we should find out who he is. He's probably just some nobody, but you never know."

Tristan agreed. He was willing to follow any lead that might get Finola worried about Liza McLane. Hell, he was willing to make up a lead. Whatever it took to get Finola to react badly.

Chapter Twenty-one

"Where do you want to go now?" Michael asked once they stepped outside of the restaurant.

Feeling a bit like Cinderella with still more time before the clock struck midnight, or in Liza's case, before the demon returned, she wasn't ready to call it a night.

"Would you like to just come back to my place?"

Michael agreed immediately. "Sure."

Raising a hand, he waved down a taxi. Once inside, he turned to her. "So you haven't told me how you came to work for *HOT!* Was working for a fashion magazine always your dream job?"

Liza didn't have to hesitate. "Yes, it always was."

He nodded as if he'd expected her answer, but more than that, like it confirmed something to him. She wasn't sure what, or really if she wasn't just reading too much into a simple nod.

"I actually was an editor-in-chief for a very successful fashion magazine," she told him, although not admitting it had actually been *HOT!* before it was controlled by demons.

"Really?"

She nodded with a slight smile, finding his surprise a little amusing, although her current situation at *HOT!* certainly did not amuse her.

"Why did you decide to take the position at *HOT!* then?"

She shrugged, then gave him the most honest answer she could. "Finola White made me an offer I couldn't refuse."

"Oh, okay," Michael said, although he didn't quite understand. Usually, the way a demon got a human to sign a soul contract was to offer them something they simply couldn't refuse. Their heart's desire.

How was moving from a position as editor-in-chief to one working under Finola Liza's heart's desire? Unless she was just determined to work for *HOT!*, which, as he'd come to understand it, was the most successful of all the fashion magazines out there. Maybe that had been enough of a lure. Or maybe Finola had promised her something more than Liza had actually gotten. That was a breach of a soul contract, but he was sure a powerful demon like Finola White could find a way around such technicalities. Not to mention, she had no problems breaching contracts anyway.

Still, who signed a contract with the devil that got them less than what they already had? That was strange.

"Anyway," Liza said, pulling him out of his thoughts, "I plan to be free of Finola soon. I'm hoping anyway."

Michael wondered if Liza was aware that help was out there. In fact, right below her every day in the mailroom. He knew he couldn't risk asking in case she didn't know. Revealing anything about the DIA could be detrimental to the agency's work.

So instead he decided to simply reassure her.

"You definitely will. Sometimes you just have to be patient and bide your time."

She glanced at him, her eyes roaming over his face. "I hope you are right."

Michael knew he was right. No matter what, she would be freed from that contract. Whether it was by DIA's actions or his own.

But discussing the issue any further wasn't going to fix her problem right now, and frankly Michael wanted an evening when they could get to know each other without demons being a part of the equation. If that was possible.

"So you've never told me where you are from," he said.

She smiled, and he was glad to see her relax a little. "Not far. I grew up in Connecticut. My family still lives there, although you'd think it was a thousand miles away, considering all the times I get there. Working for *HOT!* keeps me awfully busy."

He nodded, imagining that was very true. But again, he wasn't going to let the conversation revolve around *HOT!* or Finola.

"How about you?" she asked.

"I'm from all over, really. I've traveled a lot."

"Because of your special forces work?"

Man, it was hard to avoid their demonically ruled lives, wasn't it?

"Yes," he said. "That was a good portion of it." There was also the fact that he'd been alive for many, many decades.

"That must have been a very exciting career. And dangerous."

"It was." He wasn't even lying when he used the past tense. He wasn't a slayer anymore. At least for the time being. But he would be again, if he had to.

"Why did you decide to get out of it?" she asked.

"I didn't decide to—it's more like my unit was de-activated."

"They can do that?"

Michael sighed. "Yeah. They can do that." As much as he wished it wasn't true.

"You sound disappointed."

He nodded. "I am. I like to think that our unit was one of the most elite and effective teams they had."

"That must be hard."

Michael nodded. "It is, and I'm hoping the higher-ups are making the right choices. I'm honestly not convinced they are."

Liza didn't know exactly what he was talking about. She certainly didn't do anything as dangerous as special ops, but she did understand how it felt to be taken out of a job she loved and how helpless that made her feel. Sure, she still did most of the work an editor-in-chief would do, but now she worked for someone who made her job more difficult and took all the credit for the good things Liza did.

Not quite the same, but still as frustrating.

"So how did you come to be working in a mailroom after a career in special forces? That definitely doesn't sound like a natural progression," she said, giving him a sympathetic smile, since she didn't need him to even say it to know the mailroom wasn't his idea of a great job.

"Like I said, I just sort of found myself with the job. I happened to know the mailroom manager and he suggested that I take the position. Since I didn't have any other prospects at the moment, I decided to take him up on the offer."

Liza nodded, again sympathetic. "In this economy, I guess there aren't as many options in all fields, including law enforcement."

"I really had no options," he said flatly and again Liza knew he was very dissatisfied.

Again, she understood. "I don't have any options either."

Michael turned more toward her on the vinyl bench seat of the cab, his knees brushing hers.

"But things will change for you," he said, reaching for her hand. His thumb rubbed back and forth across the back of her fingers, his touch soothing and arousing at the same time. "I can promise you. You just have to be patient."

She looked down at their joined hands, loving his touch and believing his reassurance, although she wondered how she could. She didn't know if things would ever be okay, whether she'd ever be free of Finola and Boris, but she wanted to believe him.

And something about the way he spoke seemed to say that he totally understood what she was going through even though he couldn't possibly.

What would he know about possession? Or demons. He'd fought evil and villains, but they'd been the human kind.

"Here we are," the taxi driver said in a heavy Middle Eastern accent.

Michael caressed his thumb over her fingers one last time, then reached for his wallet.

"Let me," she said, but he had already given the driver several bills.

"I have the unglamorous job of mailroom clerk, but the gig pays surprisingly well."

Liza found that hard to believe, but didn't argue. She appreciated his gentlemanliness.

She stepped out of the vehicle onto the sidewalk, feeling warm even though there was a chill to the night air. Michael always had that effect on her. As well as making her heart race in her chest.

She even felt a little light-headed as she waited for him to follow her out of the cab. Very light-headed actually.

She swayed, but before her knees buckled, Michael was at her side, his strong arm around her back to steady her.

"Liza, what's wrong? Are you okay?"

She nodded, although her vision now blurred too.

"I think maybe the wine went to my head more than I thought," she told him, then blinked and smiled. "Or you have."

He raised an eyebrow, offering her a lopsided smile of his own. "I'm not sure that is a compliment. You look pretty pale and woozy."

"I'll be fine in a moment," she assured him, but when she moved to take a step, she wobbled sideways and only Michael's hold kept her from toppling over.

"Whoa there." He pulled her tighter against his side.

She smiled, starting to be a little worried that maybe something was really wrong. The dizziness wasn't going away, and she could hear her heart beating in her ears. The combination made her feel slightly ill.

"I think we need to get you somewhere to lie down," Michael said.

She could hear the concern in his voice even over her pounding heartbeat.

"I look that bad?" she asked, trying to sound airy, even as she was getting more concerned herself.

"A little," he said, not giving her the answer she necessarily wanted. Then he further concerned her by hoisting her up in his arms.

"Michael," she cried, her arms wrapping around his neck as a wave of light-headedness hit her.

"Shh, just let me carry you."

She felt silly, but at the same time she also felt protected and cared for, which she had to admit was a wonderful feeling.

This strange light-headedness wasn't so wonderful however. She groaned slightly as he headed up the steps to the apartment.

"I don't understand what is wrong," she said to him, letting her head drop on his shoulder. "I was feeling fine and now . . ." She moaned again.

"Maybe we should go to the hospital," he suggested, his voice thick with worry.

"No," she said immediately, knowing if they did any blood work or an examination of her now, a doctor might discover the amount of allergy meds in her system. Which had to be what was making her feel this way. Although this was not how she normally reacted to the meds.

It had to be the pills combined with the two glasses of wine she'd had with dinner. That was it, she was sure. And it would pass.

"I'm fine. I really think the wine just went straight to my head," she told him, trying to sound firm, which wasn't easy when she felt so woozy.

"Maybe it was that tuna and seaweed salad,"

Michael suggested in jest, and she managed a small laugh.

"That is it," she agreed. "Definitely."

Then she fell silent, the dizziness and rapid heartbeat making it hard to focus on anything else.

In fact she wasn't even aware that they had reached her apartment until he asked her where her keys were. She fumbled with her small purse, trying to locate them, which seemed like a colossal undertaking.

Finally he set her down, careful to keep her pinned to his side, and got the keys from one of the pockets of the leather purse himself.

She heard the door unlock, rather than seeing because she had her eyes closed and she was trying to force her heart to calm down.

"Are you sure we shouldn't just go to the hospital?" Michael asked again and this time she made herself open her eyes and look at him.

"No," she answered, willing her gaze to hold his, even as the edges of her vision closed in to a tunnel with Michael's handsome face at the center of it.

"I will be fine in a minute," she repeated, not feeling certain of that fact, but not willing to go to the hospital. "I just need to rest for a moment."

He still looked like he wanted to argue, but he nodded again and led her into her apartment and directly to her bedroom.

She groaned in relief as he helped her down onto the bed. She draped an arm over her eyes and tried to keep her breathing even and slow.

Beside her, she felt her mattress dip under Michael's weight, and he slipped her shoes off. She heard them drop to the floor.

"I'm going to get you a warm cloth to put on your forehead," Michael said softly and she nodded. She wasn't sure if that would help, but at this point, she'd try anything.

She wasn't aware how long Michael was gone, but after some unspecified amount of time, she felt the bed shift again and a warm, damp cloth replacing her arm on her forehead.

"How does that feel?"

She remained still for a moment, then slowly opened her eyes. She felt better, although she didn't think it was the warm cloth, but rather that the spell had simply passed.

"I feel much better," she said, glad to feel that her heart rate had calmed and her head had stopped spinning. She was even more relieved that she could see Michael clearly.

She smiled at him and noticed relief on Michael's face too. He'd been truly concerned. But it had to be the combination of wine and meds.

She smiled wider and reached up to touch his cheek. "I think you were right. Definitely some bad seaweed."

He smiled, but he still didn't look totally convinced she was fine.

She found his concern sweet, especially since she hadn't had that kind of attention for a long time, and certainly not from a man who could be so fierce and so tender all at once.

She carefully elbowed herself up, moving gingerly in case her head wasn't totally okay, but found the action didn't bother her in the least. Then she slipped the hand that was on his cheek around to the back of his head and kissed him.

The brush of her lips against his was sweet and lingering, but her body surged with desire, burning instantly with the need for him.

But she didn't deepen the kiss, instead just caressing his firm, sculpted mouth over and over with feathery, whispering touches.

After a few moments, she dropped back against the pillows to look up at him from under heavy, desirous eyelids.

"I've never been so attracted to anyone," she murmured.

He reached forward and stroked her hair, pushing back several strands that clung to her cheeks.

"I've never felt this way either," he said, his gaze roaming over her features in a combination of amazement, and maybe a tad of confusion.

She understood those emotions completely. But she also knew that she wanted this man. To the point she would risk anything to have him. It didn't make sense, not rationally, but when she was close to him, it was as natural as breathing.

And the kind of impulsiveness and need she felt with him was thrilling too.

"I want you to know I would do anything for you," he said softly, his fingers still toying with locks of her hair.

She didn't know exactly what he referred to, but she did know she believed him.

"How can we have this connection?" she asked, her own fingers sinking into the cropped locks of his hair, soft and thick against her fingertips.

He shook his head slightly. "I don't know. I just know from the moment I saw you, I had to be with you."

She understood. She'd felt the same way.

She rose up again to kiss him. This time the kiss was deeper, more intense, but no less filled with strange wonder.

"Baby," he whispered against her lips, "I want to make love to you."

She moaned her assent. She wanted nothing more.

"Are you really okay?" he asked, lifting his head to study her.

She didn't hesitate. "I'm absolutely fine."

There was nothing that could stop her from making love with this man. Nothing.

"Are you sure?"

She smiled, then kissed him. "So sure."

He smiled too, although she still saw worry in his golden eyes.

"I'm fine," she said again, and this time she kissed him with all the passion that swelled up from deep inside her. He responded immediately, pulling her tight against him. But even with so much desire and need tugging achingly at both of them, they went slowly. Each kiss ripe with hunger. Each touch lingering, exploring. And their whole beings focused on each other.

Bit by bit, their clothing came off, their skin touching, hot and smooth, their breath mingling, warm and damp.

After what could have been hours or only minutes, because the place where they were, lost in each other, didn't seem to be made of time and space, they were eventually joined. His body deep within her, her body cradling him, embracing him.

"Perfect."

She wasn't sure who actually said the word, her or him. But it was simply that. Their union was perfect. And she knew they both felt it. Just like they both felt

the rising ecstasy building more and more until neither of them could speak, they could only feel. Wave
after wave of pure bliss washed over them until they
collapsed in spent oblivion.

   Perfect.

Chapter Twenty-two

Michael woke as soon as he felt Liza moving beside him, but he didn't speak to her, or give any indication that he was awake.

Through barely opened eyes, he watched her slip out of bed, her form naked and pale, like a ghostly sylph illuminated by the streetlights outside her bedroom windows. She tiptoed across the room, and his first sinking thought was that she was leaving again. Her usual postcoital disappearing act.

But this was her apartment, and he was relieved when she simply disappeared into her bathroom.

He rolled over onto his side, watching the door, considering what had happened between them. He didn't doubt her attraction and interest in him. And there was no denying his feelings for her.

But yet, he still felt that she might pull away again. It was a strange feeling, and one he was very curious about. He still suspected it was her concerns about her soul contract that made her hold back a little. Part of him really did want to tell her that he knew, but he knew that wasn't the best course of action for either of them. At least not now.

He listened, hearing Liza opening and closing something, maybe the medicine cabinet. Then he heard something rattling, but he couldn't tell what that noise was. Something like crinkling plastic, but he wasn't sure.

Then he heard her faint, whispering voice. As if she was rather emphatically whispering to herself. Liza did have that quirk; she seemed to talk to herself a lot. Maybe a little odd, but Michael found himself smiling. Leave it to him to fall for a woman who talked to herself.

His smile slipped just slightly. Fall for . . . fall for . . . yeah, he was falling for Liza. There wasn't much point in denying it.

He heard the water come on then, and after a few moments, the bathroom door opened. While in the bathroom, Liza had pulled on a long T-shirt, much to his dismay. He liked watching her walk across the room, her pale skin glowing, her lithe limbs graceful.

But he was glad she was coming back to the bed, carefully crawling in beside him. He was surprised when she seemed to purposely cling to her side of the bed, making sure there was plenty of room between them.

He started to roll over to drape an arm over her, but she quickly pulled the covers tight around her, even tugging them around her head.

Why? He knew she enjoyed his touch. There was no denying that when they made love.

Maybe she wasn't feeling well again and he was tempted to let her know he was awake and ask, but then she seemed to relax, her body sinking into the mattress and pillows. Within a few more seconds, her breathing became low and even.

Was he reading too much into the way she'd gotten back into bed? Probably. He stretched beside her, letting his own fatigue take him over.

Everything was fine. Well, as fine as it could be in their world.

"Good morning."

Michael blinked, looking up to find Liza beside the bed, still in the oversized tee he'd seen last night, but now the sunlight shone through the window.

Wow, he'd slept soundly all night. He usually wasn't a particularly deep sleeper. Years of having to be aware of potential trouble. Demons often didn't sleep, so often neither did he.

But beside Liza he obviously felt safe and content. As he stretched, he did not miss the way Liza's gaze traveled appreciatively over him, admiring his chest and arms. He stretched again—just to have her admire a little more.

"What time is it?" he asked through a yawn.

"Nearly ten," she said, and he noticed that her words seemed to be slightly slurred . . . or at least he thought they were. If so, it was just a bit, like maybe she was still tired too.

She swayed on her feet, just a little as well.

"Are you feeling okay?" he asked, sitting up to study her closer.

"Definitely," she said with a sweet smile. God, she was beautiful, her black hair all mussed around her pale face. Her green-blue eyes were bright. Maybe a little too bright, again like she was tired . . . a little glazed, but she didn't look ill as she had last night. She looked stunning.

"So, want to crawl back into bed?"

She nodded, slipping in beside him as he held up the covers.

"I made coffee," she told him, relaxing against him. "I would have brought you some, but I wasn't sure if you even drink it or what you take in it."

"I'll get some in a bit." He tucked her in beside him. "Right now, I want to just enjoy waking up, holding you."

"Okay," she agreed readily, but before she could even settle in, an alarm of some sort went off.

"Darn." She slid back out of bed and went to her purse. It still lay on the floor beside the bed, where it had fallen when he'd put her to bed last night.

She pulled out her cell phone, then grimaced. But she pressed the flat screen, then held the small rectangle to her ear.

"Hello? Yes . . . yes . . . okay, I'll be right there."

Michael frowned, not pleased that it sounded like their leisurely morning together had been interrupted. He had no doubt about who the person—or creature—on the other end was.

"Finola White?" he asked as soon as she hung up.

Liza made a face and nodded. "She wants me in the office, because we are preparing an additional special edition summer issue of *HOT!* that needs to go to press this week, and she needs me in the office today to work on some of the layouts and articles."

"On a Sunday?"

"Finola doesn't pay attention to what day it is. Every day is a workday to her."

He nodded, not surprised.

"And you have no choice but to go?"

She shook her head, quirking her lips regretfully.

"No. Especially right now. She's really watching me at the moment and I have to give her the kind of work she wants. I'm actually trying to prove to her that I can give her exactly what she's looking for. And if I can, maybe it will ultimately make my life a little easier."

"But don't you always give her what she wants?" he asked, knowing she had to. That's how a soul contract worked. Liza gave Finola what she wanted, or Finola could claim breach of contract.

"I do," she agreed as she walked to her closet and shuffled through her clothes. "But I'm really trying to make a point right now."

He considered that, hoping she wasn't trying to find a loophole in her contract. That never worked and in most cases just ensured that a soul was cast to Hell all the sooner.

"I know you must get frustrated with your situation, but you really should just keep things status quo right now."

She stopped browsing through her clothes and turned to look at him, her expression quizzical. "What do you mean my situation?"

Damn. He'd said too much. After all, what was he supposed to know about her job? He was just the guy who delivered and picked up the mail.

"I just meant . . ." Shit, he didn't know what to say. "I just meant that you already work long hours, and you clearly haven't been feeling well, so I don't think it's good to stress yourself out even more."

She seemed to consider that for a moment, then shrugged. "I know what you are saying, but really I think I have a good plan set in place that could actually make my work, and life in general, a lot less stressful."

She turned back to her closet, focusing all her attention on picking out an outfit.

Michael watched her, really not liking what she was saying. It would be awful if she managed to lose her soul just as the DIA might be able to save her.

He'd just have to keep a closer eye on her. First he would try to stop her from making any silly moves, and if that failed, he would save her himself.

"So what did you find out?" Finola demanded, not looking away from her own reflection in the hand mirror she held. But before Tristan could answer her, she waved to the stylist hovering nearby.

"This lash isn't as long as the others," she said sharply to the woman, pointing at the offensive eyelash hair, which appeared to be on her left eye. "Replace it."

The woman immediately turned to the lash extensions and other tools laid out on the wheeled stand next to Finola's massage chair, which she was currently using as a salon chair.

The woman scrutinized Finola's left eye, clearly trying to figure out exactly which lash Finola found unsatisfactory.

Good luck with that, Tristan thought wryly. He was suddenly glad he was stuck with the job of tailing Liza McLane. It beat the hell out of what this poor woman had to do.

"So go on, Tristan?"

"All we've discovered so far is that Liza is seeing someone, but we don't know who he is," Tristan told her, which was what he and Dippy had finally decided to tell their suddenly scrupulous mistress. Both demon and demon dog had decided maybe they could plant enough concerns about Liza dating that Finola would do something.

"Well, I'm not concerned with her dating as long as it doesn't affect her work or her behavior," Finola said, taking that calm, rational stance that seemed to be her new thing.

Oh, to have back crazy, impulsive, unpredictable Finola. Damn, he'd never thought he'd say that.

Suddenly a loud, irritated hiss filled the room.

"Damn it," Finola said in a low, angry voice to the woman working on her eyes, "be careful or else."

"Sorry, Ms. White," the stylist said quickly, nervously.

Tristan glanced at Dippy. Hell, maybe this woman with her eyelashes and glue would be the one to bring on their coup. Maybe they didn't even need Liza. Or Peaches.

"Well, we are rather interested in this man," Tristan continued casually as if Finola hadn't just threatened a female human over an eyelash.

"Why?" she said absently, clearly more concerned with her sweeping, seductive lashes than the task at hand.

"Can Liza really date without eventually drawing attention to her little—inconvenience? It's just that anyone who is seeing her would eventually have to find out that she's possessed. After all, she isn't that great at tuning out nasty little Bartoris. At the very least, this man will think she's crazy. Do you want some guy telling everyone that one of your editors is insane—or worse, actually believing she's possessed? Now that might draw a little unwanted attention, mightn't it?"

Finola didn't answer for a moment, and for a moment, Tristan wondered if she even would. But finally she said, "Yes, find out more about this man. But again, we aren't going to act rashly."

No, of course we aren't going to do anything rash. Not now. Not when I actually want rash behavior. Damn it.

"I will see what I can find out."

"Good."

The stylist finished replacing what Tristan knew she was really, really hoping was the right eyelash. Tristan rather hoped she hadn't. He didn't wish the woman ill, but he was tired of waiting for Finola to snap.

Tristan glanced toward Dippy, who perched on the edge of his doggy bed, watching and waiting. Tristan knew the demon dog was thinking the same thing. The stylist could be their easy fix.

The stylist handed Finola the hand mirror again, and then everyone in the room waited with held breath—of course not all for the same reason.

Finola carefully inspected the new work, tilting her head one way, then another. Finally, she nodded.

"That looks much better. We are done."

The stylist sagged in noticeable relief. Tristan and Dippy deflated with disappointment.

Tristan watched as the stylist, quickly and wisely, gathered up her things. She scurried out of Finola's office, before her exacting employer could change her mind.

Finola rose from her massage chair, still admiring her newly extended lashes.

"I need a glass of champagne," she said, her tone weary, as if having her lashes done was utterly exhausting, as if she hadn't just lain there.

But as always, Tristan obediently went to the wet bar and poured her a glass of her favorite bubbly. Her everyday champagne was only $150 a bottle. Cheap, really, by Finola's standards.

"I agree that you do need to find out more about this man Liza is involved with," Finola said after setting down her mirror and taking a long sip of her champagne. "We do need to be careful."

Tristan nodded.

A knock sounded at the office door and Tristan crossed the room to answer it, even though he could see it was Peaches through the glass walls, and he could have just waved her in. But he himself was feeling agitated, and desire rather than champagne was his preferred method of unwinding.

As soon as he opened the door, Peaches's attraction to him wafted over Tristan, and he breathed it in deeply like pulling in a particularly potent and intoxicating form of opium.

Peaches's gaze fell on him, hungry despite her natural agitation at being near any of them. In the company of demons.

For some reason, the fact that she still wanted him even though she didn't trust him, made that lust of hers all the more delicious.

He wanted her, that was for sure.

She regarded him for a moment, almost as if she was helpless to do otherwise.

"Yes," Finola finally said, clearly impatient with her assistant's hesitation, "what is it?"

Peaches snapped out of her daze and slipped past Tristan, making sure to keep as much space between them as possible.

She placed a folder onto Finola's glossy white desk. "Here are the mock-ups for the special summer edition of *HOT!* Ms. McLane just dropped them off at my desk."

Finola frowned, reaching out to slide the folder in front of her. "Why didn't she bring them to me herself?"

Peaches shifted slightly, clearly uncomfortable. "She said she wasn't feeling well and needed to go home."

Finola stared at her assistant for a few moments, long enough to make Peaches's nervousness almost more palpable in the air than her desire.

Then Finola turned her pale, pale gaze on Liza's work. She flipped through each page, pausing, studying, then moving on. Finally, after scrutinizing every page, she closed the folder.

"What do you think?" Tristan asked.

Finola flicked her wrist toward Peaches, dismissing the woman.

Peaches spun on her chunky—and so not in fashion this season—heels and hurried from the room, but not before shooting Tristan one more look.

Tristan felt himself harden painfully, his testicles drawing up tight against his groin. But he pushed his desire away, focusing on what Liza had just presented to Finola.

Again his hopes rose. Maybe the work was such garbage that Finola would finally lose her temper.

"So what do you think?" he asked, the question a little breathy with anticipation. And his lingering arousal.

Finola flipped open the folder once more and browsed through the layouts again and then, much to Tristan's dismay—and Dippy's too, Tristan was sure— she smiled.

A true, pleased smile.

"Well, Liza may be feeling off, and perhaps distracted by a new lover, but neither is affecting her work. These layouts are exactly what I wanted."

Tristan forced a smile of his own. Of course they were.

Chapter Twenty-three

"Whoa there," Simon said as Michael entered the employee break room.

"Whoa there," Michael said back, giving the Brethren a puzzled look. "How are you today?"

"Not as good as you," Simon said, elbowing Michael as he passed him on the way to his locker.

Michael gave him another quizzical look, confused by his friend's knowing little smirk. "So what's the skinny with you?"

"I think I should be the one asking you that question." Simon then did a little dance that was more like a goofy sort of shuffle.

Michael chuckled, still completely confused by his friend's ridiculous behavior.

"Come on," Simon said when Michael just shook his head and opened his locker to hang up his jacket and messenger bag. "Spill."

"What do you mean?" Michael asked, looking away from his open locker toward his friend.

Simon gave him another expectant look, then did his little dance again, this time adding a few pelvis thrusts that managed to look more silly than sexual.

Simon had always been the most outrageous of The Brethren, but he was acting particularly silly this morning.

Gabriel strode into the room, followed by John.

"Good morning," Gabriel said.

"It's a better morning for some of us than others," Simon said, grinning and jerking his head toward Michael.

Michael frowned again, truly not understanding Simon's behavior. What the hell was he talking about?

Gabriel studied Michael for a moment, then lifted a surprised eyebrow.

Michael raised his own eyebrows questioningly. Why were they all acting this way?

"Well, damn, you sly dog, you," John added, clearly understanding what was happening while Michael was still in the dark.

"Okay, guys, why don't you let me in on what you are talking about?" Michael demanded, not enjoying being the only one in the room who had no idea what was going on. Especially when they were talking about him.

"It's just like they say it is," Simon chuckled. "The poor sap who's bonded is always the last to know."

Michael stared at Simon. "Bonded?"

His gaze moved from one of his Brethren to the next, waiting to see them all laugh at their little joke. But while each of them smiled, it wasn't the look of a shared prank, but rather almost like proud papas.

"You are bonded, brother," John said, stepping forward to thump him on the back.

"Unreal," Simon said, shaking his head. "Frozen in time for decades, back for only a short amount of time, and now bonded. You are a man with a wacky life."

His life was something all right, but Michael wasn't

sure *wacky* was the right word. Bonded? Was he really? Wouldn't he be the first one to know?

No. That wasn't how bonding worked. He knew that. Bonding just happened, sneaking up on the male before he realized.

But he definitely did know whom he was bonded to. Liza. Suddenly his intense feelings of desire and protectiveness and affection made sense. How could he not know? It was so obvious.

"So who is the lucky female?" John asked.

Michael blinked, coming out of his reverie, to see all his Brethren still staring at him like he was some kind of novelty. Which he supposed he was.

"Umm—" He shook his head, trying to think of something reasonable to tell them. He was reluctant to admit she was a woman who worked for *HOT!* A woman who had a soul contract on her.

He'd bonded with a woman who had a soul contract on her. The enormity of his dilemma was huge. She was the least likely female he'd ever guess a Brethren member would, or could, bond with. In fact, the only person less likely to be a Brethren member's soul mate would be a possessed female.

Now *that* would be a huge problem.

"You—you don't know her," he finally offered rather lamely.

"But we'll know her soon enough," Simon said, grinning widely.

Michael knew that was true, but he wasn't ready to tell them yet. He needed to sort through his own emotions before he had to explain who she was to his brothers.

John clapped a hand on Michael's shoulder again. "We should take you out tonight to celebrate. This is a big deal."

"Michael is bonded. Michael is bonded." Simon began his ridiculous gyrating dance again.

John laughed and Gabriel smiled, but he also watched Michael closely. Michael smiled too, although he suspected the gesture looked forced. He still couldn't wrap his mind around what they were saying, even though he knew it was true.

After a little more ribbing and several smacks on the back, The Brethren left him to finish putting his stuff away and get ready for the day.

Only when he closed his locker and turned around, did he realize Gabriel still stood there.

"Are you okay?" he asked.

Michael nodded. "Just a little—overwhelmed I guess."

"Well, it isn't every day that we find ourselves bonded to another person. It's pretty intense."

"Yes, it is. Even though it feels perfectly natural and right when it's happening, the realization that that is what has happened . . ." Michael shook his head. He didn't even know what else to say. It was strange, because he was pleased and sure Liza was the woman for him, yet he was also—well, terrified.

"It's definitely a lot to take in, but you'll be surprised how easily you will come to accept it. And soon you won't be able to recall a time before this woman came into your life." Gabriel's voice was low, and filled with a haunted quality.

Then Michael remembered why. How could he forget?

Clearly Gabriel hadn't forgotten all the emotions of being bonded, although Cecilia had been taken away from him decades ago. Their bond seemed as strong today as it had been when Cecilia was alive.

That idea frightened Michael even more. What if

Liza was taken from him? What if the DIA couldn't protect her soul—or worse, get her soul back if the contract was broken?

The idea of losing her stole his breath away.

"It's a wonderful thing," Gabriel said then, as if he sensed his friend's panic. "I wouldn't give up a day with Cecilia. She was the best thing that ever happened to me."

Michael stared at his friend, then nodded. He knew Gabriel was right. He wouldn't trade a moment with Liza either, even with the threat of her soul being taken away.

He would just make sure he did everything in his power to keep her safe. A soul contract wouldn't stop his love.

"This plan isn't working," Dippy muttered from where he sat at Tristan's feet.

Tristan leaned against the wall, arms folded over his chest, watching Liza work through her slightly open office door. He'd only been tailing her for two days, and already he was bored. Aside from having a mysterious boyfriend, Liza did nothing interesting.

It was becoming hard to believe that Liza would make much of an impact if she was cast to Hell. Liza McLane was boring. Hell, even Bartoris didn't seem to be bothering her these days.

"We have to pick someone else."

Tristan still didn't answer. He knew who Dippy would choose, and call him selfish, but Tristan just wasn't willing to part with Peaches yet. At least not until he got to sample a little of that lust he felt in her.

He shouldn't let desire affect something as important as a rebellion, but then again, he was a demon of lust. If anything was going to motivate him, it was the promise of pure ecstasy.

"I know we have to come up with someone else," he finally said. "I'm just not sure who. I think we can get Finola to flip out over someone who would make a bigger impact on the big guy than yet another personal assistant."

Dippy cocked his head. "I know you want to keep the little rockabilly minx for yourself."

Tristan frowned down at his furry sidekick, somewhat surprised that he'd guessed what was making Tristan hesitate to sacrifice Peaches.

"I'm a dog," Dippy said flatly. "You don't even want to know the things my sense of smell can pick up. But let me just say—her arousal smells just as sweet as your little nickname for her."

"I know," Tristan said. Damn, did he know.

"So who should we . . ." Dippy's question trailed off as their eyes both locked on the same thing at once. The man Liza had spent the majority of her weekend with.

Tristan quickly picked up Dippy and stepped behind the wall of the closest cubicle, peeking out to see where the man went. Sure enough, he walked right to Liza's office.

"The man she's dating is another *HOT!* employee," Tristan said. From the man's blue smock, Tristan realized he must work in the mailroom.

In fact, he vaguely remembered why the guy had seemed familiar the other night. The same mailroom clerk had been watching him while he was in the boardroom a few days ago. He'd found the man's expression curious. Almost as if the guy hated him.

But seeing him up close, Tristan had a vague feeling he'd seen him before that moment too. But for the life of him, he couldn't think of where. Maybe it was as simple as seeing the man wandering around the *HOT!* offices, delivering mail.

The man would stand out. He was rather noticeable. Tall, muscular, handsome. Not like the usual mailroom staff, who tended to be utterly forgettable.

Probably that is it, he decided, although something niggled him.

Tristan watched as Liza and the man talked. They only spoke for a few moments, then kissed, but he didn't linger. Just a boyfriend stopping by to say a quick hello to his girl.

"Can this situation work in our favor?" Tristan pondered. When Dippy didn't respond, Tristan stopped staring toward Liza's office. Only then did he realize that the person who worked in the cubicle where he was hiding had returned.

The man regarded Tristan a little oddly, but didn't say anything. Though Tristan had no clue who this man was, he knew the man was fully aware of his identity, and wouldn't cop any attitude toward Finola White's right-hand man and assistant editor.

Tristan simply gave the fellow a blasé look and strode away. So Liza was involved with another employee. Would that bother Finola?

"I need to think about this," Tristan murmured.

Dippy growled, but Tristan wasn't sure whether he agreed or disagreed. Sometimes it was good Dippy couldn't talk freely, because Tristan didn't feel like discussing this with him right now. He needed to think.

Something about Liza's boyfriend bothered him.

Chapter Twenty-four

"So tell me what you are thinking about."

Michael looked up from shredding cheese, or rather from holding the block of cheddar against the shredder. How long had he been sitting there like that, lost in thought?

Liza joined him at her small café-style table, taking the seat across from him. She offered him a smile, waiting for him to talk to her.

He wished he could tell her what he was thinking, because of course he was thinking about her. He was thinking about the thing that had been on his mind all day. He was bonded. He was bonded with her.

But how on earth did he tell her that? It would be overwhelming for her to learn what he was, but without understanding that he was a demon slayer, how could she possibly understand what he was talking about?

Still, he felt like he had to say something.

"Do you feel that there is this amazing connection between us?"

Her beautiful smile widened. "Yes."

He nodded, glad that at least she could sense that. "We have something very special going on."

Again she didn't hesitate to agree. "I know. It's been amazing."

"And it will just keep growing between us."

"I hope so," she said. "I know this is the happiest I've been in a long, long time."

She rose up, leaning across the table to kiss him, her lips lingering and sweet against his.

His intense feelings for her swelled and he wondered now how he hadn't realized what was happening between them. It was so clear.

She ended that kiss with another of her lovely smiles, then returned to the counter to work on slicing up peppers and onions.

"So that was all you were thinking about?" she asked, after a moment.

He stopped swiping the cheese over the grater, making a face at her, because he knew she was teasing him.

"Yeah, that's all I'm thinking. Nothing important." He winked and she laughed. His heart filled with a contented, joyous warmth. This beautiful, sweet, talented woman was his soul mate. He'd been so bitter to have lost all those years, frozen in time by a demon. The only demon who'd outsmarted him. But now, he didn't feel that anger. Not when he'd arrived in this place and had almost immediately found Liza. Somehow that made his lost years seem totally worth it.

"Do you find what has happened between us strange?" he asked, knowing that if she realized the whole truth, she'd really find it strange.

But she surprised him by giving him a wry look. "I've definitely experienced stranger things. What

I've found with you is simply wonderful—not strange."

She gave him another smile, but Michael noticed it faded as soon as she returned her attention to the vegetable she was cutting.

He realized the strange thing she was talking about was what she knew about Finola White and *HOT!* and her soul contract. He wished he could tell her that he totally understood. Eventually he would, but right now, he had to be careful. He didn't want to put her at risk, and he didn't want to risk his place in the DIA. Even though he still didn't agree with a lot of what the DIA now preached, he needed to be in a position to help with this rebellion. And he needed to stay close to Liza.

So right now, he couldn't find himself on Eugene's radar.

The bang of something falling to the floor brought Michael's attention back to Liza, and as soon as he saw her leaning over the counter, he shot to his feet.

"Liza! What's wrong?"

Liza heard the panic in Michael's voice, but it sounded far away, like she was at the bottom of a well and he was calling down to her, his voice echoing around her.

She tried to focus and pull herself out of the tunnel she was in, but she couldn't. Her heart raced in her chest, the erratic beating stealing her breath. Her head swirled; her mouth was hot and dry.

What was happening to her?

She felt Michael's arms around her, pulling her limp, dizzy body against him.

"Liza," he repeated. "Tell me what's happening!"

She tried to speak, but she was too woozy to get the words to form and pass her lips. Helplessly, she shook her head, then immediately regretted the action. Her head spun even more, and she felt as if her heart was going to pound right out of her chest.

"We need to get you to the hospital."

"No." The word was weak, but clear.

"Liza. Something is really wrong."

She couldn't disagree, but she wasn't going to the ER again. If she returned, they were bound to ask even more questions. They were going to do more tests. And they were going to realize what she was doing.

No, she couldn't go to the hospital.

"Bed," she managed to say instead.

"I don't know, Liza."

"Please."

She could feel Michael's hesitation, but then he scooped her up as he'd done before—too many times before—and headed toward her bedroom.

He placed her gently amid the pillows and comforter, then sat down beside her. She closed her eyes, focusing on keeping her breathing steady and even. As he'd done before, Michael smoothed back her hair, his touch something else for her to use as a focal point. Something else to soothe and strengthen her.

"Let me get you some water."

He started to rise, but she caught his hand, squeezing his fingers with as much strength as she could.

"Don't go."

She felt his weight settle down beside her again and his hand return to her forehead, her hair, her cheek. He felt like a rock at her side, keeping her from spinning away in a tide of dizziness and panic.

She needed him. Not just now, but always.

"I love you," she whispered, her voice shaky. She wasn't even sure he would hear her. But his fingers stilled on her hair and he didn't speak for a moment.

Then he said, "I love you, Liza. So much."

Although she didn't open her eyes, afraid the room would be spinning too wildly, she did manage a smile and her fingers found his knee.

Michael watched Liza, relaxing a little as he saw more color return to her cheeks and her breathing become less rapid and stressed. This episode appeared to be passing, but that didn't make him feel much better. Not when it was becoming clear that whatever was happening to her was going to keep happening.

She had to go to the hospital. It was that simple. But he wasn't going to get her to go now, and since she was resting peacefully at the moment, her cheeks no longer blending in with the whiteness of the bedding around her, he decided to just leave the topic alone.

"I'm going to get you some water now," he told her, reaching for the hand that lay limply on his knee.

She nodded, her willingness to let him leave her side another sign that she was feeling better.

He held her warm fingers for a second, then pressed a kiss to the backs of them, and slipped off the bed.

"Could you get me a warm cloth for my forehead too?" she asked, her voice still soft, but not as weak as before. "That helped last time."

"Of course."

He headed to her bathroom, found a cup on the edge of the sink, and filled it with cool water. Then he turned on the hot water, letting it run as he turned to retrieve a clean washcloth from the small hanging shelves that served as her linen closet.

He started to turn back to the sink, when the small trash can beside the toilet caught his attention. Or rather the box that was in the trash.

Benadryl.

He reached down and picked up the package. Inside was the empty pill packet, all the plastic bubbles crushed and empty. Twenty-four tablets gone.

He stared at it, wondering. Could she have overdosed on allergy meds again? He flipped the packet over to read the warnings and side effects. Dizziness, rapid heartbeat, dry mouth, nausea, unconsciousness, possible seizures, coma.

He glanced toward the bathroom door, fear tightening his chest.

"Liza?"

His stomach dropped as his call was met with silence.

"Yeah?"

He released a breath. Her response was low, but her voice sounded fine, not slurred or confused.

"Never mind," he said, shoving the empty pill package in his back pocket, though he wasn't sure why. He grabbed a washcloth and ran it under the hot water and then wrung it out. He turned off the faucet and grabbed the glass of water.

Returning to the bedroom, he was relieved to see that her color was even better, and she opened her eyes as he approached her side.

"Thank you," she said, accepting the cup and levering herself upright enough to take a big gulp. Then she eased herself back onto the pillows and allowed him to place the warm washcloth on her forehead.

"Just give me another few minutes," she said with a weak smile. "I'll be right as rain."

He nodded, but said, "Stay here and relax. I'll finish dinner."

She opened her mouth as if she was going to argue, but then she smiled again. "Okay, I just need a few more minutes."

"No rush." He leaned down and kissed her, then left the room to head back to the kitchen. Once there, he pulled the pill package out of his pocket again and reread the back.

There was no way to know how many pills had been in this packet before she'd emptied it. She could have just taken the recommended amount. But these episodes she suffered sure did seem to go along with an overdose.

Why would she overdose on allergy medication? It didn't make any sense. He didn't get the feeling she was depressed or wanted to hurt herself. Hell, he'd never even noticed that she had bad allergies. Or even any allergies.

So why had she overdosed on them the very first time? And why did it appear that she'd done it again? More than once?

Liza listened to Michael working in the kitchen. The clatter of a pan. The sound of him stirring something. Her body now felt heavy and tired, and the familiar sounds of someone making dinner were comforting.

She couldn't keep doing this. All this medication was affecting her—possibly doing damage to her heart or liver or kidneys or all of the above.

Still, what options did she have? Would Michael be willing to be involved with a woman who was possessed? If he even believed her. More than likely, he'd just think she was nuts. Certifiably crazy.

And while it was amazing and wonderful, their relationship had just gotten more complicated. They'd told each other "I love you."

She opened her eyes and stared at the ceiling. He loved her. Her heart skipped in her chest, and this time, for real, it wasn't the Benadryl making it do so.

Michael Archer loved her. It was the best thing she'd ever heard, but it also made her already complex life all the more difficult.

How could she have Michael, and live with Boris in her body, and keep Finola happy with her work? She had no idea. Right now, taking the allergy meds was the only thing keeping her life manageable. But she had to come up with another plan, and quickly.

"We need to come up with another plan and quick. I cannot stand being Finola's huggy-wuggy much longer." Dippy paced back and forth across the office, his tone somewhere between a growl and a whine. But all Tristan was hearing was the whine. Whiny Finola. Whiny Dippy.

Someone was always complaining. And damn it, it was getting really exhausting—and annoying. And he really had no desire to stage a coup with a whiny dog. Talk about a plan that was probably doomed to fail.

Plus, right now, he was trying to think. He leaned back in his office chair and pressed his fingertips together, only to realize that gesture made him look like the stereotypical evil villain. He immediately straightened up, dropping his hands to the arms of his chair.

Something about that man, the mailroom clerk,

was vaguely familiar. He must have seen him, roaming about, delivering mail.

But something niggled him. He felt that he knew something else about the man. But what? What could he possibly know about a lowly mailroom clerk? What would he *want* to know? Something in his gut told Tristan they needed to find out more.

"I think we should report back to Finola about this 'boyfriend' of Liza's."

"Why?" Dippy spun around to narrow his dark beady eyes at Tristan from across the office. "Finola isn't going to give a shit about this guy, as long as Liza is doing her work. Which she is. Better than ever, I might add."

Dippy suddenly plopped down on Tristan's Persian carpet, and began digging at his ear with his hind leg. "Damned dry air."

"Or maybe you have fleas," Tristan suggested wryly, leaning back in his office chair.

Dippy stopped and glared at Tristan again.

Tristan sighed, realizing dissension between them wasn't going to fix their dilemma. Nor was delaying coming up with a new plan—or rather a new victim. But still his gut . . .

"Maybe we should try to frame her boyfriend somehow," Tristan said before he even realized the words were going to come out of his mouth, but now that they had, the idea did seem like a good one. At least it was a new plan, which might stop Dippy from whining—literally.

But before Dippy could respond, both of them started as the door to Tristan's office opened, and an obviously irritated Finola strode into the room. Normally it wasn't easy to sneak up on a demon, much less two demons in a glass room, which showed they had to be more careful and more aware of what was happening around them.

"There is my precious little boy," she cooed, her voice soft and silky, despite the fact that her stance still showed she was annoyed. She crossed the room and scooped up her dog, tucking him possessively under her arm.

"I am starting to wonder why my pet is always with you, Tristan. Are you trying to steal away my sweet baby?" Again, her tone sounded light, almost teasing, but her eyes were as hard as arctic ice.

"Hardly," Tristan assured her, and he didn't even have to work to sound believable. He was starting to think he wanted to plan this rebellion on his own. But now Dippy was in, and there was no getting rid of him. Not to mention the little mutt had a direct in with the big man downstairs.

"Then why is he always with you these days?" Finola sounded almost petulant.

"Good taste."

Dippy growled.

Finola nuzzled her hellish pet against her cheek. "I know, my sweet baby, Tristan isn't very funny, is he?" She gave him a hard look.

"So, I've decided there is no reason to keep following Liza," Finola announced.

Tristan tried not to look disappointed. He couldn't say he was surprised. Liza hadn't been a problem at all since they'd decided to tail her. Her work was better than it had ever been and she hadn't shown any more signs of acting up.

"I agree," Tristan said.

Finola bobbed her head slightly in acknowledgment, and turned to leave his office.

"But," he added quickly, "I'm actually a little concerned about her boyfriend. Something about the man troubles me. I have this strange feeling about him."

Finola paused, cocking a fair eyebrow as she considered his words; then she shrugged. "Check him out then."

Tristan nodded. This was a good thing. Tristan would either discover what bothered him about that man, or he would find some way to frame him, and get Finola to take the man's soul unlawfully. And while that would probably make Liza McLane quite distraught, she wouldn't be able to do a thing about it. She'd still be stuck as *HOT!*'s ghost editor-in-chief. Probably not as cooperative as she was now, but he could work around that.

At least now he felt like he had a plan. Hell, even Dippy couldn't whine about that.

Chapter Twenty-five

"You aren't eating?"

Liza looked up from her plate across the table from Michael. He was right, she'd done nothing but poke her sashimi around the plate, leaving a raw fish trail in its wake.

"I'm sorry, I was just thinking about work." Which wasn't totally a lie. She wasn't thinking about a project or deadline, but rather how long she could keep Bartoris drugged out before Finola or her lackey, Tristan, discovered what she'd been doing. Would they even care if they did find out? Neither of them had any fondness for Bartoris.

Just then her heart skipped a beat, stealing her breath. Another reason she couldn't keep up this method of demon control much longer. She was actually getting concerned about her health. But what options did she have?

"Is there a problem?" he asked, his eyes roaming her face, his look intense. Was he really that concerned about her work, or was she growing pale again? She definitely wasn't feeling well.

But she forced a smile. "Just the usual." She wasn't

sure if her tone was airy, or just disoriented. Damn, she wished her heart would stop racing.

"Liza, are you feeling light-headed again?"

She shook her head, then immediately fought the urge to close her eyes. Michael's face swam before her, but she willed her head and heart to calm down.

"I'm fine," she said, carefully reaching for her glass of iced tea. With the same sheer determination she was using on her pulse and head, she forced her hands not to shake. She took a long sip, the cool liquid calming her a little.

Michael regarded her a moment longer, then gestured to her plate of sushi. "You really need to eat. You look washed out. I think you work too hard and don't take care of yourself."

She gave him another smile, although she knew it was a weak one, then attempted to hold her chopsticks in the appropriate position. Twice she fumbled, dropping her tekka maki roll back onto the plate with a splash of soy sauce. Finally she got the rice and seaweed and tuna to her mouth, forcing herself to chew.

"Well, at least I don't have to worry about my lunch getting cold," she said after swallowing the salty, spicy mush. Another side effect of all the allergy meds. Dry mouth.

Still, she picked up another piece and popped it into her mouth. After a couple more, she was surprised to discover she really did feel better.

As if reading her mind, Michael nodded with approval. "Your color looks better. You really do need to take better care of yourself."

She did, but she also needed to take care of Bartoris. There was no way she could have a normal relationship with an annoying chatterbox demon stuck in her head.

She really had only one hope, and that was that Finola would recognize how much better Liza's work was with Bartoris knocked out, and finally Finola would agree to cast the demon out of her.

It was a long shot, but the only plan she had. Otherwise, she was going to have to continue her four times a day overdose. Or break up with Michael, and breaking up wasn't an option.

She knew it was strange, given that they'd only been involved a couple of weeks, but she couldn't imagine life without Michael. She'd never felt this way about another man. Not about another living soul honestly. It was weird, and should have been scary, but she wasn't scared, because it also felt perfectly right.

So she had to make her plan work. Somehow.

She finished her last piece of sushi and another large drink of iced tea, then smiled her first genuine smile since sitting down in their private little booth.

"I do feel a lot better."

Michael studied her a moment longer, then nodded. "I guess we should head back to work."

She wiped her mouth with the starchy white napkin, then set it on the table and rose. "Yes, I guess we should."

They walked out together, but didn't stand too close. Both of them agreed that it was better if no one at *HOT!* or in the mailroom knew they were a couple. Of course, Liza wasn't certain they were really pulling the platonic thing off, even with no PDA. She suspected they had a vibe that people could sense and probably even see.

Still, precautions were good. Michael didn't need to be mixed up in the demon drama of *HOT!* any more than necessary.

Though Liza had found the mailroom to be a rather odd place, she didn't think the workers there were a part of the demon conspiracy. Again, who sold their soul to work in a mailroom?

Once they reached the *HOT!* building, Liza paused on the sidewalk. "So I'll see you tonight?"

Michael smiled. "You know you will."

They paused there, and Liza could tell he wanted to touch her or lean in for a kiss, but he remained standing tall, his hands down at his sides.

"I wish I could kiss you," she murmured, wanting him to know she saw his need and felt the same way.

As if he couldn't help himself, he stepped closer. Only to instantly move back again, his attention briefly on something or someone behind them.

As casually as possible, Liza glanced over her shoulder to see what had captured his attention.

Tristan McIntyre was walking toward the building. He too glanced in their direction, but barely seemed to register them aside from his usual haughty look of disdain. Nothing out of the ordinary there. Then he paused, and headed in their direction.

"Oh no," Liza said in a low voice. Michael shifted beside her.

"Liza," he called in his cultured, slightly accented voice that seemed as affected as his metrosexual style. "Finola is going to want to meet with you this afternoon."

Liza had been dreading and avoiding this meeting, but it was her chance to discover if her unlikely plan would actually work.

"Sure, just let me know when."

Tristan nodded, his gaze flicking to Michael before

he spun on his Gucci loafers and headed back to work—or rather, his maniacal demonic takeover.

"I don't think he thought anything about us talking," she said.

Michael continued to watch the other man . . . male demon . . . whatever . . . stroll up the steps and disappear through the revolving doors.

"I don't like him."

Liza noticed Michael's fingers were flexed subconsciously at his sides.

"He's not the most likeable guy I've met, but he's better than Finola, I suppose."

"Just barely," Michael muttered.

Liza wasn't sure why he had such strong feelings about Finola's lackey, maybe because he *was* a lackey. Michael was a man who didn't answer to anyone, and probably had a natural disrespect for other men who did.

Then he stopped staring toward the building, and offered Liza a smile that was only slightly distracted. "I'll see you tonight."

Liza nodded. "Yes, you will."

"Man, you don't seem terribly happy for a man newly bonded."

Michael looked up to find Gabriel standing beside his sorting table. Michael didn't respond, except to bundle up another stack of envelopes and stuff them with more force than necessary onto his delivery cart. He picked up more mail, then set it back down to look at Gabriel.

"How can you stand this?"

Gabriel frowned. "Stand what?"

"Just hanging around here doing nothing. It's bull-shit."

"What is bringing this on now? You should be feeling happier and more content than ever."

Michael stared at him, conflicted in so many ways. "I'm not sure how I'm supposed to be content when I don't even understand the world I'm living in now. I no longer know what my career is, aside from sorting these." He shoved the pile of mail across the table, and several pieces slid off the table onto the concrete floor.

"And I'm bonded, but to a—" He caught himself before he admitted who his bonded mate was and that she was under a soul contract. A demon slayer could not be bonded to a woman who had signed over her soul.

Yet, he was.

"Bonded to a what?" Gabriel's shrewd eyes locked with Michael's, reading him.

Shit. What could he say now?

He grasped on to the first thought that hit him. One that was honestly concerning him too.

"I think she has an addiction of some kind."

Gabriel made a face as if he'd never heard of such a thing with a bonded mate. Imagine if Michael had told him the truth.

"What kind of addiction?"

Michael hesitated, knowing the answer wouldn't make sense. After all, who was addicted to allergy medications? But he knew she was still taking them, and he knew they were affecting her health. But why? She certainly didn't seem suicidal. And God knows she didn't even sniff, let alone have full-blown allergies. Of course, he suspected she was taking a lot of those little pink pills. It was a wonder she wasn't as dried out as a mummy.

Michael opted to play stupid.

"I'm not really sure. But I have noticed her taking a lot of some kind of medication. Maybe it's nothing."

Gabriel looked unconvinced, but let it drop, bending down to pick up the letters that had scattered on the ground. When he rose, he returned to Michael's original comment.

"I thought you were okay with the DIA's new policies, even if you didn't agree. What has you so frustrated?"

Again, Michael couldn't state the total truth, that he was worried about Liza and her close working relationship with scumbag demons like Finola and that smarmy Tristan.

Even as they were speaking, Liza could be having her meeting with those two. And what if they'd found a reason to say she'd broken her soul contract? She could already be cast to Hell for all he knew, while he was stuck down here, utterly useless.

Despite his fears, he sensed she was still here, still in the building, still with him. But for how long? And how could he go on being a helpless bystander?

But rather than speak his thoughts, he just shook his head, not hiding his frustration, even though he had to hide his true concerns. "I just hate walking around up there, seeing demons, and letting them go on causing trouble in our world."

Gabriel nodded, then surprised Michael to the core by admitting something he had yet to admit. "I hate it too."

Michael suddenly felt less separated from his once closest friend. He felt like maybe losing thirty-something years hadn't left him completely in the dust. But he still didn't know how he was going to help Liza.

All the same, he nodded at his friend, appreciating the small gesture of support.

"I don't know how long I can just watch them," Michael admitted.

Gabriel nodded again, another surprise. "I know it's hard."

You have no idea, Gabriel. No idea. The love of my life, my soul mate, is in the middle of this war. She is potentially a casualty every moment she's up there. And I have to protect her, even if it goes against every damned policy DIA has.

But Michael didn't say that. He knew he couldn't.

"Michael."

Both of them turned their attention toward the man who'd just joined them. Elton pushed his mail cart up to Michael's table.

"Are you ready to get this shit delivered?"

Michael smiled wryly. It seemed everyone was frustrated today.

"Yeah. Almost."

Michael looked back at Gabriel, who gave him another sympathetic look, but didn't say anything. Instead he held out the envelopes from the floor.

"We have to believe."

Michael stared at Gabriel for a moment. He didn't know if he did, but he would try. Even as frustrated as he was, Michael knew he couldn't put down this massive demon takeover by himself. But he could take out any demon who directly threatened Liza. He nodded, then turned to his cart.

Here we go again. He pushed his cart to join Elton. At least he could go up and check on Liza himself. He hoped her meeting with the great and evil Finola White was over, and he could see for himself she was safe, at least for now.

"Are you okay?" Elton asked as they entered the elevator.

"Yes."

Michael could feel Elton's eyes still on him.

"You're worried about Liza."

Michael's gaze snapped back to the old man beside him before he could hide his surprised look.

"Seer," Elton said as his usual way of explanation.

Michael nodded.

"It's not easy to have her up there among the wolves, is it?"

Again, Michael wondered how much the man knew, or saw, or whatever. Did he know they were bonded? The Brethren could tell if they saw them together, but did a seer know too?

"Of course, she's never free of the evil parasites." Elton shook his head. "Poor girl."

Michael frowned, opening his mouth to ask what Elton meant. Sure, Finola had Liza pretty much at her beck and call, but at least when Liza was with him, she was free of the demons that had infiltrated the magazine. But before the words could leave his mouth, the elevator doors opened.

"Thank goodness," called the blond receptionist as soon as she saw them. She came out from behind her desk, carrying a stack of Tyvek envelopes. "Ms. White wants these mailed overnight. Immediately."

Michael stepped forward to take the packages, but Elton's gnarled hand on his arm stopped him.

"I'll take it down. You check on Liza."

Michael studied the older man, still wondering what he knew.

Elton nodded, his hazy eyes wise and all-seeing. He probably knew everything. But in the old man's eyes,

Michael also saw that Elton didn't plan to say anything to anyone about his relationship with Liza.

"Go on."

Michael nodded and pushed his cart off the elevator, while the receptionist handed Elton the packages.

Despite his helplessness, Michael had to admit that he'd discovered he had more friends at the DIA than he'd realized, which might come in very handy should he have to take matters into his own hands.

Chapter Twenty-six

Liza hesitated outside Finola's office, pleased that even though all the walls were glass, her boss hadn't yet noticed her. Nor had her toady, Tristan. They were deep in conversation. Finola waved a hand in the air, then took a sip from the champagne flute in the other. Tristan nodded, sipping from his own martini glass.

Maybe their early happy hour would work in her favor, Liza thought. Maybe if they had a nice little buzz, the fact that she'd been drugging the demon who had been assigned to possess her wouldn't be such a big deal. Maybe they'd actually see she was doing them all a favor. Well, except Boris, of course.

She watched them, trying to build up her courage. Even with the wishful thinking about the alcohol, she didn't really believe Finola or Tristan would approve of what she'd done, much less see that it was a good thing to have Boris out of Liza's life—and body.

But she had to make her argument sound like a good one. And she couldn't waver. After all, it was her only hope of being freed from her possession.

She took one more deep breath and raised her

hand to knock. But before she could do so, Finola's horrible little lapdog, the real four-legged one, not Tristan, began to yip.

Both Finola and Tristan turned in Liza's direction. Liza lowered her hand to the doorknob as Finola immediately waved for her to enter.

"Were you hovering around out there?" Finola asked.

"No," Liza assured her.

"I would hope not. I don't like people skulking outside my office. Nor do I like to be kept waiting."

Liza didn't get the feeling that Finola had really been waiting. Clearly she and Tristan had been wrapped up in their own conversation, but she wasn't going to point that out. Yes, she had been rebellious, even impertinent, the last few times she'd met with her demonic boss, but today, she had to show that she could be the perfect, compliant employee, if they would just cast Boris out of her.

"I'm sorry, but I wanted to make sure this was just right before I came to meet with you."

With her head lowered, and her posture meek, Liza carefully placed a mock-up of the latest fashion spread for the summer issue of *HOT!* on Finola's gleaming white desk. Then she stepped back, her hands clasped in front of her, waiting quietly.

Finola raised an eyebrow, then reached for the pages. She looked at each of the six photos with text.

Liza waited, praying that this was some of the best work she'd ever done. She needed Finola happy if she was going to have even a hope of getting her to see her point of view.

Finola flipped through the pages again, before finally turning her pale gaze back to Liza.

"This is"—she glanced at the layouts again—"excellent."

Liza tried not to sag with relief. Okay, this was a good start.

"I've been quite impressed with your work of late," Finola said.

Yes! Maybe, just maybe, Finola would see that Liza was a better employee without Boris. Please. Because even now, her heart was racing, galloping in her chest, partly because of her nerves, but mainly because of the allergy meds. She couldn't keep taking them. Not much longer. And then what would she do? She'd have to give up Michael, that was for sure.

"I'm glad you have been pleased," she said in a meek voice. She glanced up to check Finola's expression. The demon looked almost delighted.

This could work. Liza had to believe.

Liza's gaze shifted to Tristan. He, on the other hand, looked downright annoyed with her. Why? He couldn't know yet that Boris was drugged and dormant inside her.

But he would now.

Here goes . . .

Liza cleared her throat and said a silent prayer that her plan didn't backfire completely.

"I—I have to be upfront," Liza admitted, her tone still low and contrite.

Finola set down the page in her hand, all her attention on Liza. Tristan regarded her intently too.

Liza moved nervously from one foot to the other, trying to find the right way to explain and justify her current actions.

"I have to admit something, however," she said softly.

Finola raised a pale eyebrow, waiting for Liza to continue.

"I have been drugging Bor—Bartoris so I could get my work done without his constant interruptions," she said, managing to keep her tone apologetic.

She waited, her heart thumping so hard she was sure everyone in the room could see the pulsation through her sweater.

When she met Finola's gaze again, she saw that the woman didn't look particularly mad. In fact, she looked almost indifferent.

This could be a good reaction too.

But when Finola didn't speak for several moments, Liza started to doubt the response. Maybe Finola was furious and debating what to do to Liza.

Liza's heart skipped, and she struggled to take calming breaths.

"Well," Finola finally said, a slight smile tugging at her ruby-red lips, "you have done this before. And I can't say I blame you. Bartoris can be a distracting fellow."

Liza nodded. Okay, this was good. This was a good reaction, right?

"And I believe I gave you the go-ahead to handle him, if he was indeed being a disruption. So frankly, I don't care how you manage him as long as I get the work I want." Finola took a sip of her champagne, emptying her glass. She immediately held the glass out to Tristan for a refill, and he didn't miss a beat taking it from her. He walked over to the wet bar. As he passed Liza, she couldn't miss the irritated sidelong glance he gave her.

Liza hid her frown and confusion. Why was he annoyed? Shouldn't he be just as pleased as Finola? Or at the very least happy his usually dissatisfied boss was not making a fuss? Liza suspected that made his life easier too. She wasn't oblivious. She knew Tristan did plenty of grunt work for Finola too.

But Liza let his reaction go, refocusing on a tiny spec of something black on Finola's white carpeting. A thread or something. A slight blemish in Finola's otherwise perfect world.

No matter what, Liza didn't want to be that kind of nuisance. Finola didn't take well to imperfections; she simply got rid of them.

That idea spurred Liza on.

"It does help me concentrate," Liza told her. "But I think I would be so much more productive without having to worry about him at all."

Finola regarded her, again not saying anything. Tristan returned to her side, holding out the refreshed glass of bubbly.

"I believe we've had a version of this conversation before," the diva demon finally said, after polishing off half of the golden liquid in the expensive crystal wine flute. "I'm not sure why we are discussing this again."

Liza nodded, keeping her eyes downcast, but she couldn't help pushing her point further. "I know we have, but I thought if you saw how much work I could get done without him bothering me—and the quality of work—" She paused, her racing heart somehow still managing to feel like it was sinking in her chest.

Finola wasn't going to cast Boris out. She didn't care if Liza drugged him, but she wasn't going to get the demon out of her. Boris was there to stay as long as Finola wanted him there.

But still she finished, "I thought you would realize I'm more than willing to keep working for *HOT!* without Bor—Bartoris here to guard me."

Finola smiled then, a sweet, beautiful smile that was even more sinister because it was so deceptively lovely. "I know you want to get rid of Bartoris. Really, I do understand. But though I am the one in total control of *HOT!*—"

Liza paid attention to Finola, but out of the corner of her eye, she thought she saw Tristan roll his eyes. Was Finola's lackey frustrated by Finola's dictatorship too?

"—I'm not the one who can decide to cast Bartoris out of you. That decision is up to Satan. If you want me to bring the ruler of the underworld here to chat with you, and you can convince him of what you're suggesting, then I'd be more than happy to bring your possession to an end."

Liza's full attention returned to Finola. Was she really suggesting Liza talk directly to Satan himself? Okay, that she would happily skip.

"No," Liza said, offering Finola an appreciative smile that she didn't feel in the least. "I understand your situation. And mine."

Finola nodded approvingly. "Good. Although I do have one more thing to discuss with you."

Liza's chest tightened. What could Finola want to talk about? She had thought this meeting was solely about her productivity.

"Yes?"

"Tell us about your boyfriend."

Liza's breath caught and she couldn't speak for a moment. Her boyfriend. They knew about Michael. But of course they did. She'd been stupid to think they would miss anything. They were demons, after all.

But still Liza tried to play it down. She didn't want Michael drawn into this.

"You must be talking about Michael. We are really just friends—not really boyfriend and girlfriend."

Finola nodded, although skepticism was clear in her pale eyes. "Michael. Does Michael have a last name?"

Liza's chest tightened further. She didn't want Michael on Finola's radar at all. Of course it was too late for that anyway.

"Michael Archer."

Again, she noticed Tristan's reaction more than Finola's. He frowned, his eyes narrowing as if he was trying to place that name.

"He's just a mailroom clerk," Liza added quickly, somehow hoping that if they realized Michael was nothing but a lowly peon, they would lose interest.

Finola appeared to do just that. She nodded. "A mailroom clerk. How quaint."

Liza bowed her head too. "Did you need anything else from me?" She just wanted to get out of there. She was disappointed by the outcome of the meeting, and even more worried about Michael. Although she wasn't sure what to tell him about their questions.

"Just one last thing and then you can go back to work." Finola polished off the remainder of her champagne, this time setting the empty glass on her desk. "Tristan, get the mirror."

Tristan again jumped to attention, and Liza wondered how he could stand working so closely with this demanding bitch—even being a demon himself. Especially being a demon himself.

Did he ever wonder why Finola was the demon with all the power? That had to be frustrating too.

But as always, he did what he was told. He went behind the screen in the corner and wheeled out Finola's full-length mirror. Liza couldn't help thinking of the evil queen from *Snow White*.

Who's the fairest of them all?

Finola White was that literally. But mainly, she was the evilest of all, which was probably why she was the demon in control and not Tristan.

He positioned the mirror so Finola could see Liza reflected in the polished glass.

And there at her feet, curled in a fetal position, was Boris. Snoring quietly away. A sound Liza had come to hear as soothing white noise in her head.

Finola giggled then.

"I almost have to applaud you for your brilliance," she said to Liza. "Somehow you figured out how to drug a demon. It does show ingenuity, that is for certain."

Liza nodded, not sharing Finola's amusement. As the demon diva giggled again, Liza noticed that Tristan did not look amused either.

In fact, he looked positively annoyed.

Chapter Twenty-seven

Michael knocked on Liza's office door, but his rap was greeted by silence. She must be in her meeting with Finola, and a part of him wanted to stride right back to Finola's glass maze and find his soul mate. Protect his soul mate. That was his job. But he knew that wasn't a possibility. Not right now. Still, he wasn't going to leave until he saw for himself Liza was okay.

He glanced around to make sure no one was watching. For all he knew that pompous ass demon, Tristan, was lurking. He was clearly Finola's eyes and ears, and Michael didn't trust the guy, which was really an unnecessary statement since he was a demon. He didn't trust demons or the possessed. Period. No matter what the DIA's new policies might say.

A few employees bustled around, but they were too focused on their work to give a lowly mailroom employee even a cursory glance. So he opened Liza's office door and slipped inside.

Her office was small with one window that looked out at the street below. She had two chairs facing her desk and her office chair on the other side. The desk itself was scattered with photos, printouts, and pages. He wandered over to see what she was working on. From the photos, it looked like a fall fashion spread. Maybe winter. In truth, Michael wasn't much up on his fashion. Then again, he'd come from a world where bell-bottoms and platform shoes and huge lapels were the height of style.

He had to admit he definitely didn't miss some stuff about the seventies.

He reached to pick up one of the pages, an article on how to create a romantic getaway on a budget, but when he picked it up, one of the fashion shots slipped off the desk and drifted to the floor.

He bent down to grab it, only to become distracted by a plastic shopping bag under Liza's desk. The white bag was labeled with the name DUANE READE.

Even though he knew he shouldn't, he ignored the fallen picture and reached under the desk to pull out the bag. It was light, but definitely had a few items inside. He suspected he already knew what was inside, but he opened the bag, making the white plastic crinkle.

Just as he thought. Inside were four boxes of allergy medication, clearly just purchased. More allergy meds.

Why? Why was she taking these? And if she was buying so many packages at once, it was definitely likely she was taking too many. Of course, he knew she was. And he knew it was affecting her health.

Again, why?

Behind him, the doorknob rattled, and without hesitation, he wadded up the plastic bag and shoved it into the back of his pants waistband. His hideous royal blue smock fell into place, covering the bulge of the bag.

He turned and waited, glad that he'd managed to hide Liza's contraband before whoever was coming in to the office saw that he was stealing it.

As Liza had walked back to her office, she'd let her disappointment go. She'd known getting Finola to cast Boris out of her had been a long shot, and at least the diva demon wasn't angry that she'd been keeping the annoying little demon drugged. Nor was she particularly interested in Liza's relationship with Michael. And in truth, that was the thing that mattered most to Liza. She didn't want Michael on Finola's radar. No good would come from that.

Now she twisted the handle to her door, still lost in her own thoughts, only to jump when she realized someone was in her office. At first all she registered was a tall figure near her desk, his back to her. Then very quickly she realized it was Michael.

"Oh my gosh," she said with a surprised laugh as she pressed a hand to her chest. "You startled me."

Michael, who had turned to face her now, gave her an apologetic smile. "I'm sorry. I didn't mean to. I was just waiting here to see how your meeting with Finola went."

Liza's smile slipped slightly. "It went pretty much as I expected. But overall pretty well."

"What did she want to discuss?"

Her smile vanished, becoming a wan grimace. For a moment she didn't speak and he thought maybe she wasn't going to answer, but then she said, "Well, she wanted to know about you."

"Me? Why?"

Liza shrugged and sighed. "Finola feels like she needs to be a part of all her employees' lives. I'm sure she just wants to be sure nothing is distracting me from my work."

He was sure that was true, but he couldn't help wondering if the demons were suspicious of him or, worse, suspicious of the mailroom, although he hadn't done anything to draw attention to either himself or the DIA.

Other than bonding with Liza. Could any of the demons sense that? As far as he knew, only other Brethren could sense a bonding.

Except he got the feeling Elton knew. What if the demons did too? He'd have to talk to Gabriel about this. Except he would have to reveal who he was bonded with, and that might cause problems for the DIA.

Damn.

"It really isn't anything to worry about," Liza said, her hand touching his shoulder reassuringly, then sliding down his back. He shifted before her fingers could make contact with the bag tucked into the back of his pants.

She frowned slightly at his sudden movement, but he quickly leaned in to kiss her as a way of distracting her.

"I just don't like the idea of your boss controlling so much of your life," he said once the kiss ended.

"I don't either," she said with another sigh. "But for the time being there isn't much I can do to change it. And I'm just happy she isn't trying to interfere any more."

He nodded, knowing she couldn't tell him anything more about her relationship with Finola. And he supposed she was right. As long as the demon diva didn't ask any more questions, they were probably both safe.

And in truth, he was more worried about why Liza was taking these allergy meds, but that wasn't something he was going to question her about now.

"I guess I'd better get back to work," he said.

She gave him a disappointed little pout, but then nodded. "I'd better get to work too. We don't want her thinking our relationship is a problem."

No, they didn't want that.

"But I will come up after work and maybe we can go out to dinner."

Liza smiled, one of her true, genuine, beautiful smiles. "That would be nice."

He smiled too, although he still wondered if Finola was more suspicious than she'd revealed. And there was the meds issue. He'd get to the bottom of that one tonight, even if Liza tried to avoid the topic.

He gave her another kiss. "See you in a bit."

"Can't wait."

"Are you going to continue that pacing? It's positively irritating."

Tristan stopped, pausing in the middle of Finola's office, but rather than looking contrite, he frowned. "Something about Liza's mailroom boyfriend is bothering me. I can't put my finger on why, but I keep feeling that something about him seems familiar."

Finola looked completely uninterested as she debated over several pairs of shoes that he'd actually placed before her minutes ago.

"Well, if there is something we should know about the man, I'm sure it will come to you. Right now I have far more urgent matters at hand. Which of these shoes should I wear to the gala tonight? And I haven't even contemplated an evening bag."

Tristan fought the urge to roll his eyes at Finola's idea of a crisis.

"I like the Jimmy Choos," he said without really looking.

Finola remained silent for a moment, then shook her head. "Too predictable. I'm going with the Delilah Jameses. She's fresh and I like the femininity of her style."

So why ask, he wanted to say to her, but instead he made some comment that flattered her choice, then went back to his own thoughts.

Michael Archer. That name really did seem so familiar. But where—where did he know this man from?

"I'm not sure why you are letting this bother you so. Liza McLane seems more malleable than she ever has. I'm pleased with her work. I'm pleased that she no longer seems rebellious." Finola paused, studying the Delilah James shoes closer, then nodded to herself. Apparently her decision was official.

"I suppose I should be upset with her treatment of Bartoris," she finally continued. "But to be honest, I find it amusing. It makes me actually admire her. And I so rarely admire any human."

Tristan couldn't argue that. Finola rarely admired anyone but herself.

"So overall, I'm willing to allow things to go as they are. If Liza stops pleasing me, then I will rethink her beau and her treatment of Bartoris. Otherwise, I have bigger issues to focus on."

She rose from her desk, going over to a clothing rack that one of Finola's many peons had wheeled into the room. She sorted through the evening bags hanging there beside her white, crystal-encrusted evening gown.

He started to move, to pace again, but caught himself. Instead he wandered over to the wet bar and poured himself a martini.

"I can see you are still agitated," she said, not looking away from the small drawstring bag she studied.

He added several olives to his glass, then turned to look at his mistress.

"I just have this feeling something is not right. And it goes beyond Liza's handling of Bartoris. I'm with you on that count—as long as she's doing her work, I can't blame her for silencing the little demonic pest."

She smiled, clearly still finding Liza's trick amusing.

"But I do feel we are overlooking something big here. Something to do with that boyfriend."

Finola nodded again, choosing a classic clutch in white silk. Then she finally turned to look at Tristan.

"Well then, my dear, feel free to watch the man further. I don't mind as long as it doesn't interfere with your work for me. Like getting me another glass of champagne and then helping me into my dress."

"Of course," Tristan agreed, gritting his teeth, wondering if this was really what Satan had intended his job to be as Finola's right-hand man.

Liza stretched, leaning back in her desk chair, her neck and back stiff from being bent over her desk for so long. The latest layout she was working on looked darned good. It was amazing how well she could work when Boris was silent.

But as if on cue, Boris yawned, the deep groaning sigh seeming to go right along with her own stretching. If only the sound was coming from her, rather than echoing inside her.

She stopped her own stretching, and gently brought

her arms down to the arms of her chair as if she could lull him back to sleep by remaining still.

Of course that didn't work. And as usual, Boris did not wake up on the right side of the bed.

Bitch.

She smiled. "Sweet talker."

A low growl echoed through her head and she laughed. Even though the medication was making her feel awful. Really awful at times, it was worth these moments. Moments when she knew she was in control. Even when he was awake, she was more powerful than he. And she had more allergy meds right under her desk to knock him out again.

Bitch.

"I think the days and days of unconsciousness are making you less than articulate. What's wrong, no pithy, sarcastic comments now?"

She knew she probably shouldn't taunt him this way. Nor should she allow him to fully gather his senses before she drugged him again, but she couldn't help feeling a little smug.

"I should probably let you in on a little something that happened while you were asleep today."

She paused, waiting for him to comment. But Boris actually remained silent. Even though he wasn't saying a word, she knew he was seething. He was one angry, angry demon.

Maybe she shouldn't be so bold, so ready to tease him. But in one regard today had been a very good day. Finola White didn't care what she was doing to Boris, so that meant she could keep doing it.

And Boris could complain, but it wouldn't matter.

"I'm sorry that your own kind don't seem to care what's happening to you, but Finola doesn't mind that

I'm drugging you. In fact she gave me props for actually figuring out a way to keep you quiet."

She's a bitch too.

Liza laughed. "Well, I will pass that along to her, if you like."

He growled again. Poor Boris.

Bartoris, damn it.

She chuckled slightly, then glanced at the clock on the corner of her computer screen. It was almost five o'clock. She couldn't risk letting Boris get any less groggy. She needed to take her Benadryl and knock him out again. In fact, she'd pushed this little moment of torment too long as it was. Michael might arrive at any moment.

She pushed back her chair and leaned down to feel around under her desk for the bag of meds she'd purchased earlier today. But the bag wasn't where she thought she'd left it.

She leaned forward, peering underneath. The bag wasn't in view.

Maybe she'd put it in her purse. She grabbed her satchel purse, placing it on the desk and disregarding her work as she unzipped it. She rooted around inside the bag, standing as if a higher sight line would suddenly make the bag appear. It didn't.

"Where is it?"

In her head, she heard a chuckle.

Damn it, where was the bag? It had been here.

She sat back down, leaning so far under her desk she was practically crawling underneath. But there was no bag.

Just then she heard a knock on her office door, and she didn't have to look up to know who it was.

"Liza, are you in here?"

Michael. She remained still, hoping somehow she could simply hide under her desk and he would leave. But no such luck. She heard his footfalls coming into the room.

"Liza? What are you doing under your desk?"

Boris chuckled louder.

Wow, it's amazing how quickly I'm feeling better. No wrong side of the bed for me today.

Chapter Twenty-eight

Michael walked over to the side of Liza's desk, peering down at her bottom and feet poking out from underneath.

"Liza? What are you doing?"

She didn't move for a moment, reminding him of a child in a game of hide-and-seek who thought because she couldn't see him, he couldn't see her.

But after a moment, she backed out of her hiding spot, looking up at him with an expression somewhere between confused and wary.

"I—I just dropped something under my desk," she finally said with an awkward smile.

"Did you find it?"

She nodded, although he noticed she didn't appear to have anything in either of her hands. But then he already suspected she wasn't looking for something she'd dropped, but rather something she'd lost. And she didn't actually lose it—he'd stolen it. She'd been looking for her bag of allergy medication. He was certain of that.

But rather than confront her about it now, he held

out a hand to her. "Are you ready to go to dinner? I know I'm kind of early, but you've been working so many long hours, I figured one early night couldn't hurt."

She stared at his proffered hand, making no attempt to take it. In fact, she regarded his open palm and extended fingers like they were a nest of poisonous snakes.

What was wrong?

"Are you okay?"

She instantly nodded, but actually almost crab-walked to scoot away from him. Only then did she use the edge of the desk to pull herself to her feet. She brushed her hands down the front of her skirt to smooth down the fabric.

"I'm fine. Just a little preoccupied with this project I'm working on. In fact, maybe you should give me a little longer to work on it."

Michael regarded her. She was pale, he noticed, and she seemed to be breathing in shallow puffs. Was she having one of her spells again?

He thought about the meds he'd tossed out earlier. What if the medicine wasn't causing these strange bouts, but actually helping them? But if that was the case, wouldn't she explain her problem to him? He wasn't sure.

"Liza, you don't look well."

To his surprise, she agreed. "I'm not feeling well. Maybe you could get me some water."

He hesitated, not sure he should leave her. "Okay, but please sit down." He started to come around the desk to help her, offer her an arm to keep her steady, but again she moved away.

Like she had before in this very office. She didn't want him to touch her. But why? And especially now after all the times they'd been intimate. After the hours they'd spent in each other's arms.

"I'm fine," she said, holding up a hand.

He studied her for a moment, then decided to let her reaction go. "Okay. Wait right here."

She nodded, shifting around the far side of the desk and back to her chair, clearly avoiding him.

He waited until she was seated, then headed toward the door, but once outside, he didn't head to the water cooler just a few cubicles away from her office. Instead, he stepped to the side and listened.

For a moment, he heard nothing. Then he thought he heard her murmur something. He leaned a little closer, being careful that she couldn't see him.

"Oh, shut up."

Michael frowned. Who was she talking to? Herself?

Again he remembered she'd also talked to herself earlier in their relationship, although she hadn't done so recently.

So what had triggered the return of these behaviors? She didn't want to be touched. She was talking to herself.

"You just wait. You won't see the light of day for the next year."

Michael frowned again. Who the hell was she talking to? And what did she mean?

He peeked around the corner to see she'd laid her head on the desk, almost as if she were terribly weary. He used that moment to slip back into her office.

Using his slayer stealth, he crept closer to her, stopping right beside her chair.

"Where are the pills?" she muttered without lifting her head, and only then did he touch her.

"Liza, they are gone. I threw them out."

She started at his touch and words, but he didn't let

her go, using his other hand to tug her up out of her chair so he could stare directly into her eyes, her wide, shocked eyes. Actually, she looked more than shocked. She looked terrified.

"Liza, what's going on?"

Liza couldn't speak for a moment. Michael was touching her, and Boris was seeing him. The one thing she'd never wanted was happening. Boris was now a part of her relationship.

But instead of lewd comments about Michael's good looks, or suggestive ideas of what the three of them could do, Boris only said two words.

Michael Archer.

Liza frowned. She wasn't sure if he'd ever heard Michael's name before or not, but the way Boris said his name didn't sound like he was simply repeating a name he'd heard her use. Instead, he seemed to be saying Michael's name like he recognized him. But how could he?

Michael Archer, the demon slayer.

"Demon slayer?" What was he talking about?

"What did you say?"

Only then, as Michael stared at her with almost hard eyes, did Liza realize she'd said the words aloud.

"I—I don't know," she sputtered, her answer not untrue. She really didn't know what she'd said. She'd just been repeating Boris's words.

I thought I'd seen the last of this demon-killing bastard.

Liza couldn't understand what Boris was talking about. Michael didn't kill demons. He delivered mail. He didn't even know demons ran *HOT!* magazine. Did he?

Deliver mail? Hardly. This man is a demon slayer. A very

dangerous one. One I thought I'd put out of commission indefinitely.

Liza shook her head. She had no idea what was going on.

"You said demon slayer? Why?" Michael's eyes searched hers.

I should have just killed him.

"No," she said, again not catching herself. And this was why Boris needed to be drugged at all times. She couldn't not react to the commentary in her head. Of course, this particular commentary was crazy.

Michael, a demon slayer. Boris had to be delusional from all the hours of being drugged.

Hardly. I know the slayer I once defeated. And will defeat again. I will tell Finola, Tristan, anyone who will listen. Michael Archer, demon slayer and member of The Brethren, will be killed at last.

"The Brethren? Killed? No," she stated, fear filling her, even though she didn't understand what was going on.

Suddenly Michael's hold on her arms tightened, almost painfully.

"How do you know about The Brethren? What do you mean killed?" he demanded, his voice taking on a tone she'd never heard him use with her before. More fear filled her. Whatever Boris was talking about, Michael knew something about it too.

"I—I don't know," she repeated.

But I do. I know your boyfriend very, very well. And he knows me. I was once his worst nightmare.

Liza shook her head, not wanting this to be true. She'd believed Michael knew nothing about the demons around them. She'd wanted to believe he was no part of the demon takeover.

But he is.

Boris's voice was the one that was taunting and smug now.

Michael frowned, trying to understand what was going on. Liza stared at him as if she were staring at a monster. And she kept saying things that sounded as if she knew what he was, except each time she said something like "demon slayer" or "The Brethren," the terms had question marks after them as if she didn't even understand what she was saying. As if she was just repeating the words.

She twisted again in his hold, clearly wanting to get away.

"Liza, tell me what's going on," he demanded.

"I don't know," she repeated. "I don't understand."

She winced, but he didn't believe it was because of his touch. He wasn't holding her that tight, but he did release her. He didn't want to hurt or scare her.

She stumbled away from him, and her hands went up to her ears, covering them as if to block out something only she could hear. She squeezed her eyes closed and shook her head.

"You are lying," she said, shaking her head.

"Lying about what?" Damn it, what was going on? She knew something about him, that much was certain. But what and how and why couldn't she just tell him what was going on?

"You have to bring her with us."

Michael turned then to see Elton standing just inside the door; behind him was Gabriel. More confusion bombarded him. He didn't understand what was going on at all. Was Liza somehow psychic? And was she going crazy or something?

When he looked back at her, she also looked toward

the door, seeing the other men. She looked confused too, but then she flinched again and her hands went back to her head.

Something was definitely wrong with her.

"We aren't going to hurt her," Elton said, stepping farther into the room. Gabriel shut the door and stood guard there. He nodded as if to confirm what the old man said.

"But she does need to go with us," Elton said in his gravelly, yet almost soothing voice. "For her protection as well as yours."

"Tell me what's going on," Michael demanded, casting another worried look toward the clearly overwhelmed Liza. She scrunched her eyes shut again as if to block them out, although Michael sensed it wasn't the people around her that she was trying to shut out. It was someone else.

"We need to do this quickly," Gabriel said, shifting to look out the small window in the door. "We can't risk discovery now."

"Michael, this has to be done," Elton assured him, giving him an almost fatherly look. He then rushed over to Liza with more speed than Michael would have imagined the old man capable of. Michael charged forward too, not sure what he intended to do. But before either he or Liza could react, Elton pressed a small rectangle against the side of Liza's neck, and she started to crumple to the ground.

Michael caught her before she fell.

"What the hell," Michael growled.

"It didn't hurt her and the effects aren't long-lasting, so we've got to move," Elton said, his tone leaving no room for argument. "Now."

"The coast is clear," Gabriel said from his position peering out the door. "Let's go. Now, Michael."

Michael looked down at the unconscious Liza, and decided he had to trust that his fellow DIA members had her best interests at heart, as well as his own. The truth was, he had little choice.

He followed Gabriel, and Elton followed him. They rushed to a set of doors that led to a back hallway and a freight elevator.

"Do you think anyone saw?" he asked Gabriel.

"No. We were lucky." He herded them onto the elevator.

"How did you know about all of this?" Michael asked, looking down at Liza, concern and confusion at war inside him. "How did you know she would recognize me?"

"I've been watching her," Elton said. "I've been watching you both."

"Why?" Michael had no idea what was going on.

"We will explain once we are all safely downstairs," Gabriel said.

Michael wanted to keep asking questions, but knew there was no point. Not now. He'd have to wait to get the answers to his questions. He just prayed they were the answers he wanted.

"Finola was right," Dippy said. "Your pacing is pretty annoying."

"Well, so is the constant licking," Tristan pointed out.

Dippy lowered his back leg. "It's grooming."

"Whatever." Tristan strode across the carpet of his office, pausing to look out at the city skyline.

"I don't see what you are fixating on," the dog said. "I mean, the whole Liza and boyfriend thing is a bust. I've been saying right along we need a new plan, and now we officially do. Finola is just hunky-dory with both of those humans."

Tristan nodded. "I know, but I keep feeling I know something about that guy—that what's-his-name."

"I believe he's named Michael Archer."

Tristan nodded again.

"But let's face it. If Finola is fine with Liza drugging the drool out of Bartoris, she's not going to have any further interest in this Michael Archer. Even if we manufacture something about him. At this point, what could we make up that would be bad enough to get Finola's attention?"

Tristan knew the hellhound had a point. What could they make up about Michael Archer? He then thought about poor, silly Bartoris—that demon would probably rather go back to Hell than exist the way he was now. He was an annoying little weasel of a demon, always bragging about this and that, but even Bartoris didn't deserve to exist in a comatose state.

"I guess we'd better think of something . . ." Tristan stopped his comment as his mind suddenly pieced together the niggling feelings that had been bugging him.

He suddenly remembered how he knew that name. He spun around to Dippy.

"Michael Archer is a demon slayer."

Chapter Twenty-nine

When Michael stepped out of the elevator, he saw his other Brethren mates waiting, as well as Eugene. They didn't speak, but rather fell into step beside him, leading him toward a hallway where he'd never been before. The area reminded him of an asylum, except instead of cells with padded walls, these rooms were lined with copper. Copper was a metal demons couldn't vanish through; it held them captive.

But why were they bringing Liza here?

Finally they reached one of the copper-lined cells, actually two rooms separated by a wall of glass.

Eugene unlocked one of the doors and stepped aside to allow Michael inside. Michael hesitated for a moment, trying to read Eugene's expression, but as usual he couldn't see anything on the man's bland features to help him understand what was going on.

"Liza is in no danger," was all his superior said, then waved a hand for him to enter.

Michael did, crossing over to a comfortable enough looking sofa. He carefully placed Liza's still limp body on the cushions, then straightened, taking in each detail of her features. Her pallor, her expression, whether she displayed any signs of distress.

"She is fine," Eugene assured him again.

"You know I wouldn't hurt your mate," Elton added.

Michael turned to stare at Elton, his gaze then moving from Eugene to Gabriel and back to Elton. "You all know that Liza is my bonded?"

The three men nodded.

"It's my job to know everything that is going on both in the DIA and within the *HOT!* offices themselves," Eugene said.

Michael didn't speak. Damn, it would have been nice if he'd known that they knew.

"We didn't say anything until now," Eugene added, "because you two seemed to be safe. But I've been noticing some strange behavior from Finola's assistant, Tristan. He'd been following you."

"So why this intervention?"

"I just had a feeling that things were getting too complicated and we might be outed if we didn't step in."

"Outed by whom?" Michael didn't understand.

"Let's leave Liza here to rest. She is perfectly fine," Eugene assured him again.

They left the room only to go across the hall to what looked like an employee lounge with a table and two sofas. Eugene walked over to the small kitchenette and poured himself some coffee.

"Can I get you any?" he asked, his tone as even and unconcerned as ever, which only served to agitate Michael more.

"No, I just want to know what's going on."

Eugene finished preparing his coffee and then sat

down on the sofa. Michael stood by the door, while Elton and Gabriel sat down too.

Eugene took a sip of his coffee, then held the mug
loosely in both hands as he regarded Michael with his
eerie blue eyes.

"We've been following you and Liza," Eugene said.

Michael opened his mouth to ask why, but his superior continued, "Not really to keep tabs on you, but
to keep tabs on Tristan McIntyre. He was also following you."

Michael had had a sense that he was being watched.
And he'd never liked Tristan, but just the same, he felt
the fool. He'd been followed by two people without
knowing it. That was not like a member of The
Brethren. He was trained to be aware at all times.

"You can't be too hard on yourself," Eugene said
after another sip of coffee. "You are newly bonded.
That alone is distracting. Plus you've been getting
readjusted to everything. Definitely a lot of things already on your mind."

Michael couldn't disagree, but it still didn't make
him feel any better.

"So why do you think Tristan was following me?"

Eugene took a deep breath. "I'm not a hundred
percent sure. But I know we can't risk his finding out
about you. And then with Liza losing control today, we
just decided it was time for intervention."

"Losing control?"

"She was doing a pretty good job of maintaining a
relationship with you and keeping the demon subdued,
but we knew she couldn't keep it up. Not indefinitely."

Michael frowned, totally lost. What the hell were
they talking about? Subdue the demon?

"I'm lost," he finally said, even though the admis-
sion made him feel even more like a total ass.

This time it was Elton who answered in his low, gravelly voice. "Liza is possessed."

Tristan tried Finola's cell phone again, but the call went right to voice mail. She'd clearly decided that she didn't want to be bothered tonight, but as the head of a demon rebellion, she should have realized there was no such thing as a night off.

Especially not tonight. She needed to be made aware that they had a demon slayer in their midst, and that might very well mean there was more than one as well.

"Damn it," he muttered after punching the button to hang up.

"You know," Dippy said from his spot on Tristan's office chair, "this could be our moment."

"How so?"

"Well, what if we go directly to Satan and tell him that we've discovered a slayer in our midst, and Finola was oblivious to the whole thing—right down to not answering her cell phone now."

Tristan tilted his head, considering that idea. Satan wouldn't take kindly to Finola's oversight. And he would very likely be impressed with him—and Dippy, sort of—realizing there was a threat.

"Definitely not a bad plan, but it would be even better if we caught this demon slayer."

Dippy nodded. "That would be even better."

"Let's go see what else we can find out."

Possessed? Michael stared at the old man, trying to understand what he was being told. It couldn't be true. He would never be attracted to, much less bond with, a possessed human. The possessed were only a few steps above actual demons. Liza wasn't demonic in any way.

"Liza has been possessed for a little over three years," Eugene said.

Michael stood then, unable to hear any more. This wasn't true. It couldn't be. He'd shared private, close moments with Liza. They'd been intimate. They'd talked and laughed. They'd spent hours and hours together. He'd fallen in love with her. He couldn't do that with a possessed soul.

But he had to go see her for himself. See the woman he loved. He knew they had to be lying to him.

He stepped out of the lounge and headed to the room where they had her locked up. John and Simon stood guard outside the door, and both men regarded him with sympathy as soon as they saw him. But not because he was bonded to a possessed female. He refused to believe that. They just felt bad that . . . that what? His bonded female had gone mad? Was ill?

God, something really was wrong here, wasn't it?

He stared at the men for a moment, then instead of going into the room where Liza was, he entered the room next to it, the one with the glass wall.

He entered, almost afraid to approach the glass, as if he were about to see the woman he loved with her head spinning 360 degrees on her shoulders and green bile spewing from her mouth.

Instead she still lay on the sofa where he'd placed her. She looked as lovely as she always did. She was a little pale, but otherwise she was the woman he'd known.

Then she shifted, regaining consciousness. She blinked, sat upright. She peered around, confusion furrowing her brow. Then her gaze found him. She spoke and started to rise, only to realize he was watching her from behind a glass window.

She frowned, tilting her head, clearly bewildered by the fact he was not with her. He should be with her.

Then she sat back down heavily, and her hands returned to her head. Her lips moved again, and this time he realized she wasn't talking to him.

She was talking to the demon inside her. Like she'd done before, but he hadn't understood. She finished her debate, her battle, and looked back at him. He saw pleading and a need for comfort in her eyes, but he couldn't look any longer. He couldn't accept what he was seeing, so he simply turned and walked away.

Liza stared as Michael turned and left the adjacent room without looking back.

He knew the truth, and he couldn't handle it, just as she'd feared.

A demon slayer is hardly going to fall for someone possessed. They kill people like you. Like us.

"I'm not like you," she almost yelled, her distress so high, she could barely contain her emotions.

In his eyes you are.

Her eyes filled with tears, both because she knew Boris was right, and because she was afraid of what was going to happen to her. She didn't even know where she was or what was going on. But she did know Michael had just had the chance to tell her, to reassure her, and he'd walked away.

She'd never felt so alone. So deserted.

But you always have me.

Liza curled in a ball and silently began crying.

Chapter Thirty

Michael didn't return to the employee lounge and the others, nor did he even look toward his other Brethren mates at Liza's door. Instead he turned down the hallway, not even sure where he was headed. He just had to get away.

He walked until he saw a sign for the men's room. Inside, the tile walls were cold and stark. He walked over to the sinks, stopping in front of one of them, bracing his hands on the sides of the sink, staring into the mirror.

How had things gone down like this? How had he lost all those years, found himself in a life he didn't understand, and now in love with and bonded to a woman he would have probably killed in his past life?

What kind of cruel, damned joke was this? He turned then and punched the bathroom stall door, needing to lash out. The metal door slammed against the stall wall, the sound loud and echoing around him. But that didn't satisfy the anger inside him. He punched it again, this time bloodying his knuckles with the force of his blow.

He wound up to punch the cold metal again, his

rage blind and powerful, but his swing was caught from behind, and he found himself whipped around and shoved hard against the cold tile wall. His breath was forced from his body at the impact, but even that felt good. The physical pain actually felt better than the pain in his heart.

When his head cleared slightly, he realized Gabriel held him pinned to the wall.

"Stop it," his friend yelled at him. "Stop it."

Michael glared at him, but he didn't speak.

"I know you are upset by all this. Shaken. But you need to get yourself together."

"Do I? For what purpose? To stand by helpless as usual?"

"No, to be a man for your woman, damn it. Liza needs you."

Michael's gut wrenched as he recalled her vulnerable look right before he'd walked away from her. She had wanted him in there with her. But he couldn't.

"She's not who I thought she was. She's polluted by that thing inside her."

Gabriel stared at him, and Michael could practically feel his disgust. He was disgusted with himself, but he couldn't help how he felt. He'd seen the possessed before and they were always tainted by the evil inside them.

"She is the woman you love," Gabriel said.

"She is the woman I thought I loved. How can you possibly expect me to love her now? You know what happens to the possessed."

Gabriel stared at him for a moment longer, then nodded. "I do know some possessed can't be saved, but I also know now some can. I've seen it myself."

Michael laughed then, a harsh, disbelieving sound. "You just told me earlier that you didn't believe in all this PC crap that Eugene and his new DIA are spouting."

Gabriel sighed, releasing his grip on Michael's throat just slightly. "I don't believe it all. And I understand your frustration. But in this case, I believe what the DIA claims they can do. I have to believe that you wouldn't bond with a woman who was lost, who was evil."

Michael didn't speak.

"I have to believe you would have seen that evil in her. That Elton would have seen it."

Michael considered his friend's words, and for a moment, he wanted to believe that too. But he just wasn't sure. He didn't know what to do.

"You are bonded," Gabriel said. "That much you and all the Brethren know. So that means you need to stand by her. Whatever the outcome. We've lost a lot of our power, that's true. But we haven't lost our loyalty and our honor. And both of those things belong to her."

Gabriel released him then, and left the bathroom.

Michael remained leaning heavily against the wall, torn up by his words and the memory of that look on Liza's face.

But still he didn't know what to do.

"I have to admit," Tristan said, wrinkling his nose at the stench of smoke and brimstone, "I don't really like this plan. I find it best to avoid the Prince of Darkness as much as possible."

Dippy pranced ahead, seemingly not at all daunted at the prospect of bringing bad news to their exalted leader.

"This is the right move. Just you see."

Tristan glanced over his shoulder warily at the cry of yet another tortured soul echoing up from the fiery abyss.

"I think I'll let you do all the talking."

Dippy made a noise somewhere between a growl and a laugh.

They entered a long hallway riddled with stalactites and stalagmites. As they wove their way through the maze, Tristan saw that they were approaching an open cavern with an ornate throne carved into the stone. Satan's official greeting room.

Welcoming, Tristan thought wryly.

"Who approaches?" came a booming, almost deafeningly deep voice.

Dippy didn't even hesitate. "Me, master. Dippy."

Satan appeared then in his full, demonic glory. Red skin, bulging muscles, cloven hooves, and thick, intimidating horns.

Tristan had seen Satan this way, but the sight never ceased to impress and terrify. Not to mention that pants of some sort would have been welcome.

Tristan averted his eyes.

"Ah, my little helpers of the demon rebellion. What brings you here? Not another problem with Finola, I hope."

Tristan kept his head bowed and waited for Dippy to answer that one.

"I'm afraid to say it is, in a way, master," the dog said.

"Explain."

"We have discovered that a demon slayer has infiltrated *HOT!* magazine's employment via the mailroom."

Tristan wasn't sure he liked the phrasing of "we," given the fact that it wasn't Dippy who'd recognized the slayer—nor had he even wanted to deal with the man in the first place—but he let the comment slide, partially due to good sportsmanship, and partly because he still felt nervous in the Prince of Darkness's presence.

Satan was silent for a moment; then his voice boomed again. "How did you discover this?"

"We—" Dippy started again, and this time Tristan didn't think he could accept sharing the credit. Satan needed to know who was really responsible.

"I recognized the name," Tristan said, his voice calmer than he'd expected it to sound.

Dippy glanced at him, narrowing a beady dog eye.

"Yes," he then agreed, offering a wolfish smile to their master. "Tristan did recognize the name—"

"And the man," Tristan added.

"Yes," Dippy agreed, his voice becoming a low growl. "But I was the one who suggested we come to you."

Satan glanced back and forth between the two of them, looking unimpressed. Finally he nodded. "I'm pleased that you discovered this threat and decided to come to me. It would seem that between the two of you, you have one decent brain. And I'm disappointed to see that Finola is not with you. Is it safe to say she doesn't know about this threat?"

"We've tried to contact her, but she was not available, so we decided to come directly to you," Dippy said.

"Again, a wise choice," Satan said. "I want you to go back now and find out what you can about this slayer. And about the mailroom. I think it's safe to say, this slayer might not be the only one. I will deal with Finola. Again."

Both Tristan and Dippy nodded.

"Go," Satan ordered. They didn't need to be told twice.

* * *

Liza paced the room, realizing that she was essentially in a prison, and she had no idea what her captors intended to do with her. In fact, she wasn't even sure who her captors were. She recognized them as some of the mailroom staff. She certainly recognized Elton, but she now realized he wasn't just a mere mailroom worker. Her captors still hadn't come to talk to her, but she'd seen them coming in and out of the room on the other side of the glass wall.

Definitely not just mailroom staff. They know demons.

Despite herself, she found herself asking Boris, "What kind of place is this?"

This room is copper. As is the one on the other side of that glass.

"What does copper do?"

It keeps me trapped here.

Interesting, Liza thought, watching as several other people came in and out of the neighboring room, clearly preparing for something. But then, all of a sudden they were gone. And she still hadn't seen any sign of Michael. Why wouldn't he come see her? Had he only been interested in capturing her all along?

She didn't want to believe that. But his last look at her through the window had been anything but loving and kind. He'd appeared disgusted.

I'm telling you, slayers have no use for demons or the possessed. He's done with you.

"Shut up," she muttered, pulling her knees up to her chest and resting her head on them. She didn't know what to believe and she could hardly think with Boris back. She just wanted to understand what was going on. And she wanted to see Michael again too.

She wanted him to tell her what was happening. She thought he owed her at least that much.

"We are going to have to put a hold on things," Eugene said to the group he'd called over to the employee lounge. "It appears that our worst fear has been realized, and we've gained the attention of Finola and her demons. Tristan has been down to the mailroom asking about you, Michael."

Michael didn't know why he'd garnered Tristan's attention. In fact, he'd thought he'd been playing it very safe. But then again, he hadn't known he was dealing with a possessed woman either.

"So before we handle the situation with Liza McLane, we are going to have to run interference upstairs," Eugene told the DIA members who'd been working on Liza's "situation" as they kept calling it. "That means that none of you know Michael Archer. He wasn't a real mailroom employee, and he must have somehow sneaked in here for reasons none of us could possibly imagine. This memo has been sent out to all of the mailroom, and it's imperative that everyone stick to the same story. Michael Archer was never a real employee—at least not to our knowledge."

Michael didn't need to be told directly that this meant he was relegated to an even less important job within the DIA.

Fucking great. It was pretty much like he didn't exist already.

"Okay, let's make this go away," Eugene said by way of a rally cry. The members nodded and disappeared from the room, each busy with some sort of task.

Michael had none, obviously.

Then Eugene, who still stood by the door, turned

back to him. "And you, Michael, will be in charge of Liza."

Michael immediately shook his head. "I don't think I'm the best choice for that."

"I think you are the only choice, because we need to keep you down here out of sight along with her. You also know her and can keep her calm. As calm as she can be right now."

Michael didn't want to even keep watch outside the door. He didn't want to see her at all. It was too painful.

But Eugene was his superior, at least for now, and aside from quitting, which he wasn't willing to do, not when he was the cause of all this upheaval, he had to do what was requested of him.

"I'm hoping we can have this all sorted out very quickly."

Michael nodded, not sure which problem he was referring to. Although he supposed they were all sort of one. A domino effect of problems.

Michael pushed away from the counter where he'd been leaning and followed Eugene into the hallway. John and Simon were gone from their posts, probably working security in the actual mailroom now.

Michael positioned himself where they'd been.

"I think you'd be able to watch her better from the other room," Eugene said. "We don't have reason to believe that the demon will make her do something destructive to her surroundings or herself, but it's better to play it safe rather than sorry. You can't enter the room, but you can call for help if you feel she needs it."

Michael stared at his boss for a moment, suddenly very tempted to walk out. He couldn't do this task. Any other one, yes. But not this. Would he really have a job when all this was said and done anyway?

But he simply nodded and walked to the next door down. Taking a moment to brace himself, he opened the door and stepped inside.

He couldn't even bring himself to look at the window until he was in the center of the room. Once there, did he manage to gaze through the glass, telling himself that the person over there wasn't the person he'd believed her to be.

But even with his mental pep talk, his determination to steel his heart, the sight of her tore at him.

She sat curled up on the sofa, her knees drawn tight to her chest, her head down and her shoulders shaking as she sobbed. She appeared as heartbroken as he felt.

But she was possessed. He knew this behavior might not even be Liza, but rather the demon conning him.

Then he noticed what looked like a speaker near the window and a switch along the bottom of it. He carefully approached the window and flicked it; suddenly he could hear her. Her strangled sobs.

"No," she whispered amid her tears. "No, Michael would not let that happen."

Michael moved to the wall where she wouldn't see him if she lifted her head. He wanted to listen without her being aware that he was there.

"Shut up," she pleaded, her voice cracking with dismay and actual fear. "I don't care if he's a slayer, he won't kill me. He won't."

Michael's heart sank in his chest as he realized the demon was telling her what slayers did to the possessed. And the demon was telling the truth. Or at least what used to be the truth.

"Michael loves me."

He listened to her fight. Her desperate fight not

only with the demon, but her fight to believe her own words. He closed his eyes, wondering again, could this just be a ploy by the demon to make him let down his guard? But he could feel Liza reaching out to him. He could feel her love. A love that was wavering with her fear, but a love that was still there. They were still connected.

He stepped out from his place against the wall, and lightly tapped the window. Almost as if she didn't quite dare, as if she was afraid of what she might see, she slowly lifted her head, swiping her disheveled hair away from her pale, tear-streaked face.

"Liza," he said and placed a hand on the glass. She hesitated, as if she wasn't sure she could trust him. But then she slowly uncurled herself and walked toward the window, her expression that of a scared animal. She paused just on the other side of the glass, and then tentatively she placed her hand up to his.

"Everything is going to be okay," he said loudly, not sure if she could hear him.

She frowned, focusing on his lips.

"You will be okay," he repeated louder, and this time she nodded, giving him a small, tremulous smile.

He didn't know if what he was telling her was true, but he needed to offer her some reassurance. Some comfort.

"He's telling me all sorts of awful things," she said, her own wording slow and loud because she didn't realize he could hear her. "He's telling me that he can't be exorcised from me. That the only way to get rid of him is to get rid of me."

Michael didn't need any more clarification of what the demon was saying to her, he already knew. This demon wasn't holding back. He was panicked too and playing hard ball.

Michael shook his head adamantly, determined to make her believe she would be all right even if he didn't quite believe it himself.

"You will be fine," he said loudly.

She nodded, her blue-green eyes pleading again, desperate.

"He says you don't really believe that. He says you have killed plenty of possessed people just to kill the demon within them."

Michael felt sick to his stomach, not knowing how to handle this. He didn't want to lie to her. In truth, he didn't know what the DIA would do with her now to fix this. But he couldn't try to explain his past through a wall of glass.

"He's lying," he said, trying to reassure her. "He's trying to scare you."

She nodded to let him know she understood his words, but then she paused as if she was listening. To that evil being inside her, filling her with more fear and doubts.

"He says you are the one lying. He knows you are, because he knows you."

He frowned, shaking his head. What demon would know him?

Was it a demon who'd heard of him? That must be it, because there was only one demon who had ever escaped him.

Suddenly his blood went cold.

"He says to tell you that the demon inside me is named Bartoris."

Bartoris.

Chapter Thirty-one

"So what you are telling me is that you've never heard of Michael Archer?"

The man named Eugene, whom Tristan had never seen before in his life and whom he disliked instantly, shook his head. "No, I can go through my employment records for you again if you would like, but I don't see anyone by that name. In fact, I didn't see a single Archer, period."

"So how do you think this man got a mailroom smock, a mail cart, and an identification badge?"

Eugene again shook his head. "I don't think it would be too hard to obtain either the smock or the cart. They are readily available anywhere down here. As far as the ID, I'm sure in this day and age of computers and high-end printers, our badges could be forged. Not a comforting thought, that's for sure."

Tristan really didn't like this guy. He had an answer for everything—well, except for how and why Michael Archer had been here. And he had been. There was no doubt about that.

"One of our employees, one of the *HOT!* editors actually, admitted to dating this man, so he was around for some time. I can't believe none of your employees saw him or spoke to him."

"Perhaps they did, but just assumed he was a new guy or something. I do know that I never saw him down here, so maybe he was focused on the magazine itself."

Tristan studied Eugene, the mailroom manager, for a few moments. He hated to admit that the man's suggestions made sense. After all, why would a demon slayer want to hang out down here? No self-respecting demon would be caught dead in the mailroom. Michael Archer had just needed an easy way to get up onto the fifteenth floor.

Still, Tristan didn't like how easily Eugene was explaining away all of his questions and concerns.

"I suppose you are right, but I think I should talk to some of your staff anyway. Ms. White would want me to be thorough."

"Of course," Eugene agreed readily—just as Tristan had known he would. A man who had nothing to hide. Tristan never trusted men like that. "Just let me know if I can help you in any way."

Tristan rose from the folding metal chair that served as the mailroom manager's office furniture and exited the square of plyboard walls that served as his office.

Again, Tristan couldn't imagine a demon slayer really hanging out down here, even if he was just biding his time while waiting to get up to the *HOT!* offices where the demons dwelled. But he wanted to be totally sure.

After all, now Satan was involved, and Finola was going to be livid that he was, so Tristan needed to prove he'd followed every lead he could.

Tristan walked into the mailroom proper, rather

amazed that this department was so large. It seemed excessively big, really. But then again, what did he know about mailrooms?

"What do I want to know about mailrooms?" he muttered to himself as he regarded all the odd-looking people and machines around him.

Still he stayed focused, talking to the least offensive-looking of the employees. Perhaps not the best way to get information, but better than Finola's approach would be. She wouldn't even set foot in a place like this. Concrete floor, drab gray walls, and strange people. It was an aesthetic mess down here.

Tristan didn't discover anything new about Michael Archer. His only hope was that the man would return, not realizing Tristan was onto him.

His other option was to follow Liza McLane. She might lead him right to the demon slayer.

All Tristan knew, even as he left the mailroom with no more information than when he'd entered, was that he would discover something, and that would be enough to make Satan realize he was the one who should be in charge of *HOT!* and the demon rebellion.

Michael told Liza to stay right near the glass and to ignore the demon—Bartoris—as much as she could. He told her he would be right back. That he wasn't leaving her.

She nodded, trying to look confident, but he could tell she was afraid. Afraid he would disappear again. And he couldn't very well blame her, if his previous re-action had been any indication. But in this case, he was leaving to get help. To get someone who understood what the DIA did with the possessed now.

He hurried down the hallway back toward the elevators. There was a lobby area and a receptionist of sorts there.

"I was told if the woman being held back there got upset or was at risk, I should contact Eugene."

The woman, who was not only the receptionist, but could double for a female gladiator, bobbed her head, then reached for the phone. She pressed a series of numbers and waited.

"He's not answering," she finally said in a voice that reminded him of a cat. Husky but silky and strangely out of place.

"Could you try again?"

"If he's available, he always answers."

"Can you call Gabriel?"

The woman nodded as if she found his question a little ridiculous. She picked up the phone and pressed another sequence of numbers.

The woman spoke in her odd purring voice, telling Gabriel that he was needed down below, which Michael guessed was code for where they were.

She made a few more clipped, cryptic comments, then hung up.

"He will be right with you."

"Send him down to the room where—" He couldn't bring himself to call Liza "the possessed." "Down to the rooms where we have the woman."

The receptionist/pro-wrestler nodded, then busied herself with something on her computer as if he'd never been there.

When Michael rushed back into the holding cell, he found Liza right where he'd left her.

He immediately went back to the glass and placed his palm against it. She did the same, her small hand disappearing behind his.

They stayed that way for a moment, until he noticed her wincing again. Bartoris was talking to her, that evil bastard.

He couldn't imagine anything worse than the woman he loved being possessed by the demon who'd cursed him. It was more than a coincidence. It was fate.

This time, he swore, the demon wouldn't walk away from Michael's sword. But he had to believe the DIA could exorcise him first and leave Liza unscathed.

He had to believe that.

"Michael?"

He turned from the glass to find Gabriel in the doorway, a stunned look on his face. His gaze flicked from Michael's hand to Liza's, and then an almost relieved look softened his features.

"What's going on?"

"We have to do the exorcism, or whatever they do now, as soon as possible," Michael told him. "It's Bartoris inside her."

Gabriel didn't react for a moment, although that softness left his features. "What are the chances?"

"I know," Michael agreed. "This is fate."

Gabriel didn't argue.

"I can call the team down to handle this," Gabriel told him, moving to pull out his cell phone.

Damn, Michael thought, he kept forgetting he had one of those too. He hadn't even needed to leave Liza, had he? He could have called Gabriel directly.

He listened as Gabriel instructed the exorcism team to assemble.

"We will save her," Gabriel assured him.

Michael nodded, again having to believe his beloved would be safe and untouched by Bartoris's evil.

Within minutes, the room was filled with a group of

people who, in Michael's opinion, looked like a yuppie dinner party.

"Where is the priest?" Michael asked, frowning as a man passed him in a button-down shirt and argyle vest.

"We've discovered that religion isn't a necessary factor in an exorcism. We've learned that good Samaritans work just as well and are easier to find. Not to mention, they work for cheap. They are good Samaritans after all."

Michael frowned, not sure this whole twist on exorcism was making him feel that confident, especially when he already had his doubts.

But he knew they had to move on this. He looked over at Liza. Her face was strained and her eyes scrunched closed. Bartoris was torturing her. And Michael had seen other possessed humans crack under the constant talking and pressure of a demon.

Liza needed to be free. She needed to be his.

"We're going to send seven people in with her. One person of pure virtue for each of the deadly sins. Another trick we've learned," Gabriel explained. "Demons always embody one of the sins."

Michael nodded, praying this worked. He had to admit, Gabriel's explanation made sense. Finola embodied greed. And he suspected Bartoris's sin was envy.

Michael watched as the team entered Liza's chamber. She cast him an unsure look, scared by the sudden appearance of the others.

"I want to be with her," Michael said, heading toward the door. But Gabriel caught his shoulder as he passed.

"You can't go in there unless you truly believe. It is necessary if the exorcism is to work correctly."

Michael frowned. "But faith has always played a huge role in exorcisms. We've known that for centuries."

Gabriel nodded, but then said, "Faith is good and powerful. But what I'm talking about is belief. Belief in the goodness of the person you are exorcising. Belief that the people surrounding her can save her, and belief that we can contain and help the demon who leaves her."

Michael was totally on board until Gabriel's last request. How could a creature like Bartoris be contained and helped? Okay, he knew he could be contained, but helped? How? Michael was willing to believe the possessed could be truly saved. Hell, he needed to trust that fact, but demons were evil through and through. What could be reformed inside them?

He glanced back to the other room. The good Samaritans were leading Liza away. She kept looking over her shoulder toward Michael. His bonded mate needed him and frankly he'd probably have said anything to be able to go to her.

"I believe," he said to Gabriel, who didn't react right away.

"I believe," Michael repeated, more adamantly.

Gabriel hesitated a moment longer, then nodded. "Go to her."

Michael was out the door even before Gabriel finished speaking. He went to the other door and knocked. One of the team opened the door a crack.

"I'm her mate," Michael said, then wondered if this person would even understand. To his surprise the young man on the other side of the door bobbed his head slightly, then swung the door open just enough to allow Michael inside.

"Michael," Liza cried as soon as she saw him moving toward her, his motions still hesitant and unsure. He knew he needed to be certain. Gabriel said he had to believe, and he did. All but that last part. Doubts still niggled about Bartoris, and the fact he could be helped once he was out of Liza's body.

But Liza looked at him pleadingly, her blue-green eyes glistening with tears and fear. The team had placed her onto a long rectangle, boardroom-type table like it was an operating table. She twisted her head to watch only him as he came to her.

"Michael," she repeated as if focusing on him was the only thing keeping her calm. Maybe it was.

"I'm here," he assured her, stepping up to the table and clasping her hand in one of his, while the other touched her face, brushing the tangle of messy hair from her cheeks and forehead.

"I'm scared," she whispered, but he could already tell she was much calmer than she'd been while he was in the other room.

"Just focus on getting this bastard out of you."

She studied him for a moment, then nodded. She tried to relax against the hard tabletop, her eyes closed, and one of the team members, a woman who looked more like a schoolteacher than an exorcist, told everyone to lay their hands on Liza.

The woman began to repeat simple things like "Leave." "Be gone." "You are not wanted, or able to stay in this good, kind, sweet woman."

The rest of the table repeated whatever she said, and Michael had no trouble going along with these words. They were how he felt too. Bartoris needed to be out of Liza.

But the more they talked and demanded, the more agitated Liza became. Her head twisted from side to side. Her limbs twitched.

"Liza, please, let him go. Let this demon exit you," he murmured to her, his hand still stroking her hair.

Suddenly her face jerked toward him, her head off the table.

"You don't believe," she hissed.

"I do," he told her. "I do."

She laughed then and Michael knew he wasn't talking to Liza. Bartoris wasn't just stuck inside her, taunting and teasing her. He was the one smiling up at Michael.

"Michael," the demon said in a distorted version of Liza's pretty voice. This voice wasn't pretty. "I thought I got rid of you."

"Obviously not," Michael stated. "You just slowed me down a little, but I'm here. And you are here. It would seem this is my time to finish what I started."

"Or time for me to finish you." Liza's hand yanked away from the young man on the other side of her and she started to turn toward Michael. The young man reached for her, to renew his hold, but Liza was strong, mostly because of Bartoris.

Michael didn't flinch or struggle as Liza's hand curled around his throat and squeezed. All around him, Michael was aware of the team, trying to regain control, their voices growing louder and more emphatic.

"We believe. We believe."

Michael said it too, but he wasn't sure what he was saying he believed anymore. He did want Liza safe. More than anything, but his desire to war with this demon also was strong.

Suddenly Liza—or rather Bartoris and Liza's body—started to sit up. The demon didn't seem to be leaving. He was just growing stronger and he was

solely focused on Michael. On this fight they had yet
to finish. Liza's fingers squeezed even tighter. Her
beautiful features were barely her own, her mouth
contorted into a sneer, her eyes blazing with hate.

She was off the table then, walking Michael backward.

"What are you going to do, slayer?" Bartoris demanded in that mocking version of Liza's voice. "You
can't hurt me without hurting your beloved. Are you
willing to kill her to kill me?"

Michael realized the team was no longer chanting.
They hadn't seen this before. But Michael had. This
was the point when the evil in the demon tainted the
human host.

Michael struggled to look around at the others.
This was what he'd been assured, even by Gabriel,
wouldn't happen.

Panic filled Michael for the first time. Not for his
safety, but for Liza's.

"Go ahead, slayer. Get me out of her body." Bartoris shoved Michael hard, and Michael realized he
was pinned to the glass of the other room. He also realized he couldn't breathe. The air barely wheezed
past Liza's strong, strangling fingers.

"Bartoris."

Liza's body actually stopped, almost immediately
frozen at the sound of the voice behind her. Or rather
Bartoris froze.

Then the possessed body slowly turned. Michael
followed Liza's gaze.

There in the doorway was Eugene. Eugene with his
calm demeanor and average looks. Nothing about
him strong-looking or striking. Except for his eyes.
And now his eyes glowed a brighter, more vivid blue
than ever before.

"Let the man go, Bartoris," Eugene said evenly, more a suggestion than a demand.

Bartoris continued to stare. Then the demon said something. A word Michael didn't understand.

"Do as I say," Eugene said, moving closer.

Michael felt Liza's body flinch.

"I believe," Eugene added, and a low noise escaped Liza's throat. But her hand no longer held Michael with that superhuman strength she had even moments before.

"I believe," Eugene repeated.

Another strange noise, and another shudder of Liza's body.

"Leave her," Eugene demanded.

The demon within Liza repeated that word again. But he released Michael, moving backward away from Eugene.

"I believe," Eugene informed the demon as if he was discussing the weather. "I believe."

Liza then jerked violently, almost as if she was going into a seizure; then she started to crumple to the floor.

But Michael was there, his arms catching her before she hit the ground. Her head lolled against his shoulder, her whole body limp.

Michael immediately worried that this was too much for her. She'd had her episodes before. What if this was another one? What if the medications she overdosed on had made it too hard for her to deal with an exorcism? What if her body couldn't take it?

"She's fine," Eugene said from beside him in his usual conversational way. "The exorcism is done, and she is tired. That is all. It's very normal."

Michael frowned at his boss. The exorcism was done? No way. Exorcisms could take hours, days.

But by way of explanation, Eugene jerked his head toward the glass partition of the other room. There on the other side of the glass was a diminutive man, who looked like he could be someone's rather geeky uncle.

"Bartoris," Michael said, recognizing the demon's human form right away. The demon growled and pounded the glass, clearly furious to still be trapped.

Michael frowned at Eugene. "How did you do that?"

"I didn't," he said simply. "Not alone. The others helped too."

Michael then noticed the others still circled around them. Michael didn't understand. He hadn't seen anything like this. Maybe the others had helped, but he knew Eugene had done the majority of the exorcism.

"Let's get Liza out of here. She needs to lie down and rest," Eugene said. He gestured to one of the others in the room. "Hannah, show Michael to the room down the hall where Liza can rest."

Hannah nodded, waiting for Michael to follow. Michael wanted to ask Eugene more. He wanted to understand what had just happened, and what would happen to Bartoris now, but he had to take care of his mate first.

Liza was his first priority. Always.

So he followed Hannah out of the room.

Chapter Thirty-two

Liza woke slowly, stretching her aching muscles. Even though she didn't know where she was, or what had happened, she had a strange feeling something was very different.

"Liza."

She blinked repeatedly to find Michael beside her, his strong hand holding hers.

"Where am I?" she asked, her voice hoarse. Her throat a little sore.

Michael hesitated, and she instantly got the feeling he didn't know how to answer her. She squinted, trying to remember. Then she did. She'd been brought somewhere by the mailroom staff. Or people who had pretended to be the mailroom staff.

They'd locked her in a strange room. And Boris had told her they were going to kill her in order to kill him. But she wasn't dead.

She braced her arms to lever herself up. Michael immediately helped her.

"I feel strange," she said, touching a hand to her head. She didn't feel sick exactly. And nothing hurt. She just didn't feel quite right.

"Do you want some water?"

She nodded absently, still trying to figure out what felt so different.

Michael made sure she was safely upright, then moved away from the bed to a counter with a sink. He brought her a paper cup filled with cold water.

She took a long sip, then looked around her again. The room looked rather like a hospital room although she didn't think she was in a hospital.

"Where am I?"

Michael glanced around too. "Under the basement of the *HOT!* building."

She stared at him for a moment. "And you are a demon slayer."

He studied her for a moment, then nodded. "I am—at least in theory."

She considered that for a moment. "And the mailroom is just a cover for people who are here to fight the demons?"

He nodded again. "Yes."

She thought about that, then took another sip of her water. Then she slowly lowered the cup, realizing what was different. She stared at him with wide eyes.

"He's no longer here."

Michael returned her gaze, then smiled slightly. "You're right. The demon is gone."

A laugh bubbled up inside her. "He's gone."

She flung herself at him, and he caught her, laughing himself.

"Oh Michael, I'm finally free."

"You are," he agreed, hugging her tightly. "But not completely."

She pulled back, her laughter dying on her lips. "What do you mean?"

"Finola and Tristan are still in control of *HOT!*, for

now anyway. So you need to go into hiding. They can't find you or me or discover that Bartoris is gone. We have to go into hiding to keep you safe."

Liza hugged him again, pressing her face against his chest.

"Sort of like witness protection," she finally said.

"Yes."

The idea was overwhelming, but it certainly wasn't any more overwhelming than the last few years had been. And she was finally free of Boris.

"Will you go with me?" she asked without lifting her head from his strong chest.

"Yes. If you want me."

She looked at him then. "Of course, I want you. I feel like I couldn't go on without you by my side. That's scarier to me than the idea of having to hide or even being possessed, which was no picnic."

She gave him a smile and was pleased to see him smile back.

"I can only imagine," he told her. "Was that why you took all the allergy medicine? To somehow subdue the demon inside you?"

She nodded, then smiled a little proudly. "It knocked him out cold."

"But it was also hurting you," he pointed out and she nodded again.

"But it was worth it. It allowed me to have an almost normal relationship with you. And I had to have that."

Michael kissed her then, just a brief brush of his lips against her mouth. He rested his forehead against hers.

"I do have one more thing to tell you. I hope you will be pleased, because I'm not sure there's much we can do to change it."

She waited, feeling a little nervous. She was already hearing so many odd things. Things that would change her life forever. What else could he tell her?

His gaze searched hers, his golden eyes uncertain in a way she'd never seen before. He was nervous too.

But finally he spoke. "I am a demon slayer, and I have been for centuries."

She frowned. "Are you immortal?"

He shook his head. "I just age differently from normal humans. But I am human. I don't have any powers or anything except for the fact that I was chosen, by God or some higher power, to battle demons. My only special skill is that ability."

"So will you kill Finola?"

"No. Things have changed and now the DIA—the Demon Intelligence Agency—is handling demons much differently than they used to."

She nodded, not totally understanding, but getting the basic gist.

"But that's not the main thing I want to tell you."

"Okay," she said slowly, finding it a little hard to believe there could be more.

Again she got the feeling he was nervous.

"Another part of being a slayer is that we—we sort of mate for life."

Liza stared at him, her stomach tensing with dread. Was he saying what she thought he was? She pulled away from him, trying to prepare herself for the answer to her next question.

"Are you mated with someone then?"

He nodded, but his expression seemed almost amused. She couldn't find anything funny about that. She'd been involved with what was in essence a married man. Definitely not funny to her.

"Who? Does she know about us?"

He nodded again, and she couldn't miss the amusement there now. Really? She couldn't find anything humorous about this at all.

She pulled away even more, but his hands on her shoulders stopped her before she could break all contact.

"Please, Michael, let me go."

But he didn't. Instead he caught her gaze with his. "Liza, it's you. I'm bonded to you. You are my soul mate."

She searched his eyes, suddenly realizing what he'd said was true. How could she not know that? She could feel it now.

"We—we're soul mates." Her words were spoken more as an agreement than a question.

"Yes. Does—does that bother you?"

Now it was her turn to be amused. "After everything I've been through in the past day—in the past few years, do you really think being with the man I love is going to shake me?"

He stared at her for a moment, then laughed, pulling her tight against his chest.

"I love you, Liza. We are going to be just fine."

"I know we are," she said, really feeling that things would be okay for the first time in years. She had Michael, her very own demon slayer. Who could want more?

Epilogue

"Are you two all set?" Eugene asked.

Michael held up the plane tickets to London. The DIA had set up a place for Michael and Liza to live in England. They even had jobs. Michael would work for the DIA over there, and Liza would work for a publishing company. Working on children's books, which pleased her. She'd had enough of the fashion industry, that was for sure.

"We are good to go," he told his boss. His old boss.

"You will be safe there," Eugene said.

"We will be fine." Michael had no doubt about that. As long as he and Liza were together, they would always be good.

Eugene nodded as if he agreed with Michael's thoughts.

"Thanks for your help," Michael said. "I'm sure we will be in touch every now and then."

"Yes."

Michael nodded again, not quite sure what to say to the man who'd been in some ways his nemesis and also his savior. But he felt the need to say something.

"Thank you for saving Liza."

Eugene smiled, and even his smile seemed rather bland. "It's my job."

Michael nodded again, still not sure exactly what to say. Still wanting to ask something he didn't actually think he'd get an answer for. But he was leaving, so he had to try.

"How did you cast Bartoris out of Liza like that?"

Eugene looked as if he wasn't going to answer, but then he shrugged. "I have a very good understanding of how to deal with demons."

Michael no longer doubted that, but still he had never seen anyone exorcise a demon so easily. Only another demon could do that.

He studied Eugene for a moment, wondering about that very possibility, not for the first time.

Eugene gave him a look that he couldn't quite decipher, then nodded slightly as if agreeing with what Michael was thinking. But Michael didn't ask the question that had been swirling in his mind. *Are you a demon?*

Maybe he really didn't want to know.

He waved the tickets in the air once more as a good-bye. "Thank you again."

Eugene nodded. "Thank you."

Michael left Eugene's underground office and went to Liza, where she waited in the reception area.

She smiled as he approached and he no longer considered how Eugene did what he did, or what he might or might not be. He was headed to his future, and he was just glad it was with the love of his life by his side.

For once, Michael didn't need any other answer than that.

Finola's office, a week later . . .

"So what you are telling me is that not only can you not locate a demon slayer who somehow made it directly into our midst, but now you have lost a possessed human and the demon that possessed her?"

Finola gave Satan a pained look, then nodded. "Yes, that is what has happened."

Satan, who stood in the center of her office in his older man guise, tapped his cane on the floor, clearly frustrated. Tristan didn't want to know what he'd rather be doing with that cane.

"I'm not pleased about this," Satan said, his voice booming off the glass walls.

"I know, master." Finola lowered her head, contrite. She knew she was in deep doo-doo. She'd already angered the Prince of Darkness once. Most demons didn't get too many second chances, much less a third one.

"I did tell Tristan to follow both the human and the boyfriend," Finola said, throwing him under the bus as usual. He wasn't surprised.

But he was also hopeful about Satan's response. Tristan was counting on the big boss to see the truth about Finola. She hadn't even been aware that there was a demon slayer in their midst.

And Satan didn't let him down.

"The only reason I'm aware that there is a breach in our security is because of Tristan. You didn't even know," Satan stated. "That is why I've decided that Tristan will now be in charge of this magazine and this takeover."

Finola looked like she wanted to argue, but she remained silent.

Satan turned to Tristan. "I expect you to do a much better job than Finola has."

Tristan nodded. "I will, master."

Oh, he would.

Did you miss the first book in the series?

Devilishly Hot

And you thought your job was hell . . .

Annie Lou Riddle had a plan: Move to New York City. Break into the fashion industry. Work her way to the top. Nowhere in that scenario did she expect to accidentally sell her soul in exchange for a job at *HOT!* magazine. Oops.

Demons, it seems, aren't big on letting mortals off the hook. Now Annie is stuck working as assistant/personal slave to Finola White—diva extraordinaire and glamorous she-devil. Whatever Finola wants, she gets, and she wants Annie to match her up with Nick Rossi, the gorgeous detective investigating shady doings at *HOT!*

Frankly, Annie sees the appeal. Nick is effortlessly sexy, rugged, charming—and the one man Annie should definitely not be flirting with, or kissing, or . . . Oops. But some loves are too devilishly hot to resist.

Books by Bestselling Author
Fern Michaels

Available Wherever Books Are Sold!
Check out our website at www.kensingtonbooks.com

Romantic Suspense from
Lisa Jackson

See How She Dies	0-8217-7605-3	$6.99US/$9.99CAN
Final Scream	0-8217-7712-2	$7.99US/$10.99CAN
Wishes	0-8217-6309-1	$5.99US/$7.99CAN
Whispers	0-8217-7603-7	$6.99US/$9.99CAN
Twice Kissed	0-8217-6038-6	$5.99US/$7.99CAN
Unspoken	0-8217-6402-0	$6.50US/$8.50CAN
If She Only Knew	0-8217-6708-9	$6.50US/$8.50CAN
Hot Blooded	0-8217-6841-7	$6.99US/$9.99CAN
Cold Blooded	0-8217-6934-0	$6.99US/$9.99CAN
The Night Before	0-8217-6936-7	$6.99US/$9.99CAN
The Morning After	0-8217-7295-3	$6.99US/$9.99CAN
Deep Freeze	0-8217-7296-1	$7.99US/$10.99CAN
Fatal Burn	0-8217-7577-4	$7.99US/$10.99CAN
Shiver	0-8217-7578-2	$7.99US/$10.99CAN
Most Likely to Die	0-8217-7576-6	$7.99US/$10.99CAN
Absolute Fear	0-8217-7936-2	$7.99US/$9.49CAN
Almost Dead	0-8217-7579-0	$7.99US/$10.99CAN
Lost Souls	0-8217-7938-9	$7.99US/$10.99CAN
Left to Die	1-4201-0276-1	$7.99US/$10.99CAN
Wicked Game	1-4201-0338-5	$7.99US/$9.99CAN
Malice	0-8217-7940-0	$7.99US/$9.49CAN

Available Wherever Books Are Sold!
Visit our website at **www.kensingtonbooks.com**

More from Bestselling Author
JANET DAILEY

Calder Storm	0-8217-7543-X	$7.99US/$10.99CAN
Close to You	1-4201-1714-9	$5.99US/$6.99CAN
Crazy in Love	1-4201-0303-2	$4.99US/$5.99CAN
Dance With Me	1-4201-2213-4	$5.99US/$6.99CAN
Everything	1-4201-2214-2	$5.99US/$6.99CAN
Forever	1-4201-2215-0	$5.99US/$6.99CAN
Green Calder Grass	0-8217-7222-8	$7.99US/$10.99CAN
Heiress	1-4201-0002-5	$6.99US/$7.99CAN
Lone Calder Star	0-8217-7542-1	$7.99US/$10.99CAN
Lover Man	1-4201-0666-X	$4.99US/$5.99CAN
Masquerade	1-4201-0005-X	$6.99US/$8.99CAN
Mistletoe and Molly	1-4201-0041-6	$6.99US/$9.99CAN
Rivals	1-4201-0003-3	$6.99US/$7.99CAN
Santa in a Stetson	1-4201-0664-3	$6.99US/$9.99CAN
Santa in Montana	1-4201-1474-3	$7.99US/$9.99CAN
Searching for Santa	1-4201-0306-7	$6.99US/$9.99CAN
Something More	0-8217-7544-8	$7.99US/$9.99CAN
Stealing Kisses	1-4201-0304-0	$4.99US/$5.99CAN
Tangled Vines	1-4201-0004-1	$6.99US/$8.99CAN
Texas Kiss	1-4201-0665-1	$4.99US/$5.99CAN
That Loving Feeling	1-4201-1713-0	$5.99US/$6.99CAN
To Santa With Love	1-4201-2073-5	$6.99US/$7.99CAN
When You Kiss Me	1-4201-0667-8	$4.99US/$5.99CAN
Yes, I Do	1-4201-0305-9	$4.99US/$5.99CAN

Available Wherever Books Are Sold!

Check out our website at www.kensingtonbooks.com.